EVERYONE WAS FALLING

A novel by

JS LEE

Pent-Up Press
ISBN-13: 978-1-7320943-5-2

This book is dedicated to
all the badass women of color
holding each other up in a world
that keeps knocking us down.

THERE WAS BLOOD

I'm shattering like glass. Coming undone, bit by bit. I hold myself together, arms crossed with a squeeze.

"Whenever you're ready," he says, hitting record. The overhead light deepens the hollows under his eyes. Though it's sharpened with time, I remember his face. I peer down at his badge that reads: WHITLEY.

"I was talking to this guy. Ben." The normalcy of my voice startles me. "He was doing all the talking. I was distracted. His facial hair was . . . It had, like, this pattern." I'm brought back to the moment now forever imprinted in my brain. It moves through me like hallucinogenic honey. But Whitley is bouncing a pen on his knee. I get to the point. "And then he just . . . fell."

His pale eyes fixate on my upper arm. I look down and notice a speck of blood that the hospital missed. Without thinking, I rub it with a wet thumb, as if it were my own. He leans forward, patience waning. "Was anything out of place?"

"Everyone was falling. There was blood—"

He cuts in. "Before that."

I shiver, gripping my crossed arms tight, pressing away the terror. "I'd never been to one of those things before, but it seemed like what I would've expected—until . . ."

"Did you have anyone with you?"

"No," I say, louder than intended. "Thankfully."

"Did you recognize the shooter?"

I gaze up at the ceiling, blinding myself with fluorescent lights. It's like a makeshift shot of whiskey—a numbing. Shifting

1

my unfocused eyes back down, I say, "I think he was wearing some kind of mask—a ski mask, or what do you call them—baklavas? Balaclavas? Not sure if my mind's just putting it there since it's such a cliché."

"You say he. You could tell that it was a man?"

I lift my eyes to his. "Aren't they all?"

His face tics. "You suspect anyone?"

"I haven't really been in touch with anyone here since I left. I can't imagine why . . ."

His pen stills. "They all have their reasons, none of 'em good."

"Could there be a good enough reason?"

He raises a shaggy white brow. His eyes bounce left and right as if trying to somehow calibrate my face. I suddenly wonder how it looks. Shocked? Scared? He asks, "Whose idea was it to hide in that closet?"

"I don't know . . . But when I saw Donna, I knew it was where she was going." As if on a transparent screen between us, I see her running ahead in an emerald-green dress.

"How's that?"

"We used to meet down there sometimes."

"Y'all friends?"

"Sure?" I scrunch my face, ruminating on the word "friend." "I don't really know her now. We were close years ago."

"And Christy? How'd she end up with you?" There's an inflection to the words "she" and "you." Christy's a town treasure, unlike Donna and me.

"I saw her on the floor and grabbed her. She was friends with us, too . . . back in the day."

His face contorts. "Did she say why her husband wasn't with her?"

I shrug. "We weren't in the frame of mind for catching up."

"And Donna's?"

I shake my head, face flushing under his quickening succession of questions. My fingers find each other, twisting and intertwining for comfort. "I'm surprised she came at all."

He squints. "Why's that?"

"Being the only Black kid in town didn't seem easy."

He tilts his chin down. With an air of disbelief, he says, "Strange she moved back if that's true."

"Yeah?" A chill rushes up my spine, fanning over my skin. I feel somehow betrayed by this new information. "Well, there you go. I never understood this town or anyone in it."

FRACTURES

The house is empty. When I saw the note earlier, I had wondered what kind of mother begs her daughter to visit and then leaves for the night. Well, that would be Margaret. But now I'm relieved. I welcome the silence.

Heading upstairs, I marvel over how everything's as it's always been in this house and this town. I could win a scavenger hunt blindfolded; I could draw a map from memory. Bixby's unchangeable. Or it was.

I peel my clothes off and toss them to the floor, unable to shake how everything was so normal—almost painfully so— every second before. No warning. Just bullets. So many bullets. And then came the screams.

A hand that doesn't feel like my own twists the shower dial all the way to the left. I let the hot water scorch my skin to burn through any splattered memories of other people's DNA. Eyes open or closed, I still see them falling. I still see their bodies looking like no bodies should.

My back connects with cold tile, jolting me awake to the moment. I acknowledge where I am and that I'm alive—for which I'm both guilty and grateful.

Lucky Lucy.

I squat in the shower, letting the hot water mist down upon me.

People called me lucky so much it became my first English word and nickname. I was three years old when I first came to Bixby. They said I spoke gobbledygook. Most likely, it was

Korean—all of which is forgotten. Overwritten.

Lucky Lucy. I say it again in my head.

This time I didn't wait around to be saved. My eyes scanned the room. I saw Christy. I grabbed her. We ran. We came upon Donna. They'd both lost their bags, but I had my phone in my pocket. Not wanting the shooter to hear me call 911, I silenced my phone and texted Alexis our location so the police could find us. They did.

I'm still lucky. The three of us are.

I try to make sense of time.

The reunion started at six thirty. I arrived at a regrettable seven. The shooting broke out soon after. The three of us must've been holed up in the closet for twenty minutes or so. After that came hours at the hospital, then another hour at the police station. They drove me home since no one was picking me up.

A wave of fatigue engulfs me. My body feels heavy and tired, yet there are things I need to know. How many of us made it out? Who did it and why? Is he dead or on the run?

I push the white curtain aside. The patrolman appears to be sleeping. Being able to sleep in a car is a sense of security I don't comprehend tonight.

Desperate to connect to something from Before, I grab my phone and scroll through an earlier conversation with Alexis. It feels like a lifetime ago.

> Me: I'm here and I'm queer!
> Alexis: And I miss your face.
> Me: Kind of wishing I asked you to come but glad I spared you the horror.
> Alexis: I would've totally gone!
> Me: Communication FAIL!
> Alexis: Absence makes the heart grow like Jane . . .

Me: Fonda <3

Alexis: Have fun tonight. You'll have to tell me all about it tomorrow.

Me: If I survive! ;-)

My eyes revisit the words "horror" and "survive." I wonder if on some level I knew this would happen. I remind myself that I'm not psychic and put down my phone.

Who'd open fire on a high school reunion? A disgruntled classmate? A former teacher? Sports rival? Jealous lover?

I keep nodding off, not realizing I've fallen asleep until I wake in a panic. As my eyes adjust to the dark, I see the Nirvana and Lost Boys posters tacked to the floral wallpaper of my youth. Each time, I remember where I am and what happened. Each time, I wish that the next time I wake it will all have just been a bad dream.

TOO MUCH TOO SOON

I wake again to my mother's melodically riled voice. It's as if her tongue's on a mission to escape her mouth. "Well, I can't believe it! The one night Henry and I chose to disconnect . . . Thank you for keeping our baby safe! What is this world coming to?"

The front door opens and slams shut, rattling my nerves. I hear two sets of footsteps charge up the stairs. My door swings open, my mother's hand jutting out to stop it from bouncing back in her face. She rushes to me in her powder-pink sweats. Her chestnut-brown hair swings down, tickling my neck.

"We just heard about it in the car! I left my phone here, and your father's ran out of juice. We got here as quick as we could. I'm so glad you're alive—thank the Lord! It's my fault, isn't it? I beg you to come home—and now this! I'll never forgive myself."

I wriggle out from under her. My father nods from the doorway in his blue-and-gold Bixby cap.

"It's not your fault." I inch up the bed and sit back, lifting my knees to my chest. "No one could've known."

"I can't believe you had to sleep all alone after that."

"I'm fine."

"What can we do, honey?" She pats my thigh twice. "What can we do for you now?"

"Well . . . My girlfriend's on her way out. I'd like her to stay here—with me, in this room. Would you be cool with that?"

Her upper half swivels towards Dad's hopeless shrug for a moment. "Well, okay. You're a grown woman, I guess."

The landline rings. Dad mumbles something unintelligible in

the hallway and returns with a strained face. "Your friend's on the phone." He holds out the cordless receiver.

Mom asks, "Who is it?"

"Christy Fox."

"Christy Fox *Tilden*," she corrects him, grabbing the phone. "I'm giving you to Lucy but just wanted to say I'm so glad you're alive! I can't believe what all happened! We were down at the lake—of all nights . . . Anyway, here's Lucy. God bless!" Handing me the receiver, she mimes that they'll be downstairs.

I rise to shut the door and collapse back onto the bed. It's too much too soon. I just want to rewind, to be back in San Francisco and never return.

"Hey. This is crazy, right?"

"Yeah," says Christy. "I woke up thinking it was all a bad dream. If only."

"You slept?"

"I was out cold. You?"

I mumble, "Here and there."

"So, I'm calling to thank you."

"For what?"

"I would've died if it weren't for you."

I pause. "Well, we don't know—"

"Look . . . I'm two hundred percent certain I'd be dead if you hadn't reached out to me when you did. I was a sitting duck."

I hold my breath a few beats and exhale. "I just did what anyone else would've done."

"But they didn't. And now they're all dead." Chills rush up my spine and down my extremities. She goes on. "They said on TV we're the only ones who made it out—just us three." The silence between us endures half a minute. "You were brave. I didn't know what to do."

"No one did. It was luck. We were lucky." I think, *Lucky Lucy*

& Co.

She says, "You're a hero." I cringe. My fingertips go white from gripping the phone so hard. "I'll never forget it," she continues. "My family's indebted to you. For life."

I snicker from nerves. "Oh, come on."

"Please. Don't be like that."

"I'm sorry. It's all so—"

"Much? I know. Listen, why don't you come over tonight? Donna, too. We should talk."

"Tonight? Oh . . . My girlfriend's flying in. I can't leave her."

"Bring her. Donna's husband will be here. They need to process, too."

"Maybe tomorrow."

"We need this."

"It can't wait one more day?" I chew on a broken fingernail, trying to smooth its cracked edge.

"If it has to . . . Look, I know you're not into God or anything, but I've got this really strong feeling."

"Well," I say, sighing loudly. "Okay." I hang up and go back to sleep.

IT'S COMPLICATED

I stir to a commotion downstairs, tuning my ears to Alexis's voice. Leaping out of bed, I wipe the oil from my forehead with the back of my hand, finger-comb my hair, and gallop downstairs in my pajamas. As I round the corner, Alexis drops her bag. Tears roll from her eyes. We clumsily clutch one another like a pair of drunken, seasick lovers.

"I thought I might never see you again." She brushes the hair from my eyes.

My mother's voice interjects. "I'll make some tea. Come. I want to learn all about you, Alexis. How was your flight? It must've cost an arm and a leg to get here so fast. And the bus isn't pleasant. You must be exhausted. Do you want to lie down?"

Alexis pulls out a stool and slides onto it. "I'm okay, Mrs. Byrne."

"Please . . . Call me Mrs. B."

From a stool across the kitchen island, my father scans Alexis with his eyes. "You're not what I expected."

She asks, "What were you expecting?"

"Maybe one of those girls who looks more like a man."

"Henry!" Mom scolds.

"Never made sense to me." He shrugs. "Why not just date a man then?"

"Because it's the whole person, not just the shell." Alexis grins and takes the mug from my mother. Her eyes shift back to my father. "Sex and gender aren't so black and white."

My eyes widen. "Can we not talk about sex with my parents right now?"

"Great idea," chirps Mom.

"They want me to be social, but then they don't like what I have to say," grumbles Dad.

"I think it's nice you show interest," says Alexis, pawing his forearm. His body awkwardly responds to her touch. "We've all gotta start somewhere."

"How 'bout some eggs?" Mom grabs a carton from the fridge. "I know it's late, but Lucy hasn't eaten all day. Scrambled? Over easy? Over hard?"

"Anything's fine with me," says Alexis. "Thanks."

I nod in agreement, unable to focus on the mundane. Reaching into the bread box, I break off a chunk of a fresh country loaf.

"Alexis, what do you do in San Fran?"

"No one there calls it San Fran," I tell my mother.

"I teach. Third grade this year. First grade before that. It's a big jump at that age. I'm excited." She pops the bread in her mouth and moans with delight. Dad smirks embarrassingly at her pleasure.

"I'll bet." Mom nods, cracking eggs. "I remember those years fondly." She peers over at me with an easy smile.

"I love kids. Working with them is so rewarding."

"Can I ask another question, or am I gonna get in trouble?" Dad glances at Mom.

Alexis says, "Ask away."

"Why would someone who loves kids so much choose to be in a lesbian"—he wags his finger between Alexis and me—"whatever you call it?"

I drop my forehead to the counter.

Alexis says, "It doesn't mean we can't have kids. And being

14

a lesbian isn't a choice—just like being hetero wasn't a decision for you or Mrs. B. You probably grew up knowing you liked the opposite sex. I grew up knowing I liked girls."

"Well, Lucy didn't." Dad points to me. "She liked boys for a while."

"I'm a lesbian. Lucy's pan."

Dad scrunches his face. "Pan? Like Peter Pan?"

I wish I had the energy to explain All the Things, but I settle for saying, "Hello? I'm right here. Can we please not do this today? I just can't."

"Lucy's had a rough night," Mom reminds them, scrambling eggs in a bowl. "It's not a good time, I don't think."

Shaking my head, I speak words that I can't believe are the truth or need saying. "I just survived a mass shooting, and you want to talk about my sex life."

"We know, honey. It's okay." Mom glares at Dad, and he lazily shrugs.

"No, it's not," I remind them. "All those people are dead—from one man with one gun. I don't even know how many were there, but they're gone. And I was there with them."

"On the radio, they said fifty-six. Thirty-four were Bixby alumni," Mom says quietly.

Dad chimes in. "Too bad there was no armed guard there on duty."

I lift my hand in protest. "Not now."

"I'm just sayin'."

"Please!"

Alexis rubs my back, and I shake it off. She stares at the plate my mother slides in front of her and says, "You're right. It's not real to us. We're over here talking like it's just another day."

"It doesn't feel real to me, either," I confess. "I keep wondering: How can it be? It's like I'm trapped in a nightmare or tangled up in a book . . .”

Mom walks around the kitchen island and kisses the top of my head. “None of it makes sense. Not everything does.”

“I keep seeing things.”

Dad nods. “That’s the PTSD. We all got it after the war—those of us who made it home alive.”

I tilt my head back and talk to the ceiling. “I need a shirt that says ‘I survived a mass shooting and all I got was this dumb PTSD.’ ”

Alexis smiles. “Good to see you’re still in there.”

Dad takes off his cap and tousles his frosted, sandy-blond hair. “I may not be good for much. But I’ve seen my friends killed. I’ve dealt with the guilt, the flashbacks and shit. My advice to you is to stick with the others. No one knows it like them. They’ll help see you through.”

I reach for Alexis’s hand and give it a squeeze. “We’ve gotta go to Christy’s tonight. I couldn’t get us out of it.”

Alexis nods. “That’s fine. I’m not here on vacation. I’m here for you.”

FIREWORKS

The pale yellow ranch with white trim looks exactly like the house Christy dreamed of as a child. She drew it over and over, sitting outside her trailer while her mom sat on a fraying chair drinking cans of Bud Light and smoking cigarettes to the nub.

Colorful flowers outline the lawn. We walk past a mini sun-bleached pink convertible, its door open from what looks like a fast getaway. A tan lounger you'd find by a pool sits under a yellow sun umbrella. New age music seeps through the window on the right. I knock on the door, pause, and ring the bell.

The white door flies open. Christy throws her arms around us both at once. "Thanks so much for coming!" Holding Alexis by the upper arm, she says, "Welcome to Bixby! It's so nice to meet you."

Alexis hands her a bottle of rosé. "I feel like I'm intruding."

"Nonsense!" She ushers us in. "Make yourselves at home. I'll be back with the cookies."

"Nice skirt," Alexis calls as Christy walks away. The teal gauze sways to a stop.

"Thanks!" Christy flashes a smile. "We sell 'em at the yoga studio. Come on by." Her head tics to the left. "We'll get you one."

I suck on the insides of my cheeks, wishing I'd never agreed to this. It feels like a regular house party in an alternate reality.

We move into a dimly lit room with shaded lamps and flickering gardenia-scented candles. Jars of wildflowers are scattered about. There's a wood-framed amateur painting of Jesus above the mantle, and I struggle not to laugh. It reminds me of that hilariously botched restoration in Spain a year or two ago.

A tall Black man rises with his hand outstretched. "Jacob." His voice is surprisingly deep for someone with such a soft, boyish face.

"Lucy. Nice to meet you."

"Alexis."

Jacob cocks his head with surprise. "I thought it was just three."

"Alexis is my girlfriend from San Francisco."

His lips morph into an awkward smile, and he sits back down. "How nice."

From her seat, Donna nods. "Nice to meet you, Alexis. Lucy. Glad to see you under better circumstances."

"This is weird, right?" I lean on one leg, sweeping a hand to the side.

Donna blinks slowly and nods. "Thank the Lord for keeping us safe."

Christy enters the room with two empty glasses in one hand and a tray of freshly baked cookies in the other. "I'm a devout believer in Christ, but this girl right here's the one who saved us." After placing everything down on the wooden chest in the center of the room, she rubs my back. "She dragged me out from the chaos. I'd never have made it without her."

My eyes dodge contact with the others. "It was luck."

"I don't believe in luck," says Jacob.

Christy motions to the couch. "Sit down. Help yourselves to whatever."

As I pour two hefty glasses of wine, I'm aware of Jacob's watchful eye. I pull a small twig of grapes off the bunch and feed one to Alexis.

Footsteps come thundering down the stairs, and a White

man with a chiseled jaw and bulging upper body enters the room. "She's out like a light," he tells Christy. Noticing us on the couch, he leans in, holding out his hand. "I'm Mike. You must be the gays from San Fran." Christy whacks him on the tricep, her eyes wide and glaring. Mike retracts his arm and asks, "Was that a bad thing to say?"

"It's nothing I'm ashamed of," I tell him.

"I love gays—especially pretty ones," Mike says.

Christy rolls her eyes and sits down. "Michael . . ."

"It's all right," I tell her. "I love me some good-looking heteros."

A few chuckles release some of the tension from the room.

"I'm just glad you all came—the gays and the Blacks," Christy says giddily, to a dumbfounded room, before bowing her head in shame.

"I'm offended you left out Asian," I joke.

Her face squinches. "Well, pardon the awkward start. I'm so glad you came. When I woke up this morning, I felt thankful to be alive. Hugged my girl. Made love to my man." Donna and I exchange a quick, horrified glance. "Then I prayed. God told me to have you all here. That's why I called—in His name."

"Praise the Lord," commands Jacob.

"Praise Him," says Donna.

Christy says, "Is it any coincidence that the three of us survived by hiding in that same old spot? God brought us back together."

"But wouldn't that mean God left the others to die?" I ask.

"That would've been the Devil," says Donna.

"Cool," I say. "Blame my nemesis for all the bad things I do."

Jacob clears his throat. "Has anyone heard anything about the shooter?"

"He's nowhere to be found," says Mike. "One of my buddies

in the BPD said he wasn't among the rest."

"I feel like we shouldn't say 'the rest.' " Our eyes connect. "It's like lumping him in with the people he murdered."

Mike nods. "Fair point."

Alexis uncrosses her legs and leans forward. "He didn't shoot himself at the end?"

"At least not at the school," Mike says.

Christy gathers her wavy blond locks to the right. "How can you live with yourself after something like that?"

Heads shake and mouths move in silence.

"Just trust the cops now," says Mike, giving us a confident nod. "They'll get to the bottom of this."

"Pfft." Donna turns her head and glares out the window. "They made me feel like a suspect."

"No!" Christy says with a gasp. "They couldn't have!"

"Asking me whether I got along with everybody, as if maybe I had some twenty-year gripe."

"You must have misunderstood," insists Christy. "They can't think you had anything to do with it. You were with us!"

Donna sighs. "Did they ask either of you how well you got on with the others?"

"No . . ."

"Nope."

"Well, see? They singled me out—after all my daddy's done for this town. He practically built that whole station. And Bixby High? He gave them plenty, too, but you never saw so much as a room with his name."

"Your family's given a lot." I nod. "They still in Bixby?"

"Retired to Florida."

"Well, I wouldn't be so quick to make it a race thing," Mike interjects. "Maybe they just didn't know who you were or who your father was. You said he's in Florida."

Donna's volume goes up a decibel, but she stays controlled. "We're the one Black family to have ever lived in Bixby—in my lifetime, anyway. We moved here when I was in diapers. He knows who I am."

Christy jumps in. "This kind of thing doesn't happen here. They don't know what to make of it. The biggest scandal was when that farmer mistook his own daughter for a thief and shot her as she sneaked back in. Remember that? All the real crime happens down in the city. Not here at home."

"Can't say that now," I tell her.

"Guess not."

"In the city, where all the Black people live." Donna groans.

"I didn't mean it like that," says Christy.

Donna nods, unconvinced.

"At my church in the city, I preach about loving thy neighbor—no matter what color he or she happens to be," says Jacob. "We're tolerant of other religions, too. What matters is that someone's got God in his heart."

"Is this a bad time to mention I'm atheist?" I smile awkwardly. "How does your church feel about queers?"

Jacob readjusts his seat. "We believe you deserve to be saved, too. You seem like good people. I'd open my church to you both if you ever come down."

Alexis and I exchange wide-eyed looks. "Saved from our queerdom?" I ask. "I wonder . . . Who's worse? A non-murderous queer atheist or a hetero believer who shoots up a school?"

"I mean saved as in we all deserve saving," Jacob clarifies.

"We don't know that the shooter was Christian," says Christy.

"Or hetero," adds Donna.

"I'm just curious—in the eyes of God—who's worse: atheist queers or Christian killers?"

"Well, I can't speak for God," says Jacob. He chuckles

nervously. "All I'm trying to say is that now, more than ever, we should set aside our differences and come together. We need love in this world."

"Hear, hear. I can get behind that." Christy nods and takes a big gulp of wine.

"Tell that to a certain presidential candidate," mutters Alexis.

Christy's hand rests on Alexis's forearm. She leans in. "He's not so bad. Don't listen to all that nonsense. Give him a chance. You'll see." She nods cheerily.

Bang! Bang! Bang!

The room freezes.

Bang! Bang! Bang! Bang! Bang!

Wine spills as we crash to the floor. My heart beats through my chest.

Mike rises to his feet and approaches the window.

Christy shrieks, "Get down, Mike! Get away from the window!"

Donna mouths a silent prayer.

"It's okay," reports Mike. "It's just fireworks. Tomorrow's the Fourth."

"Are you sure?" squeaks Alexis.

"Sure as I'm standing."

Everyone finds their way back to their seat.

"Fucking hell," I grumble.

Jacob looks to Donna. "You okay, babe?" Donna looks ill, but she nods. "How's everyone else doing?"

"Not great," remarks Christy.

Alexis asks, "There was only one shooter, right?"

"As far as I could tell," says Donna.

"I only remember bullets coming from one direction," I say.

"Who do you think it could be?" asks Mike. "Some nut from the city?"

"Why again with the city?" says Donna.

Mike shrugs. "The gun—was it a semi-automatic?"

"I don't know much about guns," I admit, "but the bullets fired fast and steady like a shootout in movies."

"Probably an AR-15 or AK-47," says Mike with a nod of pride.

"Who'd want to kill so many people?" asks Christy.

Donna says, "Someone ungodly, anyhow."

My eyes find hers. "Ungodly?"

"Most of us were Christians—one form or another."

"It was probably the Muslims," says Mike. "From the city, like I said."

Jacob shakes his head. "The bulk of mass shooters are White. Either disgruntled or mentally and spiritually ill."

"Let's not make this about race now," blurts Mike.

"When you say Muslims, I don't think you mean the White ones," Jacob replies. "I'm just saying the crime, well . . . It's no secret that these shootings tend to be by White men."

"Except that one Asian," I say before anyone else can.

"Hey—why weren't you there?" Mike sharpens his eyes on Jacob. "You stayed home, didn't you?"

Donna jumps in. "What does that have to do with anything?"

Mike shrugs. "I just want to know."

"Donna asked me not to, so I stayed home and looked after our boys."

"Why didn't you want him there, Donna? He's a good-looking man. And a pastor, no less," says Mike.

"I . . . well . . ." Donna looks flustered.

"Christy says you hated the class."

"Mike . . ." pleads Christy. "It's not necessary."

Mike paces the room. "I think it is."

Donna sighs. "It's true. I wasn't fond of the class. Wouldn't have gone if we weren't back to sell the old house, but I guess I was curious. They treated me terribly when I was a kid. I was either invisible or too visible. I wasn't sure how they'd react— how I'd react. And anyway, I didn't want my husband there for it. Even an apology can be humiliating."

"Yeah. I get it," I tell her. "I didn't want Alexis there, either."

"Or," Mike says, stopping in his tracks, "maybe you'd planned to have everyone killed and didn't want your husband to get shot. No one appreciated your daddy. Right?"

"This is getting out of hand." I shake my head, rising. "Donna—you don't have to listen to this."

"Come on, baby. Let's go." Jacob helps his wife to her feet, but she subtly shakes him off and stands on her own.

"I'm sorry." Christy rises, too.

"You're sorry?" Mike shouts, not settling down. "Didn't you tell me she almost didn't let you and Lucy in the closet? And how'd she get such a head start? She planned this! How clear does it have to be? She wanted revenge! She's looked uncomfortable here all night!"

"We just survived a massacre," I remind him. "How are we supposed to look?"

"And where were you, Mike?" Jacob steps up. "I heard you weren't there, neither."

"Oh, don't give me that!" Mike scoffs. "I defend my country. I've saved more lives than you've saved souls."

"I'm just saying," Jacob continues, closing in another inch, "you fit the demographic better than she. So if you want to go around pointing fingers, I suggest you give it more thought."

"Is that a threat?"

"Nah, I don't do threats. I believe in peace, not war."

"Yeah?" Mike tightens his fists and spits, "Well, peace ain't free. Don't forget who's out there putting their lives on the line as you stand within your safe walls and preach."

"Donna, Jacob—let's go," I plead. "Nothing good will come of this."

Jacob nods to Christy and says, "I appreciate your hospitality, ma'am."

"I'm sorry," she repeats, shaking her head.

We file out the front door.

Bang! Bang! Bang!

I tug Alexis to the grass. Jacob jumps in front of Donna, pushing her into the bush. A moment later, we realize it's the fireworks again.

We climb into our cars without speaking. Christy waves apologetically from the steps, but no one waves back.

LIFE GOES ON

Sometimes it's hard to tell the difference between wanting closure and wanting someone to blame. The ones who are honest might admit to the latter, while the rest rush to force the former.

I imagine the shooter lurking behind what he presents to the world when he's shopping among us, living and breathing among us. Although no one's said it, the scariest thing about him is he's likely one of us. And so, in the same way that people tend to draw Jesus and Santa like themselves, they paint the bad guys as foreign. I suppose I'm not above it, but I have no choice since there's no one here like me.

When Alexis showers, I busy myself with my phone. One of the reunion non-attendees from our graduating class has created a Facebook group called I Reach Out to You. I take a quick glance at the page. Upon invitation, I was automatically added. Half the deceased show as joined. It's unsettling. I close the app, not ready for it.

I shudder at the realization that my hometown will forever be known as the site of The Reunion Massacre. They keep finding another person who wasn't there and putting their face above the chyron. Each willing Bixby resident goes on about how awful and frightening it is, but they don't know the half of it. The reporters on TV speak in grave tones, but their removal shines through their unchanged faces.

The papers report the terror as if it's something the whole town owns—but only Donna, Christy, and I truly know what it's like to survive it. I resent them for using it as an item of interest, sandwiching it between the ridiculous and the mundane: "Who raised the fattest swine?" and "Another petty theft occurred at the gas station over by the highway."

It's been twenty years since I knew the victims, and we never truly connected, but they were there for half my life. Shouldn't I feel something? Or is it like before? Instead of letting my next thought materialize, I shut it down and file it away.

Sucking on the insides of my cheeks, I stew in the knowledge that the worst of the worst can happen, and like it or not, life goes on. It's cruel and unfair. In the midst of the terror, you beg to survive, not fully grasping that the life you had is already gone.

JUST LIKE OLD TIMES

The summer concoction of freshly cut grass and barbecue smoke fills the air. Dad's in the yard, manning the grill in a white polo and navy shorts. His thick hair is combed and secured neatly to the right. He cracks open a can of Bud Light.

Mom's in a navy-blue sundress, white belt, and red hair scarf. After admiring Alexis's dress, her face doesn't hide her disappointment when she glances in my direction. "Is that what you're wearing? Your father didn't risk life and limb for you to be disrespectful."

I'm wearing a black tank with black shorts. I've never been the festive type or the doll she hoped to dress. I tap the blue-and-silver necklace on my chest. "A splash of color," I joke.

"Well, I guess you're in mourning." She sighs. "Go on outside, and I'll bring out some vodka lemonades." When she does, they're adorned with raspberries and blueberries on a miniature USA umbrella, of course.

Dad slides his aviators down his nose. "Didja get a good sleep?"

I lean back and stretch in my chair. "I don't think I'll sleep through the night again."

"Give it time." He nods, nudging his glasses back up. "Going up against death like that and seeing it all around you. It heals on its own time—not yours."

He's never mentioned grief or the deaths he's witnessed till now. He's never spoken about much with this level of realness. It may be the first time either of us has understood a thing about the other.

"Officer Brown brought the car back this morning," he continues. "Said it was all clear. They're working overtime to get things back to people."

"Good to hear." I scoop a wad of hummus onto a pretzel. "We're heading back on Wednesday. I called the detective to let him know."

"Are they any closer to finding him?" Mom places a fruit platter that's arranged into an intricate fireworks pattern on the table.

"I don't think so."

She tweaks a few berries and melons that shifted. "Sure you don't want to stick around for the services?"

"You couldn't pay me to stay. All the questions, the stares, the pity . . ."

"They're canceling the fireworks and parade out of respect for the families," Mom says.

Alexis smooths the front of her blue polka-dot dress and kicks up her white ankle boots. "Some kids were playing with fireworks last night. It was awful," she tells my parents.

"I'm sure you'll hear more tonight," says Dad. "They can't stop all the fun."

I grab one of Mom's cocktails. "I thought it was the shooter coming to finish us off."

"Oh, honey!" cries Mom. "Maybe it's best you head back after all. I don't like that on top of all you went through, you still have to worry."

I take a sip of my vodka lemonade. Mom makes her cocktails strong. I feel the muscles in my back instantly relax. "Testing out our new PTSD, just to see if it works," I say.

"There's nothing funny about PTSD," Mom scolds.

"Yeah, I know. But sometimes when things feel so bad, you've just gotta laugh."

"Amen to that." Dad raises his beer before taking a swig.

Just as I'm about to comment on the amount of food Dad's piling up by the grill, Donna and her family enter the yard. "What the . . ." I trail off.

"Oh, I didn't mention?" Mom adjusts her hair. "Christy called this morning."

Donna's face flushes upon seeing mine. "Uh . . . Is this a bad time?"

"Not at all! Have a seat—all of you," demands Mom. "Nice to meet you, Jacob. I've known Donna since she was a child. You look gorgeous, Donna. And who are these handsome fellas?"

I glare at Alexis while my parents fuss over the children. "I can't believe this," I mouth as we rise to meet Donna's boys— one a few inches taller than the other. They're decked out in blue-and-white pinstripe shorts with white shirts and red bow ties.

"I'm sorry. Christy never said—" Donna begins.

"It's cool," I tell her. "It's just a surprise. Your boys are so cute!"

"Thank you." Donna's wearing a red wrap dress. Her thick braids are delicately gathered at the top of her head. She points to each of her sons. "Jalen and Jamal. They're my heart and my soul right there. My everything."

Jacob, wearing a red-and-white gingham shirt, exaggerat-edly clears his throat. Donna pulls him near, gazing up at him adoringly.

"Are you gonna be okay when Mike shows?" My eyes switch between the two of them. "I'm assuming he's coming."

"He doesn't scare me," says Donna, but her shiver insinuates otherwise.

"He sure pissed me off. I can't imagine how you felt."

Shaking her head slowly, Donna confesses, "He got my blood boiling, all right. I had some un-Christian-like thoughts. But thinking on it later, I realized his fears got the best of him."

"Hey there," sings Christy, bursting with charm. Mike and Sophie trail behind. "Thanks so much for the invite, Mrs. B."

"Why, you look as pretty as ever," Mom says, beaming and gushing over Christy's white dress with a red cherry print. Sophie's dress is a replica of her mother's. "And the little one's the spittin' image of you! What an angel."

Donna nudges Christy. "You didn't say it was an ambush."

"What? Oh . . ." Christy glances at me as if caught. "I just felt so terrible after last night. I didn't want that to be our last conversation—with Lucy heading home soon and all."

Mike approaches Donna and lifts her hands in his. "My apologies to you and Jacob. I shouldn't have come at you like that. My emotions have been running on overdrive."

Jacob steps in to put a hand on Mike's shoulder. "Brother, all our emotions have been high."

"I appreciate your apology," says Donna.

"You know, I prepare for combat, but this was too close to home. Not knowing how to keep my wife and daughter safe . . ."

"I understand," says Jacob. "All every man wants is to keep his family safe."

"As a soldier, I feel like I failed."

As I'm studying Mike—because I still don't trust him— Christy slaps my back, spilling half my drink. "Well, it's a good thing we had Lucy." She glances down at the spillage. "Whoops!"

"It's okay." I wipe my wet hand on my shorts.

"She must've gotten her survival skills from you, Henry." Christy helps herself to a cocktail.

Dad's face lights up as he nods to Christy—who, if I heard right, just called him Henry.

32

The kids play on my old swing set across the yard that's likely waiting for my nonexistent offspring. Mom's eyes dart from me and Alexis to the kids. She smiles and looks away.

Dad pops the cooler open and announces, "Help yourselves to a cold one."

"Oh, I've got another pitcher in the fridge!" Mom rushes inside.

As I bite into a portabella burger, my eyes scan the scene. Never in a million years would I have imagined seeing my childhood friends and their families together while my girlfriend sits by my side.

"Penny for your thoughts," begs Christy.

I take a sip and remark, "The one Black, the one Asian, and the one White girl in Bixby who could stand them. Here we are after all those years."

"Who'd have thunk it?" Christy giggles, a smidge of red lipstick on her teeth.

"Not me," says Donna, deadpan.

I tilt my head towards her. "Can't believe you moved back."

"It's just temporary, thank the Lord."

"Why?" Christy asks. "What's wrong with Bixby?"

Donna and I peer at each other, feeling the weight of what neither of us is sure how to say.

"Oh, nothing." As I take another sip, I mumble into my glass. "If you're a straight, White Christian."

Donna adds, "And even two out of three is still bad!"

I nearly spit out my drink.

"What's so funny?" asks Jalen, running towards his mother for a hug.

"Oh, just grown-up talk," she tells him. "Here, let me pour you some juice."

RED VELVET

Bixby High's decked out like a cream puff pie in a bake-off at the county fair. From an aerial view, I see myself standing awkwardly in the middle of the gymnasium before Ben approaches. I can't take my eyes off the intricate design of his beard; it resembles Victorian wallpaper.

"Of course, we moved to the city," he assures me, surveying the room with a look of pity. His voice lowers as he squints. "I mean, can you imagine? These people never left! This is all they know—all they'll ever know."

I'm half listening while half thinking of aborting the conversation for that red velvet cupcake on display by the punch. I should've grabbed it when I walked in. I focus back on Ben, who's casually tugging at his bamboo earring. The left side of his face explodes. His fingers erupt, and his body goes limp as he falls to the floor.

Time freezes. I point my fingers towards the bodies. With a snap, time rewinds, and they heal back to life. They lift back upright, unaffected. The shooter backs out of the room. The Goo Goo Dolls carry on singing "Name." People are laughing and telling tales, unaware they've been spared.

Ben continues with his pomp and pity, but this time I walk off. He may be offended, but at least he's alive.

I saunter over to the long table of decadent treats. Taking the red velvet cupcake between my thumb and middle finger, I close my eyes and sink my teeth into that beautiful mound of bliss.

Eric Clapton fades in, singing about changing the world. I

think it's just fine as it is.

NOT TODAY

I feel like a ghost trapped in Purgatory. Waiting. Waiting to really be dead.

Alexis reaches for my hand as we walk into town. When I give it to her, a warm rush of shame washes over me. She swings our hands freely, as if we're a couple of schoolgirls at recess. I'm mad at myself for feeling how I told myself I'd never feel again.

She asks, "You all right?"

"As good as I can be."

Alexis was raised in the Bay Area of California, which, although imperfect, is notably more progressive than the rest of the country. She never even had to come out. Her parents claimed to know she was queer before she did. They had queer and nonbinary friends whose presence was normalizing. There were a few uncomfortable occasions, but she's never lived anywhere like Bixby.

A red pickup truck slows down, and a couple of hometown boys whistle out the window. My shoulders stiffen. Alexis waves, not making anything of it.

Entering Bixby's town center, she sighs. "Man. This town's even too White for me."

"Can you imagine being me growing up here?"

She widens her eyes and shakes her head. "No."

"I remember thinking Bixby was representative of the whole world. I thought even Korea would be full of White people—with a few like me sprinkled in."

"Didn't they teach you about Asia in school?"

"Barely." I think back to Miss Kirby's class. "And when they did, I clocked out. It was too weird with everyone staring, expecting me to know it already."

"Must've been a relief moving to San Francisco."

"Yeah. For once, I could do something and blame it on somebody else."

Alexis tugs my hand, swinging me around. She holds my head and kisses me as the rest of the world slips away. "To me, you'll always stand out from the crowd."

"Like a pimple on prom night." She rolls her eyes and smirks. "This is it," I announce, swiveling towards Master Pizza. "The best in Bixby."

As I reach for the door, an employee grabs the handle from inside. He turns the sign over and says, "Closed."

"But it's only twelve thirty," I say slowly, caught off guard. "It's the middle of lunchtime. Aren't you open till ten?"

"Not today." He twists the lock and walks away.

The sun bounces off the front window. I butt my head up against it, hand to my forehead so I can see inside. I huff. "Closed, my ass. Someone's placing an order."

Alexis mimics my pose. "This is discrimination." She sneers at a few tables of people who are snickering at the two of us standing there denied. One of the patrons makes a V with her fingers and wiggles her tongue through it. Alexis pounds on the window and turns away.

Before we can get our bearings, a large camera is thrust in my face. A blond man in a blue shirt asks, "Lucy Byrne! Can you tell us what it was like to be at the reunion on Saturday?"

"What?"

"The reunion. What was it like when the shooting broke out?"

The camera crew crowds around us. I wipe the sweat from

my forehead with the back of my hand, my eyes darting from the lens to the surrounding eager faces.

"It was delightful," I tell them. "What do you think?"

"Did you get a look at the shooter? Any idea who it might have been?"

I stare into the camera. "We've told the cops everything. This restaurant, Master Pizza, is homophobic. They just slammed the door in our faces—in the middle of lunch."

He ignores me. "Do you think it could've been organized by the Black girl?"

I snap. "The Black girl has a name. And Donna's a survivor, like me." I grab Alexis's hand, pushing past the crew with fury. "This town . . ."

Alexis shakes her head. "People are afraid of what they don't know—not to excuse them, of course."

"She grew up in this town. Her husband's a pastor in the nearest city. They could go to his church, make an effort. They don't know Black folks because they make a point not to."

"I hear you."

"Nothing changes around here." I huff. "No matter what."

Alexis bites her lower lip. "I'm with you. People make decisions based on race all the time. It's disgusting. But this thing about Donna . . ."

"What thing about Donna?"

"How well do you know her now? How do you trust her if, as you said, you lost touch?"

I take a deep breath, count to five, and exhale through my nose. I want to pick something up and throw it into the road. Instead, I place my hands in my pockets and take two more breaths. "You could say the same thing about Christy—or anyone else in this town. Donna's never been violent. Not even when she had a right to be for self-defense."

"Well, it's a popular theme: The underdog comes back seeking revenge when they're bigger and stronger."

"Donna couldn't orchestrate a slaughter."

"Yeah," she mutters. "It's just . . . Something's off."

"We're all off. We survived a near-death experience. We saw people we know get killed."

"You know it has nothing to do with her being Black," Alexis says. But her eyes don't find mine. "It's just—she didn't want to open the door? And Christy doesn't seem quite as off."

"Oh my God," I moan, trying to keep it together. "Christy was never anything but celebrated around here. You have no idea what life was like for Donna. You've never stood out in your own hometown. She got beat on and teased. A lot. She probably thought if she opened the door, she'd get shot. It was a high-stress moment. People underestimate the long-term effects of bullying and being raised in racial isolation."

"See—you have a history with her." She squeezes my upper arm. "It doesn't sound like many do. She's probably glad to have someone who understands her."

Turning towards my parents' house, reaching for the maroon door of the lavender cape, I say, "Who knows? I don't think any of us feel as understood as we'd like to be."

MAKE-BELIEVE

A tart aroma swells in the air. A note on the oven door in pink ink reads: Don't Touch!

I'm in the kitchen, cooling off, throwing sandwiches together while Alexis watches the local news with Dad in the next room. Spreading mustard on bread, I sporadically peer at the TV. A man in a loose-fitting button-down shirt stands on the side of the road in the center of town. He says, "There's always been a lot of tension between Bixby alumni."

Off-screen, a woman's voice asks, "What kind of tension?"

"You know. The ones who moved away think they're better than us. And the ones who stayed either envy or fawn over them."

"Which side are you on?"

"I'm one of the poor bastards who got stuck here, right?" He grimaces. "That's what they think. But I went off to school. Came back to help build up the town. Took over the family shop right away. I want to make Bixby better for our kids. But they don't see it like that."

"How strong would you say the tension is? Enough to open fire on a high school reunion?"

"Maybe if you're already unstable." He mimes an explosion with his hands. "It'd have to be someone who left. No one who still lives here would make such a mess."

The scene cuts to the owner of Bixby Café. "Hate to say it, but it had to be one of the locals." She puffs on a cigarette behind the building. Her dyed black hair is piled into a messy bun, exposing brown roots. She leans against an unfinished picket fence, exhaling smoke through puckered red lips.

"Why's that?"

" 'Cause why would anyone come to Bixby for nothin'? We're no destination."

My father clicks off the TV. "Opinions are like assholes. Everyone's got one."

"I don't want to talk about it," I say preemptively, hoping Alexis keeps quiet about what happened in town. I don't have the energy to explain things to Dad. The conversation with Alexis was exhausting.

I hand them their plates and sit down with my own. "At least I can escape tomorrow. Donna and Christy have to stay here and listen to this."

Half of my childhood was spent dreaming of moving away. I'd had my heart set on San Francisco since middle school, knowing college was my ticket out. I'd overheard a couple of teachers talking about it disparagingly. But it sounded like a utopia to me—a place with both Asians and queers.

The image of Ben at the reunion, with his air of superiority, comes flashing back. No wonder the locals hate us. We do look down on those who've stayed. But it's hard not to when so many are bigots.

Alexis takes our empty plates. As she leaves the room, Dad smiles at me. "Nice girl." I sigh at his show of approval. "She fits here just fine."

"Well, she passes for straight and White."

Dad's tongue trips over itself. "That girl's not White?"

"She's multiracial," I say. He struggles to pick his chin off the floor. "Her mother's Irish and Filipino. Her father's Persian and Indigenous."

"Indige-what?"

"Native American. Cherokee, to be exact."

"Oh. You'd never know . . ." He shrugs before adding, "You could pass for straight, too."

I give him the side-eye. "Not White, though."

"No one cares," he scoffs. "It's not important."

"To you. That's 'cause I'm your daughter. To the rest of the country, I'm foreign."

"It's not like you're one of them girls in Vietnam who can't speak good English."

I pull my head back and crinkle my face at the absurdity of his comment. "Why would they need to speak English in Vietnam? And what has that got to do with me?"

"You know what I mean. You blend. You speak the right language and wear the right clothes."

"There's no right way. You mean the White way."

He groans. "You're just so damn hard to talk to. It's like you enjoy being offended by everything—ever since you left home."

"I'm not offended. I just think you might want to consider your words. Aexis and I will never live here. Bixby doesn't do well with our kind."

"Then why don't you just act normal when you're out in public? Do you really have to go and do your gay thing everywhere?"

"My gay thing?" I press my hand to my head and then throw it up in the air. "You want me to pretend. That's what this town—what you all beg of me. Pretend that I'm White. Pretend that I'm straight. Don't you see what's wrong with that?"

"What does it matter?" His mouth hangs open in desperation. "You'll get what you want."

"It matters because no one else has to play make-believe to be treated right."

"Your friend—the Black girl—does. How d'ya think her dad

did so well?"

I fold forward, dropping my head to my knees. "And you think that's okay?"

He shrugs. "He's rich, ain't he?"

Mom storms in with a shopping bag, twirling to shut the door behind her. She asks, "All right. Who wants ice cream with their pie?"

BUSINESS AS USUAL

A crisp breeze sweeps in through the windows. Long shadows dance across the wood floor. I drag my dangling arm onto the bed and roll on my back. I smell the salt in the air and tune in to the seagulls of Ocean Beach.

Thank fuck I'm home.

> Alexis: Have a good first day back at work. <3
>
> Me: Thanks. <3 See you Saturday for brunch.

Beyoncé sings "Sorry" through the Bluetooth speaker perched on the back of the toilet. I stand in front of the mirror with scissors, watching thick clumps fall to the floor. Sometimes the easiest thing to change is your hair. I sing along, chopping away till I'm left with a short, messy bob.

People have done stranger things to feel effective.

Bixby's all over the news, but only two people at work know it's where I'm from and that I was just there. In the halls, people comment on my hair instead of the shooting.

All I've ever wanted is to lead a normal life. As shook as I am from the shooting, I want to put it behind me, to continue living as the alter ego I worked hard to design.

Carin, the department VP, carefully approaches my office with a solemn face. "How are you doing?"

"Fine." Leaving no time for elaboration, I ask, "How are things here? Anything need recutting?"

She shakes her head. "Lucy, if you want more time off—"

"That's the last thing I want. I need to work. Keep busy."

"If you want to talk about it—"

"Thanks," I say, cutting her off again. "But I'm fine."

"Well . . . okay. We've got some fun new projects coming through. Just for kicks, we're doing a reel for National Cat Day to throw on Insta and loop in the cafeteria. No rush. We've got months. It's an in-between project, but I figured you'd want it."

"Um, yeah!"

I used to joke that I'm allergic to love because I love cats but my body won't let me near them. My office is decorated with trinkets and photos of other people's cats. The project's a dream come true.

A little later, I'm craning my neck towards the screen to perfect a transition when there's a knock on my door. Tae-Suk jumps over the armchair and lands clumsily with one leg slung over the side. "What the hell are you doing here? Shouldn't you be glued to the couch of a shrink somewhere for the next two years?"

"You didn't tell anyone, did you?" I narrow my eyes, watchful of his expression.

"Nah, I said I wouldn't. But what the fuck?"

I nod. "What the fuck, indeed."

"So, you knew all those people?"

"Most of them, yeah. A long time ago."

"They're the ones you grew up with, right?" I see his eyes searching for human qualities he can't find.

"I don't have the words. It was awful." Shaking my head, I admit, "I'm still numb from the shock of it all."

"Were you close to any of 'em?"

In my head, I scan random kids from my youth. The girl who used to tug on my hair, convinced it was a wig. The jock who mocked me whenever I walked by, saying, "Love you long time." The rest of them laughing. No one stepping in.

I hold in a breath, afraid of my own honesty. "There was always a distance between us."

He doesn't hide his judgment when he asks, "Because they were White?"

"Partly?" I lift my shoulders and bob my head to the left. "I don't know . . . It's hard to explain." Sometimes it's frustrating trying to relate to my people who were kept and never lived in racial isolation.

Tae-Suk shrugs. "All right. Want to get pizza?" In other ways, he understands me so well.

We sit on the grass along Embarcadero, eating pizza from the box. I listen to him ramble about girls on Tinder. "It's always a gamble. You know? Some won't give us a chance, no matter what. They're upfront about it. They write 'No Asians' on their profile. Not that I'd want their sorry asses anyway."

I grab a slice with a bubble. "That's obscene."

"You know, Asian men are the least desirable demographic in online hetero dating. There was an actual study." He slurps up his soda. "What's it like in the queer community?"

"Objectification can still be an issue," I tell him. "Some fetishize us, but the queer women I've met were mostly seeking deeper connections. I've heard it's worse for gay men. Lots of rice queens. Sadly, being queer doesn't guarantee being woke."

He leans back, taking in the passersby. "I'm not trying to complain, because personally I haven't had it bad." He performs his best selfie angle, hands framing his face, hamming it up. "And you and I have a certain amount of light-skin privilege. But this aversion to Asian men is a thing I've been noticing a lot lately."

"Well, if you grew up in Bixby, you'd have noticed a lot sooner. That kind of mentality is more prevalent in Whitesville."

"You're probably right." He grabs another slice.

"Nobody talks about the social racism of Asians," I say. "Not just the casual racism, but the physical violence towards men and the sexual violence against women."

"Yeah," he says. "Sometimes it seems we're the most socially acceptable group to be openly racist against." I nod. Folding a slice in half, he continues, "So, I'm gonna be real for a minute. Are you going to get help?"

"I'm doing all right." I play coy. "It was just a few days. I'll be caught up in no time."

"You know what I mean. I don't care if they were all racist pricks. You saw tens of people die. You could've died, too."

"I don't die," I joke, trying to keep it light.

Tae-Suk pulls a face. "Ooh! The Unkillable Lucy Byrne! You'll need a catchier name."

"I'm death-defying."

He gives me a skeptical look. "You say it like it's not the first time."

I shrug. "When I was a toddler."

"Oh, shit! Is this what led to your adoption?" Tae-Suk scarfs down his slice and stares attentively. Non-adopted people can be too intrigued by the lives of adoptees. Our stories can feel like entertainment. I blame comic book superheroes and Disney.

"Never mind," I say, backing off. "Just, you know . . . When we're abandoned, there's always a chance we could die before being found. We could die in the orphanage—and even at the hands of adopters." So much for keeping it light.

He asks, cautiously, "Were your parents abusive?"

"No," I stress. "My parents were . . . okay. I'm just pointing out that being adopted means I survived something before this. Many were abandoned or stolen."

"Well, anyone alive survived birth . . ."

"It's not the same." I feel myself disconnecting as I bury my growing fatigue. I work on my pizza, gazing off towards the sculpture of the giant bow and arrow.

He grabs a third slice. "My mother . . ."

I let him take the conversation on a meandering journey through human vulnerability. He's doing me a favor. He knows I'm not ready to talk, and instead of pushing, he plays along. It's one of the many reasons why I like him. But sometimes it's a bit unfulfilling.

WHEN YOU LIE

The air in Bixby hangs thick and heavy, clinging to your skin. San Franciscan air washes over you and lets you move freely. I inhale the familiar aromas of my neighborhood. Although I don't eat seafood, the smell of it brings an odd comfort as I shop local stalls. There's an artist on a ladder painting a new mural. I smile to myself, happy to witness culture and change—two things Bixby lacks.

I brush past a few White men discussing the upcoming election. They make jokes about Trump, but I'm pretty sure he's got Bixby's vote. I swallow that probability dry, in one gulp.

At a stall register, there are three different newspapers with Bixby on the front page. "Terrible thing," notes the cashier. "And they say guns aren't a problem. Try killing that many with an ax or a knife."

I freeze for a moment, struck by a montage in my brain.

"Let's just hope we elect the right person in November," he says before patting the bag.

"Of course we will," comments another in line.

"Here you go. Have a nice day." I continue to stare at the papers, unmoving. "Here you go," he repeats.

The woman behind me places her hand on my shoulder. I jump back to the moment. "Oh! Sorry."

"It's all right." He sharpens his eyes and asks, "Hey, are you—"

I grab my things and get out of there quickly.

The wind is violent on Ocean Beach. I stare out onto the

voracious waves of the Pacific through twirling strands of hair. A handful of shiny black-suited figurines wriggle like sea lions on surfboards.

Some people hurl themselves into risky situations. Why?

I think of the plane crash survivors I've seen on TV, boasting about how every damn day post-event brims with meaning. Defying death has given them a new lease on life. I add "survivor" to the list of things I'm not good enough at being—right after gay, Asian, and adopted.

A one-armed child walks by with his dad. A ghost of him falls to the sand, bleeding from the shoulder. People are falling everywhere. My heart thumps, and my head fills with dread.

Stepping back, real life resumes. Horrified by myself, I peer around, hoping no one misconstrued my reaction. I revisit that "I survived a mass shooting" shirt idea.

The waves are relentless with their dangerous beauty. I'm mesmerized by their recklessness.

Somehow, I find myself thinking of Christy's husband. I understand why Donna didn't bring Jacob—but for Christy to not bring Mike? It's strange, and we never heard the reason. I rise, brushing sand from my jeans and shaking it from my hair.

Across from the shore, there's an overpriced bar and grill that I've never set foot in. I decide today's the day. Sliding onto the thickly glazed wooden stool, I say, "Tito's, tonic, and lemon." I scan faces around the room, wondering what's tucked behind their pleasant facades. What makes them real?

A pink-haired White woman sidles up to the stool on my left and sits. She leans in with the ease of a bestie and whispers, "What are you—some kind of artist or writer?"

"No." I tilt my head. "Why do you ask?"

"You look at people like you're studying them."

I shrug. "I wonder about other lives sometimes."

She drops her hand to my thigh. There's a certain energy vibrating through her round blue eyes that's both unsettling and captivating. She wiggles her shoulders. "I've got a life for ya, then. Bet you'd never guess by looking at me." She pats her pale pink pixie cut down the right side.

There's the failing whistle of a small straw sucking the last bit of air from the bottom of a glass. I raise my hand and nod to the bartender for another.

Turning towards the woman, I give in. "Fine. I'll bite."

Pleased to have the floor, she crosses her legs and leans against the bar. "Saw my father shoot my mother dead and blow a big chunk of his own head off. I was eight years old. My older brother became overprotective. When we got into a nice foster home, there was this other boy who liked the idea of having a new sister. So, in his own fucked-up way . . . my real brother starts touching me—said it gave us a special bond. He went to juvie a few years later when he got caught trying to burn the place down. But he was all the family I had. I couldn't just stop loving him."

She talks as if what she's saying is run-of-the-mill, no-big-deal conversation. I want to shift my eyes elsewhere but can't. She chatters on. "It gutted me—having him torn from me like that. So I ran. I survived, using men for money. Didn't know it was prostitution. Thought I was the one making off with the better deal, but an undercover decided it was child trafficking." She shrugs. "I was returned to my foster home a year later. They hooked me up with a doc. Somewhere along the way, something clicked. I learned to forgive my brother, myself . . . Went to college, got a job, met a man, got married, had a family of my own. I did all the right things. Then I realized I didn't really like men. I just didn't know there was any other way." She gives a comical shrug. "So now here I am, a middle-aged queer telling my life story to a good-looking stranger."

Sucking the air from the bottom of another drink, I shake my head and say, "You weren't kidding. Sure you're not the writer?"

She cackles, whacking me on the shoulder. "I wasn't blessed with creative genes, I'm afraid. I've got other talents." She winks.

"I don't know what's more fucked-up: your story, or that you just told it to a stranger at a bar."

She thrusts out a hand. "Hi, I'm Lynnette. There. A stranger no more."

"Well, Lynnette." I shake her hand and nod to the bartender for another drink. My eyes shift back to her. "A few moments ago I was looking around, wondering what kind of stories people hide. Never in a million years would I have guessed what you shared as their collective experience." She cackles gregariously. "You should sell your story to Hollywood," I say. "Bet you'd make millions." I grab my drink from the bartender's hand.

"Maybe I already have." Lynnette winks and smirks.

Sucking down another vodka tonic, I can't help but note her aptitude for winking. "Well then, what the hell am I doing buying my own drinks?" I ask, giving an exaggerated wink. She thinks it's a riot.

"Bartender!" Lynnette slams her palm on the bar. People swivel to look and quickly turn away. "Give me two of what this lovely lady is having! And keep 'em coming!"

"Did you really sell your story?"

"Yes, ma'am. I'm not good at anything creative. Someone else is writing it. Just happened to meet a gal in LA six or so months back. Told her my story just like I did you. As luck would have it, she's an agent. Said she could make me rich if I was fine with her taking a cut. Got an advance in no time. If the film does well, I'll be cashing royalties."

"Oh yeah?" My eyes narrow skeptically. "Who's going to

play you?"

"Jennifer Lawrence, I hope." She winks again.

"Well, I wish you the utmost success," I slur, clinking my glass to hers before sucking it dry.

After a couple of more laughs and drinks, Lynnette pushes my shoulder, swiveling me to face her. "Well, I told you mine. Now you tell me yours."

The room slowly unravels. I blink, trying to steady my vision. "There's not much to tell." I've enjoyed being an uncomplicated, unpitiable stranger again—if just for one night.

"Aw, come on," Lynnette pleads. "I ain't buyin' it. I may not be creative, but I'm good at reading people. You've got a story in there."

"All right. I'll tell you my biggest secret." I lean in and whisper, "I was raised as a White girl." I lean back, soaking in her confusion. "Wouldn't know it by looking at me either, would you?"

* * *

The sun reaches in through the cracks in the bedroom curtains, stabbing me between the eyes. I stretch and groan, grasping for my phone to check the time. Eleven thirty-seven. There are several missed calls and messages from Alexis. With my finger poised to call back, I see Lynnette walk into the room in a shirt and underwear. I jump, clamping a hand to my chest.

"Sweet dreams?"

"Um . . . no." My eyes shift around, searching for memories of last night.

"Damn. You were out cold." Lynnette smirks. "You should be more careful. You never know who's around and might take advantage." I cringe at her wink. It brings some of the night back—with the exception of what may have happened here.

Noting the look on my face, she adds, "Don't worry. You're safe with me."

I shake out my hair. "Good, 'cause I remember fuck all."

"What? You don't remember sucking on my clit for an hour? It was the best head of my life!"

"I thought you said . . ."

"Maybe we did. Maybe we didn't. Guess you'll never know." Lynnette snickers. "All right, we didn't. Happy? Shit. You're not nearly as fun as you look." The intercom buzzes. "Ooh! Did you order breakfast?"

"Shit . . ."

Alexis: At your door.

"Fuck." I groan. "It's my girlfriend."

"Um . . . You have a girlfriend?"

"Not for long if she finds you here."

Alexis: Seriously? You're not letting me in?

Lynnette heads for the window. "I'll see if she's still down there."

"No!" I stifle a shout, tugging her shirt and shooting her the look of death. "Look—I don't know what happened last night, and I'm sorry if I led you on. But don't fuck with my life. I'm going through some shit and drank more than I should have."

She rubs my shoulder. "Okay. Just let her go. You can come up with a good excuse later. But it might feel better if you tell me your troubles. People always come to me with their troubles. Go on."

I fight back tears. I don't want to break down in front of anyone, let alone this annoying stranger. "My grandmother died. I found out yesterday before we met." I've never met any of my grandmothers.

"Aw, honey . . . Was it natural causes? How old?"

"Ninety-three. In her sleep."

"That's a good age. And a good death. My maternal grandma was hit by a bus while crossing the road. I shit you not. Thank God I didn't see that one. She was only sixty-seven. My paternal grandma—who knows if she's still above ground. If there's a God, she'd have suffered long and hard. She used to beat on my daddy when he was a boy—probably why he turned out as he did. Families, eh? Feel lucky she died peacefully and lived a long life. It's all any of us can hope for, really. When I go, I hope it's in my sleep. If I get sick, I'm gonna seek out some heroin or something. Just ease my way out of this plane on a great big high . . ." She holds out her arms and nods, looking proud.

On the one hand, I wish Lynnette would stop talking. But on the other, I'm killing time, hoping Alexis will leave so I can send Lynnette packing. "People come to you with their problems, eh?"

"I'm an empath, dear Lucy. It's a blessing and a curse. They see that I care. Knowing I've been through the worst, they tend to trust me."

I bite my tongue and nod. "Mm-hmm."

"So why don't you cut the shit and tell me what you're hiding."

"Hiding?" I roll my eyes. "You're delusional."

"It's called a sixth sense. I could work as a psychic, but I'm not one to capitalize on others' brokenness."

I purse my lips, skeptical.

Alexis: Whatever. I just hope you're okay.

I shift my gaze from the phone to the self-proclaimed empathic psychic. "So, why don't you tell me what I'm hiding, if you know so much?"

Lynnette jumps onto the bed. When our crossed legs touch at the knees, I inch back. She closes her eyes for a moment, palms up—as if conjuring a higher spirit. When she opens her eyes, she says, "You've been through something big—real big. Maybe you're a plane crash survivor. You've got feelings of guilt and anger dancing in there. I see it in your aura."

Forcing a laugh, I shake my head. "Nope. But that makes for a more interesting story. And you said you weren't creative!"

Then, deadpan, she states, "When you lie, your aura goes black."

It takes a few beats to recover. "Okay. You're creeping me out."

"Now, that was the truth." She smiles. "Keep going."

"What do you want from me? I've got nothing."

Lynnette closes her eyes tightly. "I see a lot of dead bodies around you."

Leaping up, I say, "All right, time to go. This isn't for me." I lean against the window, resting lightly on the sill. "Come on. Up. Out." I flap my hands through the air.

Lynnette tiredly pushes herself to stand, looking smug. She elongates her stretch. "Okay, honey. I'm going. Hold your titties. Sheesh! Guess I hit a right nerve." With no hurry, she dresses and collects her things.

I rest my head in my hands, leaning elbows on knees.

"You should consider how lucky you are," she says. "I don't know the story, of course. I just see what comes to me. It doesn't always make sense right away. But look at you—you're alive and unscathed. I mean, I could go wallow for years over what happened with my family, but what kind of life would that leave me? Might as well follow in my daddy's footsteps if that's all I'm good for!" She makes a finger gun. "Pow!"

I shake my head and shift my eyes with feigned ennui. I

clench my muscles to keep from looking as disturbed as I feel. "I don't know how these powers of yours are supposed to work, but they're wrong."

Lynnette stops at the front door and looks back with a smirk. "Oh, honey . . . I hope one day you step out of denial." From the other side of the threshold, she peers back in and adds, "I had fun licking your vaj. But I won't tell nobody."

I slam the door in her winking face.

THE HERO, THE STAR, & THE SUSPECT

A text comes in from an unknown number.

> Hi. It's Donna. The cops found my purse and my phone. Got your number from your folks.
>
> Me: Hey. Glad you got your stuff back. How are you doing?
>
> Donna: Been reeling but pushing through. You?
>
> Me: Same.
>
> Donna: Thought you might want to see this.

I click on the link and see a close-up of Christy's face. The camera zooms out to show her seated at a forty-five-degree angle from a talk show host. Christy's yellow dress matches her hair, and its bluebell pattern brings out her eyes.

"I just kept thinking of my little girl," she says, weeping and daintily dabbing a tissue to her eyes. "She's all I ever wanted. I grew up without a father . . . Couldn't bear to think of her growing up without her mom."

The video cuts to a photograph of Sophie holding a messy bouquet of wildflowers to her chin. The audience releases a synchronized "Aw."

The host lifts a "Choose Happy" mug from the table between them. She holds it to her chest. "What else went through your mind as the bullets fired off?"

"I couldn't think clearly, you know? A part of me couldn't accept what was happening. I had on these cute shoes I spent way too much on." Christy's face eases into a smile as she looks around at the knowing nods of other women. "I was cursing myself for buying them, since the money could've been better spent. Don't know why I went there. Guess I was in shock. Lucy had a clear head, though. She made me kick 'em off. They were tracking blood. I told her to go on ahead, but she wouldn't."

"Tell me more about Lucy. Was she a close friend?"

Christy straightens her spine. "We were best friends when we were small, and we stayed close through sophomore year. And then she got into taking pictures, and I got into cheering. We sort of grew apart, but there were no hard feelings." Her breath goes unsteady. "She saw me crouched down behind a table, reached out her hand, and dragged me out. She saved my life." She dabs her eyes again.

The camera zooms in on my senior yearbook picture. I cringe at my unkempt brows and awkward smile. The sheen on my face is unflattering. Some appointed amateur took that picture behind a curtain in the hallway after gym class; I couldn't afford to get it professionally done.

"There she is," says Christy. "She's prettier now. She looks a little less Asian."

What the what?

"Goes to show you never know what a hero looks like," says the host, flashing a big, cheesy grin.

My face is on fire.

The host continues. "There's a hero among us, everywhere we go. Who knows? Maybe it's you."

I drop my phone to the coffee table. The thoughts in my head are kaleidoscopic. I rub my eyes and pick the phone back up.

> Me: WTF? > <
>
> Donna: That's our girl.
>
> Me: That was wrong on so many levels!
>
> Donna: Christy's the star. At least you're the hero. All I get are rumors and hate mail.

Me: Hate mail?

Donna: Up to 5 now. Death threats included. We've sent the boys to their aunt's in Chicago.

Me: I'm sorry . . .

Donna: It wasn't you, was it?

Me: No!

Donna: Then no need to be sorry. It's just how it goes.

Me: People suck.

Donna: Some truly do.

Me: You gonna tell the cops?

Donna: I'm a suspect according to Bixby at large. Remember?

Me: Speaking of suspects, what do you think about Mike?

Donna: Yeah, I've thought of that, too. He's the one who asked who we thought it might've been . . . and was so quick to pin it on me.

Me: And he's got a temper and plenty of access to those kinds of guns . . .

Donna: Yep. But I don't know . . . I won't rule him out, but like, what was his motive? He and Christy seem tight.

Me: Yeah . . . true.

Donna: We hopefully won't be here much longer. Nearly done with the minor fixes.

Me: Will you move back to Chicago?

Donna: Nah. Somewhere near Jacob's new church.

Me: Why are you selling it, anyway?

Donna: Daddy gave it to me, but there's no way I'd raise my boys here. Jacob didn't want to take it at all. It took two months to convince him. Had he listened sooner, maybe it'd have sold before the reunion.

Me: Oof. Imagine the guilt he'd have, had you not survived?

Donna: And on that cheery note, good night. Jacob's got the boys on FaceTime.

Me: Good night. Thanks for reaching out.

I grab my vape and inhale the sour terpenes. Leaning out the living room window, I let my exhaled smoke float over the people and dogs trotting by.

I wonder what life might have been had I been adopted to San Francisco.

UNCOMFORTABLE TRUTHS

The firepits cast a warm glow along the rear wall of the beer garden. I slide back on the oversized wooden chair, gazing up at the darkening Oakland sky. The single thing I miss about Bixby is the way the nights preserve the day's sun. Out west, sunset brings a chill.

Sipping on a hoppy local brew, I watch Alexis's figure approach. I move in for a hug, praying I don't fuck things up any worse. She half-heartedly taps my back before slipping into the seat beside me and staring absently into the fire.

I hand her a menu. "Why don't you order before we get talking."

Once the server's come and gone, Alexis sighs. "So?"

"I have some explaining to do. I don't think you're going to like what I have to say, but I owe you at least that much."

She twists her hair into a side braid. It's a nervous habit I don't think she's aware of.

"I had a few too many drinks the other night. Escapism. Predictable. I'm not proud or looking for pity."

She shrugs. "You won't get it from me."

"So, I met this rabid woman at a bar—the one across from Ocean Beach." Her widening eyes tell me to stop, but I don't. "She had this wild story. I couldn't stand her, but I don't know . . . I kind of liked being in the presence of someone who seemed more messed up than me."

"Did you fuck her?"

The server returns with Alexis's pint and walks away quickly.

Alexis takes a few sips before setting it down.

"I don't think so."

She raises one brow. "You don't think so?"

"Wish I could say, but I got blackout drunk. When I woke, I'd completely forgotten she was there. Then I wished that she wasn't."

"Is that supposed to make me feel better?"

"It's supposed to show that I'm honest—even if it doesn't help you or me."

"Honesty for its own sake ain't all it's cracked up to be," Alexis murmurs.

"When I noticed your texts, I'd just woken up. I was trying to figure things out, and then she started playing with me—" Alexis scowls. "Not physically—mentally. She kept teetering between saying nothing happened and that something did. I don't know what to believe. Now I'm wondering if everything she told me was a lie, because her story was pretty messed up and convoluted. She bragged about being some kind of clairvoyant who could see people's secrets . . ."

Alexis cuts in. "Do I need to know all of this?"

"Probably not."

"Go on anyway." She sighs, flicking her left hand into the air.

"It was one thing after the next. Then she said she could see my aura, and it was full of dead bodies and guilt."

"What the fuck?"

"I know . . . Anyway, I'm sorry for blowing you off. I just didn't know how to respond. It was too much to process. I thought she'd never leave." I take a mouthful of beer. "I wondered if it was better to lie, but then I wouldn't have been able to face you. And I wouldn't want her to resurface with me not having told you already."

Alexis nods. "I was worried about you. I've been reading

about survivor's guilt and how some people attempt suicide after traumatic events. When you didn't answer, I freaked. It was out of character for you. Then I got to your place and saw movement in the window. Couldn't tell if someone was there with you. Never thought you'd cheat. Just figured you were freezing me out."

"I don't think I would've cheated on you."

"But you don't know."

I shake my head, watching the flames dance in a firepit. "I don't blame you for being pissed. I would be, too."

"I am pissed." Alexis narrows her eyes. "At everything. I'm pissed at the shooter and the cops for not finding him. I'm pissed at the small-minded backass town you grew up in. I'm pissed at that weird fucking bitch who stayed over—and at you for letting yourself get drunk enough to not even know what happened. I'm pissed that she knows where you live. And I'm really fucking pissed at myself for not wanting to get up and walk away from you now and forever. But I love you. And I'm pissed at that, too—because I know it's not going to be easy."

"I love you, too." I reach for her cheek.

"Don't." She turns her face defiantly. "I get to have my feelings now."

"Okay. Is there anything I can do to help?"

Glancing around the beer garden, she nods. "Another pint and a pizza, for starters. And fries. I'm eating my feelings tonight."

I fight back a smile. "Should I get my own food?"

"If you want any."

It's not until later, when we're at Alexis's place undressing for bed, that she notices my hair. She runs her fingers through it. "When did this happen?"

"The other morning."

"You cut it yourself?" I nod. She says, "I mean—you're obviously going through an identity crisis, but whatever. It looks good."

"Hey . . ."

She leans on one hip. "It's okay. If anyone deserves one, it's you."

"Why's that?"

She chuckles. "Look in the mirror, and then look at where you grew up and around whom. And you're gay and just survived a mass shooting."

"That affords me a crisis?"

She stumbles out of her jeans. "At least one."

"Okay," I say, considering.

"We need to sign you up with a therapist. I just wonder if there's anyone out there prepared to handle all of your . . ." She pauses, searching the room before adding, "Human experience."

"Thanks for the optimism." I bop her on the nose with my finger.

She rolls her eyes. "It's what I'm here for."

With her limbs wrapped around me in bed, I ask, "Do you forgive me for what I'm not sure I've done?"

Rubbing my thigh, she asks, "Why must we forgive everything? And what does that do—or even mean, anyway? Why can't we just live with uncomfortable truths?"

"Because it's what we're supposed to do, right? It's supposed to be good for our conscience, allowing us to let go and move on."

"Not helping your case with those Supposed Tos."

"You're right. There are things I don't question because it's been drilled into my head to accept them. Must be the Bixby in me."

"I kind of feel that questioning those things is part of what it means to grow up."

"You're right, of course. But what if I don't want to grow up?"

"Who are you? Peter Pan? Maybe your dad was right . . ." With a shake of my head, I groan. She asks, "Why would you want to hold on to your youth? I mean—yours in particular?"

"I don't know. Maybe things were easier then . . ."

She drops her hand on my hip. "Doubtful."

I twist around and tickle that spot on her side that makes her yelp every time.

"Hey! You're on thin ice, lady!"

Pressing my belly to hers, I pull her hips against mine. I'm desperate for things to feel right again. Our tongues dance around many unspoken words.

"You're the only woman for me," I tell her.

She snickers. "You're just saying that because you fucked up."

"I'm saying it because I mean it . . . And I fucked up."

When she takes control of my body, it's rougher than usual but not without love.

NO HERO

As I'm filling my teacup with hot water in the office kitchen, Carin arrives with a huge, overcompensating smile. Her pity burns through my pores. She keeps glancing at me as she fixes her coffee and plops down at a table. "Have a nice weekend?"

"It was . . . interesting," I say, not wanting to share my possible infidelity with her.

"Oh yeah?" She cuts to the chase. "How are you handling things?"

"I know you're trying to help, and it's sweet. But I'd rather not talk about it."

She presses her lips together and raises her brows. "Did my husband ever think he'd be stuck in a chair for the rest of his life? Hell to the no. But hey—he's alive." I stand awkwardly, clutching my teacup with both hands. She goes on. "Things will never be the same again, but he's learning to make the most of it. Don't know where we'd be without his therapist. Here. I wrote down her number." I take the folded paper and shove it in my pocket. She sips her coffee. "Don't feel bad now if you want to ask. No one wants to ask, but it's human to be curious."

I nod and say, "My whole life has been answering intrusive questions, so I tend to think others want privacy, too."

"What kind of questions?"

I forgive her for missing the point and sit down. "Why my face doesn't match my name or my parents. Was my mother a prostitute. You know. Fun stuff."

"Yikes."

I shrug. "So, it sounds like you want me to ask."

"You don't have to ask. I'll tell you. It was a train wreck. Literally." She puts down her "Life Is What You Make It" mug. "We were touring India on an extended vacation after seeing Ashwin's family. He's fine, thank God. But not the same."

"How long ago did this happen?"

"Five years. The first couple were the worst. Every damn time we heard a train horn, we thought life was ending. We used to live near a station. We moved—because of that and accessibility."

"I guess I should consider myself lucky," I say clumsily.

"Nah. Don't put that on him." She shakes her head. "You're not better-off. His physical life has changed, and that makes it easier for people to see his struggle. Believe me—it's just as hard when it's invisible. Maybe worse in some ways because you can't always see it yourself."

"Well shit, Carin," I marvel, putting down my tea. "I hadn't thought of that."

"See? Give Melinda a call. She practically saved our lives. Plus, she's wise to multicultural issues."

"Maybe when I'm ready," I say, standing up. "But thanks."

As I'm syncing movie clips to music, I consider Carin's words. It wasn't her intention, but I'm left feeling like a failure again. I wonder if I'm not making enough use of my life. Maybe I should be out there using my experience to speak out against gun violence. But all I've ever wanted is to blend into a nice, simple life, to enjoy the things others grew up taking for granted. I bet it's wonderful not having to stand out—not having assumptions thrust upon you. What's that like?

Will the day come when I'm more like Carin and her husband? Do I have to be, to be worthy of being spared? Can't I just fade out and live quietly, seeking my own peace?

We all think we know ourselves, who we are, and how we'll behave. But the truth is we don't. Not till it happens to us.

Christy's hell-bent on calling me a hero, but the only reason I reacted as I did is because I'm a planner of exits. I don't think about it. It just happens—because of how I've failed in the past. I'm no hero. I just got lucky this time.

JUSTICE FOR THE DEAD

Leaving behind what happened in Bixby isn't so simple. I lie in bed, tormented, searching for information. I need something that leads to a resolution, something that'll help me let it go—or make it let go of me.

A clip on Twitter shows a large group of people picketing outside the Bixby police station. Each person holds an enlarged photo of their dead beloved.

"I won't rest till Anna's body can rest in peace!"

"Frankie deserved better!"

They march in a long, narrow circle in front of the station. A couple of officers stand guard.

A woman yells, "We demand answers!"

A man shouts, "Get to work!"

The crowd chants, "Get to work! Get to work!"

The camera pans across the group of about thirty people. I spot a few familiar faces. A former teacher. The mail lady. An old classmate who sketched racist depictions of me.

One of the officers speaks through a bullhorn. "Listen up. We know you're upset, and we're doing the best we can. Now, we'd like to get back to work, but these protests take us away from just that. Please . . . Go home and let us do our job."

"We've been waiting for you to do your job!"

Someone starts chanting, "Justice for the dead!"

The crowd echoes, "Justice for the dead! Justice for the dead!"

On the edge of the lawn, a well-groomed woman talks into the camera. "We're here live at the Bixby police station, where folks are crying out on behalf of the slain. With each day that passes with no leads or arrests, fears grow that all will soon be forgotten. Detective Whitley—care to comment?"

Whitley steps into view. "I wish there were more to say. We feel for the families and want to bring them closure. Sometimes justice takes time. I know it's easier said than done, but I ask for your patience as we work to find answers."

"So, there are no suspects at the moment?"

"None I can comment on at this time."

"And what about the survivors? Are any of them on your radar?"

"No comment except to say we have great compassion for what they've been through."

"Detective, some are afraid this was a terrorist attack. Any comment on that?"

"We have no reason to believe it was the work of a terrorist. The survivors didn't report any foreign language or features."

"Do you have any proof that it was an insider—a Bixby resident?"

"No comment."

"Do you have anything to say to the shooter if he's out there watching?"

Detective Whitley looks deep into the lens. "Listen: The best thing you can do is turn yourself in. It's the only way we can guarantee your safety. Call us, and we'll come pick you up. Or walk right through those doors behind me. You still have time to do the right thing before someone takes matters into their own hands."

"Do you have reason to believe someone will seek revenge on their own?"

"There's always that chance, Stacey. Fifty-six people were shot dead at what should've been a joyous occasion. One way or another, justice will be served. We're just hoping it happens without more bloodshed."

"Will you be going door to door?"

"We have been, already."

"Okay. You heard it here first. Thank you, Detective Whitley."

He nods and walks away. The protestors carry on chanting, "Justice for the dead!"

HELLA MONEY

The receptionist calls to alert me to a visitor named Lynnette. Closing my eyes, I exhale and say, "Sorry, I have no room for unscheduled visits."

I work with Tae-Suk on the edits for one of the big promo pieces going out later this week. I act like everything's normal— one of my best skills—laughing at his stories and keeping Lynnette locked away in a cell in my mind.

As I'm cycling home, my phone lights up. No caller ID. I click the button on my headphones. "Yeah?" My chest heaves as I push uphill.

There's a playful growl. "Did I catch you at a bad time?"

"It's always a bad time. Get to the point."

"Well, that's a shame. We need to talk."

"No we don't."

"Tough girl." Lynnette cackles. "Meet me at the bar."

"Not in the mood."

"Well, I could just meet you at your front door if you'd prefer."

"What do you want?"

"You'll find out soon. I'll save you a stool. Toodles!"

I lock my bike out front, feeling red in the face. As I stride through the door, Lynnette waves wildly from the bar. She calls out, "Nice of you to join me. What're you having? My treat."

My eyes connect with the bartender's. "Just water, please."

"On the wagon? I knew you were an alchy." I don't bother to argue. She rubs my back and asks, "Did you have a good day, honey?" I shake her off.

The bartender slides a glass of water towards me. I take a few glugs and slam it down a little rougher than intended. Several patrons glance over, but I pay no mind. "Okay. I'm here. Let's get to the point."

She traces an exaggerated frown through the air in front of her pout. "You sadden me, Lucy. I thought we were friends."

"Tell me why we're here."

"Sheesh. You're making this awkward now. It was supposed to be a special, exciting time, but your attitude's crushing me."

I put on the voice of an upper-class White lady at a yacht club. "Oh, excuse me. Where are my manners?"

"There. How hard was that?" Lynnette grins and shoots back some bourbon. "You know, you really ought to have a drink for this. Sure you don't want one?"

"I'm good."

"Okay. Suit yourself." She snaps her fingers and points to her empty glass. The bartender comes by and refills it. She shoots it back and belches shamelessly. "All right. You ready for this?"

I roll my eyes.

"You're gonna be rich!" She mimics the sounds of bells and whistles with her mouth, as if I've just won a game show prize.

I tilt my eyes up, unamused. "Um, what?"

"Rich! And not just rich . . . but fucking loaded!" She's pumping her arms grotesquely. "So much money you won't even know what to do! You can buy a huge beach house some- where—anything you want. Your life will be lit, and you'll owe it all to this girl right here." She points to her dimples. "All I want is fifteen percent, and you won't even miss it—it'll be that much."

I cross my legs and shake my head. "What are you talking about?"

"Book rights! Movie rights! Huge money! More than you can imagine!"

"Rights for what?"

"Your life! Now, don't be mad, but I did some snooping. I know enough about you now, Lucy Byrne—one of three survivors of the newly famous Reunion Massacre!" Her whole body is charged with excitement. "Why'd you hold out on me?"

I dart my eyes around the room, hoping no one overheard. "It was nice not to think about it for a minute."

"I talked to my publisher, and she's willing to make you a deal. All you've gotta do is sit with a team of writers and answer their questions. They're great at this stuff. Pros. They'll write the whole thing. And of course, with a story this hot, there'll be a movie. Hella money and fame!"

"I'm not interested."

"What? This is not something one's simply not interested in. We're talking shitloads of dough here!"

"I don't want this story marketed and sold for cheap thrills. I've got enough money. I'm happy with how things are."

"Enough money! Ha! Like that's a thing." Lynnette cackles. "You live in a rent-controlled apartment. Look—if you want writing credits, you've got 'em. But if you don't want the bother, you can just answer their questions. It won't take more than a weekend. They'll have everything laid out ahead of time. Boom. Bang. Cha-ching!"

"It's not just my story to tell."

"You want the others to join in and split? Be my guest. They might even sweeten the pot."

"Eh . . ."

"You might be okay here in San Francisco, but your friends are stuck in East Bumfuck with a mass murderer on the loose. You have the power to change that. Don't you want that for them?"

"They're happy as they are."

"That's what they tell you," she spits. "No one's happy, Lucy! It's just what people say. They're trying to convince themselves as much as you. But you know what makes 'em happier? Options. And you know what buys options? Fuck-tons of money." Her gyrating hips violate my eyes.

"You don't know these people like I do. No one's life is perfect, but happiness can exist in ordinary lives."

"Bullshit. Those are nothing lives. Those lives are the ones no one cares about until something big happens. Like this! Now you have opportunity. This is your one chance to make your life important—make your friends' lives important. Think about it. That shooting—you probably think it's the worst thing that's ever happened to ya. I'm here to help you turn it into the best thing that's ever happened to ya. Do you trust me?"

"That's so fucking crude. People died." I lean in with a snarl. "And you want to talk about trust? I met you the one night I needed to blow off some steam, and you've been trying to exploit it ever since. You insinuate we slept together. You show up at my workplace uninvited. You force me to see you. A trustworthy person wouldn't do any of those things. A trustworthy person would make sure that whatever I did was something I wanted."

Lynnette shifts about awkwardly. "Well . . . I guess you're right. Hey, I'm sorry for not going about things the right way. I don't know how to be normal. I consider that one of my charms, but I see I've annoyed you. All of that said, don't turn down the offer of a lifetime just 'cause you don't like the messenger."

I tilt my head. "If the person selling you eternal life were dressed as the reaper, would you buy it?" I watch her features settle like a switched-off lava lamp. "Didn't think so."

"Tell you what. There's no gun to your head." She puts up

her hands. "My bad. There's no need to give an answer right now. Think about it. Talk to your girlfriend or whoever. Call your friends. Just don't make a rash decision and regret it. All of your lives could change for the better."

"Then you'll leave me alone?"

"If you promise to think about it. Sure. Look, I'll give you my number, since I hid it the last time I called. Call me in a week." She picks up her phone and unlocks it.

"A week is too short."

"All right. Two. Whatever. But feel free to give a holler if you come to your senses sooner." She's furiously tapping away at her screen. "Maybe you wanna mull things over. Maybe you wanna hang out. Call me."

I tilt my head incredulously. My phone vibrates with the message.

"Never thought you'd hesitate." She sulks. "I thought you'd be praising me now."

"Did we do it or not?"

"Huh?"

"That night. Yes or no." Her lips pucker. I say, "Do you want me to consider this deal? I need to know you can be straight with me."

"Girl, I'm as crooked and queer as they come. But sure—I'll be honest. Nothing happened. I just liked having a little fun with you is all."

"Are you sure now?"

She lays a hand across her chest. "Cross my heart, hope to die."

I mumble, "If only."

"What's that?"

"You know, if I decide to go along with this—which I'm not saying I will—I'm going to need some contracts. No bullshit."

"Yeah, of course." She nods. "I'm not an amateur, for God's sake. Well, this is my first time as an agent, but I know how things go. Just leave it to me."

"Famous last words."

CONSIDERATIONS

The next day at lunch, I tell Tae-Suk about Lynnette. He slurps up his noodles, his face changing expressions like he's watching a thriller. "No shit. Whatcha gonna do?"

"I don't know." I pause to nibble on some banchan. "Who knows if she's even legit?"

He puts down his drink. "What did you dream of doing when you were young?"

"Leaving Bixby."

"What else?"

I shrug. "What I'm doing now. Working in film and photography, living in San Francisco, dating a cute girl."

He nods. "But what about the big dreams?"

"That's it. All I ever wanted was to believe a life like what I had here, before the shooting, was possible. One where I could just be me without constantly needing to worry, justify my existence, or be made aware of my race every minute. I don't need much else."

"Too easy," he says. "You're already living the dream? Nah..." He shakes his head.

"Well, what were your dreams?"

"To be, like . . . James Bond. Not White, but you know—an actor known for being suave and having super fine ladies."

I grin. "Can you act?"

"Fuck yeah!" he sings. "I was the lead in two high school plays. I thought about going to school for it, but you know . . . Gotta be a doctor or lawyer." He rolls his eyes.

"So instead you became a project manager?"

"Damn, Lucy. You cold." He tears a scallion pancake apart with chopsticks.

"I'm just jealous because I don't know what it's like to have Asian parents."

"I gave up on my dream because my father was right. There's no room in Hollywood for guys like me. He said if I wanted to act, I should go back to Korea. But I speak Korean like a third grader. I don't know. Whatever."

My heart swells. "You know what? I get you on this. I wouldn't know how to live there, either, after being adopted to White folks."

He nods. "Anyway," he says, his mouth full. "I think you should take it."

"Take what?" My lips pucker from the soondubu jjigae.

"The money! Set you and your girl up for life. Hell, if you still want to work, come to work. But make it so you don't have to."

"It sounds great when you put it like that." I lean back and sip my tea. "When you isolate the money, who wouldn't take it? But it's not just my story. And why should I tell it? Do I have a right to it more than the families of the dead?"

"Then throw them some bills! It's better than having nothing and giving nothing."

"How about giving them peace?" I look around the room and lower my voice. "If someone came and shot this place up, what do you think everyone's families would want? I'm guessing to grieve in private—not a few bucks from someone who survived and capitalized on it. It's a slap in the face."

"So you feel guilty. Got it."

"I have a responsibility. I'm still figuring out what that is, but I'm pretty sure it's not getting rich off something so many died from."

"Fuck what other people think." He drops kimchi into his clay bowl and stirs it around. "They're not you. Let them do their own story. You could've died, too. Use it towards therapy. And if you really have trouble spending it, you can be the executive producer of a film my friends and I star in." He flashes his winning smile.

"You're cute enough to be a Hollywood star. Go for it."

"And be a Taekwondo master or the butt of the joke? No thanks. That's why I need to write my own film."

"So, why don't you?"

He leans in and tilts his head. "Who's to say I'm not?"

"Thought you said you gave up on your dream?"

"I gave up on my dream to star in someone else's film—not my own."

IN BETWEEN

Alexis runs her hands through my hair as I lie on her lap on my couch. She's sipping sparkling rosé and watching funny YouTube clips. I laugh when she laughs, but my eyes are unfocused. My mind's tangled up in Bixby and the book. I don't tell her about the proposition just yet because of its connection to Lynnette. I know what she'll say: take it. She believes People of Color are entitled to what anyone gives us, having been disadvantaged for so long. She's not wrong, but this feels more complicated.

I peer up at her face, on the sly. She's already removed her makeup. I catch a rare glimpse of her freckles; they're usually covered because she thinks they make her look too much like a White girl. But I love them. They're like a secret I'm privy to that makes me feel close—despite the secrets I keep from her now.

* * *

I'm transported back to early spring.

Greta looked like an American Apparel model, with olive skin, pouty lips, and pale green eyes. We were on a much-anticipated date at the Exploratorium, but she was yawning and wandering around looking bored. She couldn't pull the phone from her face for two minutes. She wasn't snapping photos; she was monitoring Instagram likes.

I remember the moment our eyes connected. Alexis had this mischievous smile that sent my heart thumping something fierce. I turned away, blushing. And when I looked back, she smiled before doing a silly dance for the sake of the kids she had with her.

She approached me, with Greta not two feet away, and whispered, "On the off chance you might be interested, here's my number." She kept her face near mine for an awkward moment before adding, "I've gotta get back to my class!" Something magic vibrated between us.

Catching my breath, I smiled and dorkishly said, "Outlook good." I then berated myself in my head.

Alexis's eyes widened. "I love Magic 8 Ball!"

Relieved, I sang, "Me too!"

"Okay. Gotta run. Kids." She made a "call me" gesture and ran off, nearly knocking over an exhibit.

I tucked the paper into my pocket, turned around, and bumped right into Greta. "I can't believe you just picked up a girl right in front of me," she whined.

I raised my right brow. "And I can't believe you pulled yourself off your phone long enough to notice."

"So rude."

"Indeed."

"Whatever," Greta said with a huff. "Have a nice life."

I floated out of the museum and nearly crashed my bike twice while thinking of Alexis.

* * *

When she laughs, my head bounces lightly from her laughter. I laugh with her again. My desire to connect is real—but so is my distance. I don't attribute it to us but to what I'm going through.

My phone buzzes.

Christy: Hey Lucy. U there?

Me: What's up?

Christy: Not much. Just thinking of U. Wish U were still here so we could go grab a drink.

Me: Everything all right?

Christy: I guess? The services are over.

Me: Did you go?

Christy: Yeah. They were rough. Lots of tears.

Me: I can only imagine.

Christy: UR parents were there.

Me: I figured. Was Donna?

Christy: No. I called to see if she wanted 2 come but she didn't want 2.

Me: Well, she's been getting hate mail. I wouldn't want to go, either.

Christy: I can't believe she's getting hate mail.

Me: Don't you remember how things were for her when we were young?

Christy: Not really.

Me: You had your own thing going on, I suppose.

Christy: I wonder what would've happened if we'd all stayed close? I blew it, didn't I?

Me: We were kids trying to figure shit out. You had to explore other friends. We had to explore other hobbies.

Christy: Still . . . Sometimes I think if one thing were different none of this would've happened.

Me: What happened isn't anyone's fault but the shooter's.

Christy: Maybe I'm just feeling nostalgic. I wish we hadn't grown apart.

Alexis asks, "Who's that?"

"Just Christy." I sigh. "She's in a weird place."

Alexis rubs my shoulder.

Me: We're friends now. Don't worry about it.

Christy: :-) <3

Me: Hey, I've gotta run. Have a good night, old friend.

Christy: Who you callin' old? ;-)

I toss the phone onto the coffee table and laugh along with Alexis again.

Here I am, stretched between Bixby and San Francisco. I've always been split between two realms: neither Asian enough nor American enough. Not fully gay but definitely not straight. Never quite here or there.

THE UNSAVED

Something wet splats across the side of my face. A few voices cry out in desperation. People are either frozen or falling. At first I can't hear anything, but then I realize it's because everything's too loud. Those who can, run. Chairs screech. Tables topple. And somehow The Goo Goo Dolls' heartfelt throwback continues through the speakers, unaffected.

Christy's on the floor, crouching behind a table on its side. I reach out to grab her. She reaches her hand out to grab someone else and so forth. I lift us into the air, flying a chain of old classmates through the broken window. Bullets are fired, but we can't be reached.

Once everyone's landed safely atop a water tank, I jump off and away. I fly so fast that the sky makes tunnels that are usually invisible to the naked eye. I whirl through them like a roller coaster in the dark.

I'm spat out the other end onto a dark parquet floor. A woman sings a delightful melody while moving about the kitchen. I watch her bare ankles pushing gray quilted slippers across the room. Someone knocks on the door. She shuffles towards it, still singing.

When the screaming begins, I levitate, grabbing the lady's hand. I fly her through the door, up into the sky, to a secret cabin in the mountains. I tuck her into bed and fly back to the house, but the man is gone. I wait until the woman's husband comes home for his family. I grab him without explanation. I take him to his wife in the mountains, where he soothes her as only he could. She sings as he paints pretty landscapes. I dip my finger into paint and add little birds in its sky before flying off.

I soar alongside an airplane. In the windows are my former classmates—including Donna and Christy—and the man and woman I left in the mountains.

How'd they get here so fast?

The plane splits in half. I can't fly fast enough. The two pieces plummet to the ground, exploding on contact.

Swooping down to the wreckage, I search for survivors. There are none. As I'm about to leave, something pulls me back. I move in to inspect the debris. Among the dead are Margaret and Henry.

I jolt awake, panting and sweating. An eerie feeling washes over my skin as I gasp.

I was supposed to save them all. But I failed.

PLAYING NORMAL

"It's a cuisine from your country . . ." Tae-Suk waves his arms frantically, nodding and staring expectantly at his date.

Sam calls, "Tempura! Teriyaki!"

Tae-Suk shakes his head. "Some use bamboo to help roll—"

Bzzzz!

"You can't say roll!" Alexis points to the card.

"Shit."

I holler, "Time!"

"It's all right." Sam pats his arm. "We got two points."

He brushes her chin with his hand, and her body responds to the charge. "Sorry. There was a crumb."

She groans. "Oh my God, I'm disgusting."

He shrugs. "It's actually kind of cute." He moves in for a kiss.

"Our turn!" I shout, obnoxiously squeezing the buzzer and spoiling their moment.

Sam flips the timer. "Go!"

With Sam hovering over my shoulder, I say, "You put these on . . . sneakers . . . to keep them on tight."

Alexis shouts, "Shoelaces!"

Tae-Suk asks, "You can say sneakers?"

I ignore him and sing, "Pur-ple blank! Pur-ur-ple blank!"

"Rain!"

I flip the card. "These kinds of lesbians get all done up."

"Femme! Lipstick!"

I rub my thumb and index finger together and say, "Oh, I feel so sorry for you! Here's the world's smallest . . ."

"Violin!"

"They're killing us," Tae-Suk whispers to Sam.

"A crab does this sideways," I continue.

"Crawl?"

"Being called this is worse than being it."

"Racist!"

Sam laughs and shakes her head. "Damn . . ."

I look up at the ceiling and back down at Alexis. "One of the words Obama ran with."

"Change! Hope!"

Tae-Suk roars, "Time! The two of you should be separated. You're too good at this."

"But then we'll be on opposite teams," Sam complains.

"It's for the greater good, babe." He pats her back. "The greater good."

Alexis leans over and pulls my face towards hers for a kiss. "You were great!"

"We rule." I pump my fist in the air.

And this is how I play Normal. I'm good at it. While I pretend for the sake of everyone else, I normalize the situation to myself. Surviving something life-changing—life-taking—is traumatic, but life moves on for the living. I convince myself that it's what I must do. I'm more comfortable when others don't worry. But inside, I'm falling apart. I'm barely hanging on by a thread.

The guilt . . . Oh, the guilt slowly eats me alive.

Alexis places a grape to my lips. I playfully open my mouth to receive it and smile, my hand on her ribcage, squeezing her side. On the outside, we look happy. It's not fake, because I am happy with her. But I know, deep down, it's not right to keep so much from her. I wonder if she can feel it.

"Lucy, you're on my team." Tae-Suk pulls me out of my head. "Let's show 'em how it's done with the jeong."

I snarl at Alexis. "You're going down."

"Meow," Alexis says.

The four of us giggle like teens.

RIPPLES

Some days I almost feel as if there was no reunion shooting—until I remember again and get angry that I forgot. And then there are days when I make such a fool of myself.

As I'm walking through the hallway at work, Carin pulls me into a screening for a new project. I stand in the back.

A couple of teens run around a fancy apartment. Another one jumps out, heaving water from a bucket towards them. It's just a prank. But the screeches. I jump back, hit the wall, and knock papers from the board to the floor.

Coworkers turn around, laughing at my clumsiness. Carin studies my face for too long. I collect myself and make my exit, ducking into the nearest restroom to catch my breath.

When she finds me later, I beat her to it. "That was awkward. Sorry. I'm having an off day."

"There's nothing to be sorry for," she says, closing my door.

"It's just gonna take time," I lie. "I'll be back to normal soon enough."

She lifts one of the plush cats off my desk. "It takes time and real dedication. It won't heal itself."

"Carin." I hold my breath for a moment. "I appreciate your concern and what you've shared about what you and Ashwin went through. But I've gotta do this my way."

She nods. "I'm worried about you. Who do you have for support?"

"My girlfriend. She's great at knowing how much to ask and when to leave me alone."

"Who else?"

I shrug. "I've been talking to the other two via text."

"Do you talk about what happened? About how you're feeling?"

"We mostly talk about what's happening now."

She places the plush cat down. "When we left India, we thought it'd be easy to recover—being so far removed. But soon enough, we learned that just because you're not there doesn't mean it won't follow."

I push back from my desk and blurt, "A train crash and a shooting are not the same thing. One's an accident. The other's on purpose."

"I know." She steps forward a few inches. "I understand. Which is why I urge you to seek out support. You can talk to me. If you don't want to, that's fine. There are other options. Groups can be great."

"I don't want to sit around a room and get triggered by everyone's traumas." I sigh. "And I don't want to tell them about mine so they can feel pity or close to the story of the moment."

"Okay. But find something that works for you."

"Not thinking about it works for me."

"That's not what I'm seeing. If you need any help finding resources, you know where to find me."

The next day's so busy that I don't have time for a real lunch break. I run down to the cafeteria and grab one of those premade sandwich/salad combos to take to my desk. I'm standing in line for the cashier when I hear the sound of shattering glass. I bolt, dropping my tray to the floor.

Tae-Suk jumps in front of me. "Hey! It's okay."

Flushed with adrenaline and humiliation, I push past him. Soon after, he enters my office with the food I'd left behind.

I ask, "How much did you see?"

"I heard the glass break and saw you split." He sits down with his lunch.

"How many others witnessed my freak-out?"

"Um . . ." His eyes shift uncomfortably. "Don't worry. They'll forget all about it tomorrow."

I drop my head to the desk.

"Take that money," he says. "You shouldn't have to work like this."

"I love my job." I unwrap the chickpea sandwich and take a bite. "It's not fair to be robbed of this, too."

"I know. None of it's fair."

There's nothing but chomping and chewing for a few minutes. My mind wanders off to the pond in Bixby; I think of throwing perfectly smooth stones and watching the ripples they make in the water.

Tae-Suk says, "It shouldn't be so easy for one event to destroy so many and change the course of others."

"One man," I say. "With one gun."

He nods. "Well, I'm pretty shit with emotions. And I'm not the best person to come to with heavy life stuff. I'm kind of the king of avoidance, but you know . . . It's easier to tell other people how to do life than it is to live it."

I scrunch my face. "Where are you going with this?"

"I'm just saying that all that aside, you can talk to me. I guarantee I won't say the right thing, but I'll listen the best I can."

I want to tell him he's better at these things than I am; I appreciate his friendship so much, and I don't know how I'd deal with being at work without him. But instead of clumsily tripping over those sentiments, I grin and say, "Thanks. I'll keep that in mind."

FANNING THE FLAMES

I'm lying on my living room floor listening to the birds outside my window. My clothes are soaked from a K-pop workout I found on YouTube. I needed to blow off some steam and thought it'd be a fun way to connect to Korean culture. It won on both counts.

My phone vibrates on the coffee table. I reach up to grab it.

> Donna: This shit here's getting out of hand.
>
> Me: ???
>
> Donna: Someone spray-painted our driveway.
>
> Me: I'm afraid to ask.
>
> Donna: It's as bad as you think.
>
> Me: Motherfuckers.
>
> Donna: Had to disconnect the landline. People wouldn't stop calling, telling me to turn myself in.
>
> Me: It makes me so mad that they're targeting you! Is there anything we can do?
>
> Donna: Jacob wants to hire security.
>
> Me: You shouldn't have to, but maybe it's wise. I'm guessing they're no closer to finding the shooter?
>
> Donna: Not as far as I know. Have you seen Christy's vlog?
>
> Me: No . . .
>
> Donna: That interview gave her a taste.

She sends me the link to Christy's channel. There are three videos. I click on the first.

Christy's sitting on her front steps. She wears the same

blue-and-gold Bixby cap my dad wears, her long blond hair hanging down in waves. She's cropped close—from the top of her hat to her shoulders.

"Hi. I'm Christy Fox Tilden, born and raised here in Bixby. I live with my husband and daughter. I'm also one of three survivors of The Reunion Massacre. Since I'm the only one who never left, I feel it's my duty to teach the rest of the world about Bixby, since you're probably just hearing of us."

The sun gives her skin a soft glow. Her head tilts sassily. "First off, we're not some backwards town. Our people are warm and loving. We work hard to keep our families safe. We watch the news and keep up with the rest of the world. We read books and go to church. What happened here's devastating. And the fact that the killer is still on the loose is unsettling. As you can see, it's a gorgeous summer day, but my daughter's inside." She pans the camera around her backyard. "The older kids still don't know where they'll be going to school come September. The town's undecided."

Christy pauses and settles back a few inches. She centers the gold cross pendant between her collarbones. "Now, some say we've got a problem with guns, but let's be real: Guns aren't the problem. We've got several farms and shops here in Bixby. We've always had guns to protect what's ours. Aside from one minor incident years ago, this is the first time we've ever had a shooting make the news."

There's a shimmer to her eyes as she leans back in. "This country's changing fast. Small towns like Bixby are disappearing. Good people like us are laughed at, but really, we're misunderstood. They want us extinct. Some man with hate in his heart decided to send a message that we don't matter. Well, I'm here to say that we do! Bixby residents are strong, and we'll get through this. But please . . . Stop with the speculations that it was one of our own. Take it from someone who's lived here every day of her life. I know. Whoever's done this was an outsider—someone who hates small-town White Christians. Well, that's it for now. More to come, so check back here soon. Until then, God bless."

I shouldn't be surprised, but I'm speechless.

> Me: Watched the first one. What are your thoughts?
>
> Donna: At least she's kind of saying it wasn't me? I guess I should be thankful . . .
>
> Me: But?
>
> Donna: But also, it's frightening.
>
> Me: Agreed. Did she tell you about it? Her channel?
>
> Donna: No. I overheard people talking about it in town. Did you see the comments?

I brace myself as I scroll.

- Guns aren't the problem! Thank God for a girl with some sense!
- We love you, Christy! Stay safe!
- Maybe the killer doesn't hate White Christians but White people? Open your eyes! It's right under your nose.
- Beautiful, strong, and smart. Leave your husband and marry me!
- Well, the other two were the only non-Whites . . .

I roll my eyes and stop reading.

> Me: Should we talk to her?
>
> Donna: No. You know what she's like. We should just leave it be.

Christy knows she's the face people want on this thing. And she knows how to talk to her people. She's the All-American Girl they need to believe in.

I fight back the urge to call her up because I know Donna's right. You can't confront Christy. She'll turn on you. And the truth is, we need her on our side.

PENDULUM

Getting paid to sort through clumsy cat footage is living my best life. Tae-Suk picked a bad time to sour me on working. And Carin can pressure me into all the therapy she wants. This is the cure for what ails me.

But as I'm cropping, panning, and applying transitions, my mind splits in two. One half is focused on the task at hand. The other hovers over Bixby High.

It's the night of the shooting. The scene is sped up. Little dots wobble through the front entrance. Smoke rises from more dots lingering outside. After a few beats, another dot approaches the gymnasium. Glass shatters, and the windows blow out on one side. Then again on the other side. Police cars zoom in. The SWAT team arrives from a couple of towns over. The three of us are rushed from the school to the ambulance. It speeds off down the road.

When the Bixby police and the SWAT team drive off, one lone dot flees the building. I leap out of my chair and nearly call the Bixby police before realizing it's a daydream.

The phone buzzes in my hand.

    Lynnette: Hi, pretty lady. Just letting you know I'm still here.

         Me: How could I forget?

    Lynnette: *blushing* Have I been on your mind?

         Me: Been trying to keep you out.

    Lynnette: Don't fight it, girl.

         Me: > <

    Lynnette: Have you given more thought to the offer?

Me: I'll let you know when there's news.

Lynnette: I just hope you decide before someone else does.

Me: What do you mean?

Lynnette: Your names are public.

Me: So?

Lynnette: I can't control whether someone else beats you to it.

Me: If that happens, so be it.

Lynnette: Are you always so blasé about shitloads of money?

Me: Only blood money.

Lynnette: Hope you don't regret it.

Me: Sounds like a threat.

Lynnette: Not a threat. Just a friendly warning.

Me: Gotta get back to work.

Lynnette: Okay, honey buns. Call me. Don't be too long.

I twist my chair around and stare at the city. Could Lynnette have gotten in touch with Christy and Donna? Or put her people in touch with them?

As my finger hovers over Donna's name, Tae-Suk swings my glass door open. He jumps over the back of the chair. Seeing the look on my face, he asks, "Is this a bad time?"

"No?"

He smirks. "You sure about that?"

I close the door. "It's just, well—that woman with the book deal just texted. I'm still working things out."

"Like whether you'll take it?"

I nod and drop into my chair. "She's up to something—implying I might miss my chance. On the one hand, I don't give a shit. On the other, it could get ugly."

He runs his fingers through the top of his hair. It falls perfectly to the side. "You think she contacted your friends?"

"That's what she alluded to, anyway."

"Call 'em."

I play with the pendulum on my desk, pulling a cat head out and letting it go. I watch it slam, sending the other end into motion. "This would be better handled in person."

He throws a leg up onto the arm of the chair and slouches. "Aside from losing out on the money—that you're unsure about taking anyway—what's the worst that could happen?"

I lean back and suck in my cheeks, searching for the right words. "There are too many ways to exploit this, depending on who's involved and who's not."

THE BOOK

From the gate at SFO, I send Alexis a message that I'm headed to Bixby.

> Alexis: Everything all right?
> Me: Yeah. I'll catch you up soon.
> Alexis: Okay. Safe travels. <3
> Me: <3

People on the plane are appalled by Trump's latest offenses. They swear he won't get elected because everyone knows he's a bigot.

People on the bus into Bixby say Trump's street-smart but unpolished and too easily dismissed—just like them.

No one knows a damn thing.

Not wanting to bother my parents, I hop into a taxi at the bus depot. The driver says, "Well, look who, look who—Bixby's own Lucy Liu."

I glance at his pale blue eyes peering back from the rearview mirror. "You look familiar . . ." And then it hits me. "Ah. You're the artist."

Twenty-something years ago, he sketched me into one of his drawings. I was naked, bowing, in a rice paddy hat. At the time it was making the rounds, students approached with exaggerated bows, spouting made-up Chinese. It took all I had to not give them the satisfaction of seeing it upset me.

"Oscar, right?"

He peers into the rearview mirror. "Surprised you remember."

I shrug. "Well, you remember me."

"Yeah, but it's not like there are any other Chinese around here."

"Korean, but you're right. I don't blend." I pause for an apology that doesn't happen. "So, you're probably glad you skipped the reunion."

"Those things aren't for me." He shifts his body, waiting for the light to turn. "People go when they have something to show for the time. I've got nothin'. No wife. No kids."

His bitter tone sends a chill up my spine. I change the subject. "You still making art?"

"I do my own thing. No one's paying me, but I enjoy it." He fidgets with the mirror before moving on.

"That's what matters most, right?" I suddenly remember his face in the crowd from that clip of the protest outside the police station. "Hey, sorry about your friends."

"Thanks." He shrugs. "Didn't lose too many."

"Glad to hear," I mumble awkwardly.

We pull up in front of the lavender cape. "All right, Lucy Liu. See ya 'round."

I hand him some bills. "Thanks for the ride."

No one answers the door when I knock. When Oscar's cab is out of view, I reach for the stone under the bush and find the key to let myself in.

"Hello?"

No answer.

It's strange to be back here again. The floral-print sofas and the matching silk flowers on the coffee table haven't moved an inch.

As I head upstairs, I pause at each of the photographs on the wall. I wasn't able to register them when I was here last. The first is of Dad in his old uniform before he was sent off to war. The next is of Mom and Dad standing outside Bixby's Methodist church in their wedding clothes. Then there's me, six years old, hamming it up with a miniature flag on the day I became a citizen. And then Sandy—our old dog from when I was a kid—sitting in the yard. I straighten the last one, which is of me in my blue graduating hat and gown, gold tassel brushing my cheekbone. In the bottom center, Mom wrote in gold craft-store ink: Bixby Class of '96.

I plug in my phone.

> Me: I'm in Bixby. Can we meet?
> Donna: Sure. Want to swing by in 30?
> Me: See you then.

Lying back on the bed, with my eyes tracing the gritty lines of Kurt Cobain's jaw, I consider Oscar for the shooting. He's always been a little bitter, but he seemed too calm to be driving me around if he'd just killed half the class.

When I pull up in front of Donna's tan-and-brick manor, a security guard is on duty. He speaks into a device. Another guard walks up from the side as I step out of the car. I nod. They nod back, following me up the slate path to the door.

We watch her silhouette approach through the tempered glass panes. Donna opens the mahogany door in an orange cotton dress that makes her dark skin glow. She hushes the black Lab barking down by her thighs. "Philip! Enough!" I pet Philip and follow Donna through the living room and kitchen to the sunroom out back. Philip rests at our feet.

Donna hands me a glass of nonalcoholic sparkling cider. She leans back and asks, "What brings you back here so soon?"

Taking a chance, I say, "I want to talk about the book."

"You came all this way just for that?" She swirls the cider in her glass, fixated on the bubbles. "I didn't realize you knew."

Her calmness startles me. "Does Christy know?"

She shakes her head. "Just Jacob. I try to lead a private life."

I nod slowly. "So, what are you gonna do?"

She crosses her legs and turns towards me with a shrug. "People will think what they think. It's done now."

I study her face. "Was it hard to write?"

"No." She shakes her head and then takes a sip. "It kind of wrote itself. It's a bit eerie though, after what happened. But I couldn't have known."

My eyes shift around. "About what?"

"The shooting."

"Why was that eerie? Wasn't that the whole point?"

Donna sighs. "Have you even read it?"

My face twists. "I didn't know that I could."

She tucks her chin in and asks, "What in the world are we talking 'bout here?"

"The book!"

"Which book?"

"About the shooting!"

She shakes her head quickly. "It's not about a shooting. It's about a young Black woman looking for love, who—in her search—turns down a White man. But it's really a romance. I didn't plan for it to have any violence, but it's the story that came out." She flicks her hand back. "It wasn't meant to be a social commentary."

I let the details connect in my brain. "We're not talking about the same book."

She crosses her arms, still holding her glass. "Well, it's the only one I've written that has any shooting."

"You're a writer."

Donna puts down her glass and asks, "If you don't know that already, why'd you come here asking about a book?"

I smile. "A novelist."

"Of course I am." She huffs. "What do you think we've been talking about here?"

I put down my glass and fold forward, laughing. Philip licks my cheek.

"It's really not funny. I go by a pen name, but I'm not ashamed. There aren't enough romance novels for Black women. I enjoy it. And I'm good."

"That's not what's so funny," I manage to say.

"Well, you'd better tell me what's going on before I lose my patience."

I sit up. "This woman—she wants me to sell the rights to my version of what happened out here. I've been on the fence. Now she's making insinuations—probably to turn up the heat to get what she wants. I thought she might have contacted you . . . and Christy."

Donna's eyes sharpen. "Someone wants to write a book about Bixby? About the shooting?" She shudders. "Why'd they want to do that?"

"It'll make people money."

"And they're gonna ask Christy?"

I shrug. "That's what I came to you for."

Donna picks up her glass and looks away. "She'll be all over it. Her vlog's up to ten clips. She's got tens of thousands of followers."

"That's what I'm afraid of. If it's going to be done one way or another, I want to make sure it's done right."

Donna's shaking her head. "No doubt in my mind she'll say yes."

"That's why we should all be involved. Work together. Maybe the money can go towards the families and town."

Donna nods, eyes fixed on a photograph of her boys. "And

there I was, worried about my book, thinkin' someone would blow things out of proportion."

"Our own Donna, a novelist." I shake my head with both pride and amusement.

She sets down her glass and straightens her dress. "There's more to me than what meets the eye, if only people cared to look."

And I can't say she's wrong.

YELLOW TAPE

When I get to the school crossing zone, I park the red sedan diagonally at the foot of Bixby High. I lean against the car for a moment, staring up at the stars.

I wonder if he's been back. How does he feel about what he's done? Is he scared, proud, regretful? Has he run off to some bunker? Or does he stick around for the invincibility high?

Transparent images of the dead run towards me, screaming and falling. Some run straight through me. I stand, impotent, watching ghost bullets pass through my flesh.

"Lucky Lucy," I mumble.

Henry always has a sixer stowed away, even if it's crappy Bud Light. The warm beer from the trunk tastes like the last day of camping. Chugging it down, I head up the long, narrow drive.

I hear myself ask, "Who's to say what lucky is, anyway?"

There's yellow tape blocking off the school entrance. I don't want to go in, but I dare myself to stand close to where everything changed forever.

Will they reopen someday? How could anyone want to sit in there now? I consider looking into what other schools did, but I quickly think better of it. There are already enough things I can't unsee.

I work my way around the side of the school to where the bulk of it happened. The windows are broken. Most of the glass has been swept but not replaced. I see shards of it glistening under the moonlight, creating an almost mystical feel. Chills creep up my arms, and I grab onto them, holding myself together again.

Turning back towards the car, I stop in my tracks. There's a sound that stands out from the cicadas and the wind through the trees. I'm suddenly aware of my vulnerability, armed with nothing but a phone in my pocket. How much luck can one person have before it runs out? I start moving again, legs going faster with each step.

A familiar voice calls out, "What are you doing here?"

"Who's there?"

Cigarette smoke blows towards me. "Has it been that long?"

His unkempt dark hair and boyish face fade into view. A chill sweeps across the skin of my arms. I haven't seen him in years. He hasn't aged much.

For the lack of anything better to say, I ask, "You back here now?"

"City life was never my thing." He leans against his brown pickup, the blue driver's side door contouring his lean shape.

I nod. "So, what are you doing here?"

He smirks. "I asked you first."

Another chill sweeps through the air. I clench my arm muscles and say, "I don't really know. I stopped by on my way home from Donna's."

He sucks his cigarette. "It's not on the way."

I shrug. "How come you're here?"

"I live down the road. Bought a lot. Built a house."

My skin tightens. "Cool." Here he is, back where he belongs. He was never meant to leave.

"Saw the car on my way out and knew it was you. Didn't think it'd be Henry or Margaret."

I fidget with keys. "Yeah. Speaking of Margaret, I should run. She's been super protective these days."

He nods and smiles like he's in on something. "Send her my regards."

I turn to the car and then back towards Kevin. "You didn't come to the reunion."

"Best decision of my life." He drops his cigarette and twists it under his sneaker. "I'd say you dodged a bullet, but you're probably tired of that one."

It's just a tasteless joke, but his smirk is hard to bear. I suck on the insides of my cheeks and climb into the car, turning the engine.

Kevin bangs on the hood. "Wait a minute." I roll the window down a third. "I, ah . . . just wanna say . . . sorry . . . 'bout last time."

I nod and drive away.

The radio plays "Black Hole Sun." I sing along dramatically all the way home, thinking and trying not to think about Kevin.

REELING

Not ready to face anyone, I sit in the driveway composing myself.

I jump when the phone rings. Alexis says, "Hey baby."

"Hey."

"What's going on?"

"I just ran into Kevin."

"Kevin?"

"My ex."

There's muffled noise in the background. "Where'd you see him?"

"At the school."

"The school? What were you doing there so late at night?"

"I don't know . . . I left Donna's and just sort of drove there. Guess I needed to see it again."

"And why was he there?"

"He says he lives down the road and saw my dad's car. Still, it was strange. It didn't feel right. You know how sometimes the air feels charged with something? Like it's vibrating on the offbeat?"

"Yeah. That's your instinct telling you to GTFO. Why'd you break up again?"

I lack both the energy and words, so I tell her, "He never should've followed me to San Francisco. He belonged here in Bixby, and I never did."

"Did y'all have words?"

"Not many." I sigh. "I don't know. It could've been the location, that it was late and a surprise. But there was something about him this time. He changed. No, I did. I changed, and he hasn't at all."

"Funny how that happens," she says.

"Makes me wonder what's real: now or then? Maybe neither."

"Don't let it fuck with you. Your mind is sound. Trust it."

I remove the keys from the ignition and unclick the seatbelt. "You make it sound so easy."

"I know it's not easy. But I believe in you." She hums like she does when she's folding laundry or doing other household chores. "What brought you back, anyway?"

"Oh . . ." I dive into the story of Lynnette and her supposed deal of a lifetime. I explain my ethical and practical concerns, apologizing for not having told her sooner.

She sighs. "Do you trust me?"

"Yeah." My heart thumps. "Of course."

"Then why didn't you tell me sooner?"

"I don't know . . . Anything having to do with Lynnette is awkward. And I know that's my fault."

"Hell yeah it is," she moans.

"I'm sorry."

"Listen—I'm not trying to be your keeper, but when you keep things from me, it doesn't feel good."

"Okay. I'll try to do better . . ."

"I know you've got issues and shit. You're going through a lot. I just hate all this distance."

"I won't be gone long—"

"Not just the physical, Lucy." She's quiet for a moment. "We're disconnected. I expect things to be strange, all things considered. But let's work on it. 'Kay?"

Feeling like I'm failing at yet another thing, I hold my breath before saying, "You're right. Okay." As I rest my head on the wheel, it hits the horn. "Shit. I should go in before my parents come out."

    " 'Kay, babe. You've got this."

    "I don't want it."

    "Well, go get it anyway."

THE IMPOSSIBLE

My parents are lounging on the couch. They pause the black-and-white film when I walk through the door. Mom springs to her feet and rushes in for a hug. "What a nice surprise! Love the hair. We saw your note and got giddy! How come you didn't tell us you were coming? I hope nothing's wrong . . ."

I've never liked her heavy floral perfume, but I find myself fond of its comfort now.

"It's all good." I step back and examine her face. Despite her jubilance, her eyes look tired and her smile forced. I say, "I just needed to talk to the girls."

Dad's in his antique Bixby High sweatshirt. He cranes his neck to nod with approval.

"What a thoughtful gesture." Mom examines my outfit without comment. "Want to sit with us, honey? We can watch this any old time."

"I'm kind of tired—but sure. For a minute." I plop down on the matching loveseat, slapping it a few times. "How do you keep these cushions so firm? We've had this set since I was a kid."

Mom kicks off her slippers. "I get them cleaned and restuffed every so many years."

"Must be expensive. For the price, you never want something different?"

"You kids—you don't seem to care about hanging on to much." Dad laughs cynically. "It's always on to the next."

Mom squeezes his arm. "There's something nice about

constants. You know? With the way this world moves so fast."
She shakes her head. "It's good to be grounded."

"I feel like it doesn't move fast enough." I shrug. "Heard you
went to the services."

"Tragic." She clutches her chest. "Those poor people! I'm
afraid they won't get any closure. It's a terrible thing to live on
when your loved ones are taken—with no one to pay the price."
Her head shakes some more.

The little hairs on my arms rise. There are things that I wish
I felt comfortable sharing with them but doubt I ever will.

"Well, honey, you look beat. Go on up to bed. I'll make a nice
breakfast tomorrow."

"All right." I rise and head for the stairs. "Good night."

In unison, they both say, "Good night."

I plug in my phone and lie awake, ruminating on my mother's words.

There's a closeness she yearns for with me. It's as obvious as
my resistance. Sometimes I hate myself for not being able to
be—or give—what she needs. But I can't.

One day, back in my youth, I asked a few questions. She was
patient with me. She showed me where Korea was on the globe
someone had given me for Christmas. Later that night, I stood
outside my parents' bedroom door listening to her cry.

"When other kids ask, mothers point to their bellies. I have to
use a gosh darn globe!"

"Well, Maggy, we knew from the start. But you wanted to
adopt from over there. What are we supposed to do now? Send
her back?"

I froze.

"No!" She stifled a yell. "Don't you ever say that! She's mine
now, and she'll always be mine. I just wish—"

"You wish for the impossible, Maggy."

"Maybe so . . . This is just the beginning, you know."

"Of what?"

"She'll want to know who her real mom is."

"You're her real mom," says Dad. "The other one threw her away like trash. That's what they do in those countries. The women are all for the sex but can't be bothered with the kids. We all know she's much better-off here with us, in the US of A."

I sneaked back to bed and wanted to cry, but of course I couldn't. In all of my years—as far as I can recall—I've never allowed myself to cry.

I spent the bulk of my life thinking my Korean mother thoughtlessly chucked me out with the garbage. Then, in college, I started connecting with other adoptees online. I learned about birth family searches and sat on it until I felt ready. What I later discovered shook me to the core—so much so that no one in my present life knows.

But my Korean mother never treated me like trash. Learning that changed everything.

THE HOLE IN HIS MASK

Blue and gold streamers are draped across the doorway of Bixby High's gym. I drag Christy through them, tugging her hand like you would a reluctant child's. Her princess doll shoes are slowing us down and tracking blood. I tell her to lose them, and she struggles, hopping on one foot at a time. I'm growing impatient, afraid we'll be killed. She tosses them aside, and we run through the halls lined with blue and gold blocks of lockers.

It sounds like a video game hooked up through the speakers, but the speakers are playing old high school hits. It feels surreal—as if I'm trapped in someone else's bad dream.

We duck into our freshman-year English classroom. Christy whimpers. I place a finger to my lips, eyes wide. If we're heard, we'll be next.

The bullets stop. A voice wails. Footsteps retreat, followed by clicks. My untrained ears could be wrong, but it sounds like he might be reloading.

I grab Christy and bolt through the halls. Donna's up ahead. She turns back and looks straight through us. I twirl around and see the shooter standing there in all black. Through the hole in his mask, I notice his smirk.

I jump from my slumber, heart racing. My t-shirt is wet. Chills wash over every inch of my skin. I ground myself with the familiar surroundings of my old room.

Kevin . . . Could it be?

SOMETHING LIKE FIFTEEN MINUTES

Of course it wasn't Kevin.

We met on the first day of kindergarten. He sheepishly slipped onto the seat next to me on the bus. He pulled a pack of grape Hubba Bubba from a pocket of his blue overalls and offered a piece. When I told him my name was Lucy, he said, "I know."

His large brown eyes were like a retriever's. But when he smiled, there was a hint of devilishness that made him swoon-worthy. He ran with a rough crowd but seemed different somehow. While the other boys showed affection with pranks and grunts, he was sweet. He'd pay compliments and ask thoughtful questions. He was the sensitive jock.

When he asked me to junior prom, I thought it might be a joke. It didn't make sense that he'd pick me over the others vying for his attention—Christy included. His teammates would tease us both, so I figured they put him up to it. I turned him down twice. But he was persistent, and I eventually gave in.

We spent a lot of our early days together doing solitary tasks alongside one another—such as reading or homework. Or we'd go for long walks where he'd vent his frustrations. Snapping photos of farm animals and landscapes, I tried to advise and console him. It was nice, but it was more like a friendship than anything romantic.

I figured our time would end after high school and wasn't upset about it. By then, I was tiring of being his free therapist. But he surprised everyone when he followed me to San

Francisco. He worked in construction while I went to school. We weren't really aligned, but we were at peace.

One day he came to me and said, "I notice you're always checking out girls." He put his lips to my ear and whispered, "Do you ever think about doing things with them?" It was a game changer. I suddenly felt safe sharing this part of myself with someone. He knew and accepted me for who I was. We married because I felt I no longer had to hide.

When I brought a new friend home from school, I noticed his eyes following her around the room. I didn't mind. Milena was a hot city girl—an unapologetic feminist. She was bold. Hearing her talk about politics and sex was refreshing. She brought new energy to each conversation.

The three of us made pizza together, drank wine, and traversed topics such as class and gender. Kevin usually faded into the background when my friends were over, but with Milena, he made an effort. He seemed to enjoy how her sexual innuendos grew into flirtations with us both as the night progressed. When she kissed me, everything inside was awakened like never before.

Kevin snapped. Objects were flying around the room—food, bottles, and glasses. "I'm out," Milena said, and she slipped away quickly. I didn't blame her. I'd never seen him like that before. Every day I had known him, he'd been gentle and kind. But for something like fifteen minutes, he was nothing but rage. I froze. He tied my limbs to the bed frame with scarves, underwear, and leggings. He cussed me out and tore my clothes down the middle. He panted above me like some kind of hulk as I quivered, afraid of what would come next. Beads of his sweat rained down on me. Then he must've come to his senses. He backed up and off me.

I pretended to sleep while he packed his things. I knew silence would help me survive. Besides, all my words were like dried-up rivers, and my mouth was cracked mud. It took hours to wiggle out a hand. I untied the rest of my limbs, broke free, and—unable to process what had happened—put it out of my mind.

Without any discussion, I was served divorce papers. He never sent for the rest of his things. I saw him through my peripheral vision once in court and never again. Until last night.

For months, I blamed myself for putting him in an uncomfortable position. I scolded myself for allowing things to go too far with Milena. I drove myself mad wondering how such a calm, gentle man could become who he was that night. I was thankful he didn't rape me, and I used that to diminish my pain. It took me years to forgive myself and reconcile that what he did was fucked up.

But murder fifty-six people? He couldn't.

BOOHOO

As I sit on the front steps of the old house, it's like I'm fifteen again. Seeing Kevin has shaken up time and left me feeling like tossed, snake-eyed dice.

I'm lost in the fog of my brain as Donna's black SUV slows down. When I climb in, she says, "Uh oh. What's wrong?"

I grunt. "Nothing." Then I realize it's Donna. If Donna's not safe to talk to, no one is. "I ran into Kevin the other night."

"Yeah?" She glances at me. "What's that fool up to?"

"I don't know. Seeing him creeped me out, bringing back things I've tried to forget."

She shakes her head. "I never understood you two as a thing."

"Like everything from my youth, it was complicated."

She swivels towards me, wide-eyed. "Well, I hear that."

"You don't think he could've done it. Do you?"

"The shooting? Hmm . . ." She gazes out at the horizon. "I suppose he could've. But why would he?"

I shrug. "Why does anyone do these things?"

"I don't know what White men have to be so upset about, but they always find something. Don't they?" She starts up the car.

On the ride over, we decide how to frame it to Christy: Lynnette got in touch with me in San Francisco. I flew out to speak with them both but ran into Donna first. We'll insist that we both want Christy involved, or it wouldn't feel right. But when we get to her house, she's not there.

Her mother seems to have aged only in the face. "She's got a class this morning."

"Okay. How've you been, Louise?" She told us to call her by her first name when we were kids.

"Still waitin' tables and typin' reports." She shrugs. "Mindin' the little one when I can."

"She's adorable," I coo, watching Sophie decorate the driveway with chalk.

Louise looks at Donna with a tinge of resentment. "Heard you were back."

Donna acts unaffected by the lack of warmth in her tone. "Yeah. Not for long, hopefully."

Louise scoffs. "You always did think that you were too good for this place."

"Are you living here now?" I ask.

"Nah. I've still got the trailer. Not everyone can be fancy-pantsy." She lifts up her Bixby Liquors t-shirt a few inches, fanning herself. Her abdomen is still tan and tight. "Hope you're not lookin' for refreshments or nothin'. Been waitin' on people my whole damn life. I'm tired. No one ever left me no nothin' to make my life easier." Her eyes shoot daggers at Donna.

I make a pitiful attempt to change the subject. "Forgot how humid it is here in the summer."

Louise ignores me. "Once we get our country back, maybe people like me will have a chance again."

Donna cocks her head. "We've only had a Black president for seven and a half years. You think he's the reason for all your problems?"

"Nah. It was going in that direction, and he just made it worse. But to give him some credit, least he knows your people need to get some control of yourselves."

"Excuse me?"

"Shootin' each other up in the streets. Robbin' your own. All your men running off with other women or sittin' in jail—when they should be takin' care of their kids. Cloggin' up the welfare system."

I bite my tongue about her poverty and single motherhood, not wanting to stoop to her level.

"You know why?" Donna says. "Because by and large, Black people don't have the opportunities of White people. Black men get locked up for petty crimes, while White men steal from the lot of you and live unscathed in their mansions."

Louise spits on the ground. "That's funny comin' from the daughter of the richest man in town—a Black man, no less. How you think your daddy got all that money if life's so unfair to coloreds?"

"He worked ten times harder and had God-given talent. Still had to kiss plenty of White ass to be given half a chance . . ."

"I suppose he's spending his retirement cryin' in his Florida mansion." Louise puts her fists to her face and mimes a sobbing baby. "Boohoo."

Unable to stay quiet any longer, I interject. "Louise, you can't deny the systemic racism in our government and every area of society."

"Can if I want, 'cause it's all a big lie." She sneers. "You should know better, being raised by hardworking White folk."

I'm speechless.

Donna shifts to one hip. "So, White folks are the ones being held back? And Black folks are takin' over and destroying the country?"

"Well, that's the most sense I ever heard from your mouth." Louise grimaces.

"Have a good day, Louise," says Donna.

We turn to leave, shaking our heads.

Louise calls out, "I'm sure you'll have a better one."

NOT EVERYONE GETS IT

Christy joins us in Donna's sunroom with Philip bouncing by her side. "Hi," she sings. "Geez! It's like Fort Knox out there! Jacob let me in."

I rise to give her a hug.

From the couch, Donna says, "Gotta do something to protect from the vandals and death threats."

"Awful." Christy groans. "My mom said you came around to see me?" Noting our faces, she adds, "Don't mind her. She's had a hard life."

"She's racist," says Donna.

"No . . . she's . . . well . . . Sometimes she sounds like a racist, but really, she's not. She just runs her mouth a little fast sometimes." She giggles dismissively. "She means no harm."

"She thinks Black folks are destroying the country," I tell her.

"You know, it's hard for people like her. My father skipped town before I was born. She struggled her whole life to make ends meet—and now she has to listen to fools saying she's had this thing called White privilege."

"White privilege is real," Donna says.

"Maybe. But not everyone gets it."

"Yeah. Sadly, they don't," retorts Donna.

"It's just as bad as saying all Black men are gangsters. Right? I mean, if all White folks had privilege," says Christy, "none of us would have to work so hard to get by. And you see how it is. You remember how it was for us—and still is for Mom."

"I don't have the energy for this," says Donna, yawning.

I jump in. "White privilege isn't just about the material things, and it's not on an individual level. It's systemic." Christy scrunches her face. I rub Philip's ears. "Overall, White people get better access to education, opportunities, and the benefit of the doubt. It's an overarching thing, rigged to keep Black and Brown folks poor and in prison. It's legalized slavery. You should learn more about it."

She frowns. "My mother worked shit jobs all her life. She couldn't have gone to college. Who'd have watched me? Who'd have put food on the table? Don't fall for it, girls. It's all made-up language meant to divide us." Christy bends down to fawn over Philip. In a baby voice, she says, "Isn't that right? Yeah! You're black and you know!"

I sit back, feeling pained.

"Anyway," says Christy, as buoyant as ever. "What's up? What'd you come around for?" She removes a bottle of wine from her bag and twists it open. "You don't mind—do you, Donna?" Donna shrugs and flicks her head in the opposite direction.

I ask, "Has anyone contacted you from San Francisco?"

"No." Christy pours herself a glass and pauses over my empty one. I nod. She says, "What for?"

I take a sip. "This woman out there tracked me down. Her publishing house wants the rights to our story."

"A story about us?" I can see her gears spinning.

"The shooting and us as survivors—maybe with some background on Bixby. Hopefully before it's done, the shooter will be caught."

"Wow . . ." Christy's eyes sparkle. She stares off at a dream in her mind. "Do you think they'll make a movie?"

"It's possible."

"Would we be in it?"

"I . . . I don't know." I glance over at Donna, who's rolling her eyes.

"Before you get off on the idea of being a movie star," says Donna, "let's not forget fifty-six people died, and their families are grieving."

"That's why I flew out—to talk about this in person. If we do this, it's our responsibility to do it justice. It can't be some cheap action film made for ratings. It's gotta be respectful of the dead and their families."

"And you know," adds Donna, "it might have a gun angle. I know we don't all agree on that."

"I don't understand why anyone, especially now, thinks we shouldn't have guns," says Christy.

"They found two handguns among the bodies," I tell her. "They didn't get a chance to fire. What do you propose? Everyone walks around with machine guns?"

Christy shrugs. "I just think it's a bad idea for only the bad guys to have guns."

"Well, I agree with that," says Donna. "As long as the cops have 'em, everyone should be allowed. Black folks need to defend ourselves. The cops already have too much power."

"I think no one should have 'em," I say. "Cops included."

"Well, that's just senseless." Christy peers at me, surprised. "All the big men would win every time. There'd be no hope for people like you and me."

"If we're all walking around with machine guns, there's no hope for anyone."

"So, what about the money?" Christy asks. "Did they say anything about that?" Donna shakes her head. "What?" Christy puts her drink down. "Am I supposed to act like money doesn't matter? I grew up in a soup can. My mom still works around the clock. She can't go sun herself on a beach for the rest of her days. Not even with all her White privilege."

"Maybe this is too much," I concede, leaning forward with my head in my hands. "I must've been crazy to think we could work together on something like this." Philip licks my chin, but I stay committed to my disappointment.

"I'm sorry." Christy crosses her arms and twists side to side. She shakes out her shoulders. "I get a little emotional sometimes when it comes to family. I'll try to do better. But I could do with less judgment."

Donna takes a sip of cider and says, "I never said a word."

"You didn't have to."

"It's your own insecurities rising up."

Christy plays with the hem of her dress. She sits a few beats in silence, then shrugs. "Could be. I'll bear that in mind."

"Well, I guess you were right, too." Donna sighs. "I was annoyed by you asking about money so fast. It seemed crude. But I get that you've spent your life not having much."

"Let's end on that note," I suggest. "We'll reconnect in a couple of days."

WHITE, HETERO, CHRIST-LOVING ARMS

The aroma of coffee swells in the air. Alexis and I don't drink coffee, and neither did Kevin. The smell of those bitter beans in the morning's a Bixby thing. In particular, it's a "Dad's Going on a Haul" thing.

"I'm headed out a few days." He stands as if paused in an in-between frame. "Will you be here when I'm back?"

"Not sure yet. I got a one-way."

"Well . . ." He clutches onto his thermos and bag like a young boy waiting for the bus, despite his six-foot frame. "Spend some time with your mother. She gets lonely when I'm gone."

"All right. Drive safely."

He nods and heads out. I stay put for a minute, ruminating on the awkwardness that's always existed between us.

Mom's in the kitchen, tossing out scraps and wiping down surfaces. She hums to herself as she works away swiftly.

"Just saw Dad off."

"Yep. Another run."

"Any wild plans while he's gone?"

She chuckles. "Eating and watching whatever I darn well please is as wild as it gets, I'm afraid. Care to join me? We can get Master Pizza." She holds a rag to her hip and smiles.

My heart jumps to a yes, but my mouth says, "I don't want to give them business anymore."

"How come?"

"When Alexis was here, they turned us away. They pretended like they were closing in the middle of lunch."

"How'd you know they weren't really closing?"

"Because I was there." I sigh, knowing where this is headed.

She shakes her head. "Ever since you went west, you think everyone's racist. Maybe they were tired and wanted to close early? Does it have to be about race every time?"

I envision myself running laps around the kitchen fifty times before knocking myself out on the fridge and falling backwards onto a chalk outline. But I say, "It wasn't about race this time. They didn't like that we're gay."

"Did they say that?"

All of the times I came home to tell my parents that some kid treated me poorly boil up. "You know—sometimes I wish your instinct was to be on my side with curiosity and compassion. I know what it was because I was there, and I've experienced these kinds of things my whole life."

She puts down her rag and crosses her arms. "Sweetie, I am on your side. But you know—you didn't even know you were gay until when? And you can't possibly know what's going on inside other people's heads and why they do things. You assume the worst. It's no way to live."

I pick up a stool and put it down hard. My body's buzzing. My brain struggles with where to start. "Just because I wasn't ready to tell you doesn't mean I didn't know. Did you ever think maybe you weren't safe to tell?"

Her jaw drops. She stands with her mouth hanging open, shifting from one hip to the other. "I have been nothing but safe! I don't know why you'd say otherwise—except to be hurtful and mean. It's been a privilege to watch you blossom into who you've become. It hasn't always been what I expected—"

"Or hoped."

She nods quickly. "Or hoped. But you were exactly what this family needed."

"Maybe that's because I knew I had to be." I pull the stool out and slide onto it, shaking with nerves. My fingers dance off one another. "As long as I lived in Bixby, I had to be a good daughter who never questioned things. I had to be straight, White, Christian."

"No one ever told you to be any of those things—except Christian."

"Maybe not directly, but it's the message I got loud and clear. Even Dad said, last time I was here, that life would be better if I'd just keep pretending I'm like the rest of you."

"I doubt that's what he meant. He's not good with words. You know that."

I cross my arms and squeeze. "I know what he meant. He asked why I had to go around doing my gay thing everywhere, because I'd be treated better if I didn't."

"Well, he has a point."

"But don't you see?" I bounce my palms on the counter. "In order to be treated right, I have to act like someone I'm not. I don't think that's fair. As my mother, you should feel the same way."

"You're telling me how I should feel now. Is that it?" She starts spraying the surfaces of appliances, going over areas already clean. I rise to stand closer to her so she can't ignore me. She squirts some more cleaning product as if unaffected. "You think it's unfair? Well, that's life, dear. I have to act nice to Darlene, who I never could stand, in order to keep peace at church. As a woman, I have to color my grays and stay thin so I'm not seen as some undesirable hag. We all have to do things—cover up parts of ourselves. I don't like it either, but it's just how it is."

I groan, following her around the kitchen as she continues with her physical distractions. "It's not the same thing! Being a young, friendly brunette is not part of your core identity in the same way that being Asian and queer is mine."

"Maybe that shouldn't be your focus! Did you ever think of that? You're so quick to home in on what makes you different. You blame us whether we notice or not. We can't win!"

"See? You put me on the other side!" I throw a rag in the air. "Well . . . Go get your gay-hating pizza then! I hope they welcome you with their White, hetero, Christ-loving arms!"

My feet nearly trip as I run up the stairs. My heart thumps in my throat. I want to slam the door but refrain. I pull the covers up tight, wondering if I'll ever stop shaking.

WHAT IT WAS

I roll over to see The Lost Boys' cast peering down at me. I rub my eyes, stretch, and grab my phone from the nightstand.

> Alexis: How are things going down there?
>
> Me: It's a shit show. > <
>
> Alexis: What happened?
>
> Me: Mom and I had it out. Hiding in my room like a child.
>
> Alexis: It seems like she loves you so much. What'd she say?
>
> Me: I'm a disappointment.
>
> Alexis: What???
>
> Me: I wasn't what she hoped for.
>
> Alexis: Ouch!
>
> Me: I'll meet with D&C this afternoon and figure out how much longer I'll stay.
>
> Alexis: Take as long as you need, but I miss you. <3
>
> Me: Miss you so much. <3

I flash back to when Alexis and I were walking into town. It was so clear to her that my childhood would've been difficult—just after two days. Why is it so hard for my parents to see it?

And then it occurs to me: They're the reason why it was what it was.

The night I overheard my mother crying, Dad said, "But you wanted to adopt from over there." I'd love to get clarification on why two White people in Whitesville specifically wanted an Asian baby. How did something so unnatural become so normal?

Mom and Dad mean well. I believe that they love me as much as they can. But in so many ways, they don't know me—or want to. I'm not sure it's enough.

I love them as much as I can, too. Sometimes I'm not sure that's enough, either.

MAYBE THINGS WILL BE OKAY

Christy has a backyard, but she prefers to sit out front. It allows her to feel connected to the town. Cars drive by with friendly beeps and waves. Her face doesn't hide how much she enjoys it.

I ask, "Is it always like this?"

"Yeah." Her face glows with an unconcealed pride. "It happens much more since I started my vlog."

I take the opportunity at hand and say, "Tell me about your vlog." Suddenly, the color drains from her face like she's just seen a ghost. Turning my head towards the street and back, I ask, "You okay?"

She exhales, blowing air over her face. "Yeah."

"What was that about?"

"I'd rather not say." After I shrug, she huffs. "I had a fling. Okay? Mike and I were on a break." She glares expectantly.

I tell her, "I'm not here to judge."

"I hate when they get so attached . . . Anyway." She shakes it off. "About the vlog . . . I saw the need for Bixby to be understood. Things I heard about us on Fox News were disturbing."

"Many things on Fox News are disturbing," Donna says.

I purse my lips, high-fiving her in my mind.

Christy continues. "It sort of took on a life of its own."

"I saw the first one," I tell her. "Guess I should check out the rest."

"Yeah! Don't forget to give a thumbs-up!"

I force a nod and a smile.

Christy reclines in her chair, slipping on a pair of oversized pink sunglasses. Lounging under the yellow umbrella, she looks like a Hollywood star.

Donna sits in an upright woven fishing chair. I use the pink plastic blow-up seat that farts when I move.

"By the way," I say, my eyes studying Christy. "Why wasn't Mike at the reunion?"

"Oh, he had a thing with his army pals," she says dismissively.

"I know he was a few years ahead, but it was your twentieth reunion. You were a big deal in our class. But he had other plans?"

"We were dealing with some stuff at the time. Hence the affair." She shrugs. "Figured it was better-off."

I nod my head to the side as if I understand. But if they were fighting, it makes him all the more suspect.

Donna says, "All right. So let's make this list." She opens the laptop and works away.

The chair announces me before I speak. "We might as well talk money first. Get it out of the way."

Donna peers at me. "Anything you care to share?"

"I propose we give most—if not all—to the families and town."

Christy scoffs. "What about all the time off work?"

"We can do what we need on off-hours," I suggest. "According to Lynnette, it shouldn't take much. She said it's just answering questions. We could probably do it via video chat."

"Still." Christy slides one leg up the lounger, raising a knee. "Our time should be worth something. Not to mention the emotional toll. Every hour on this is an hour away from our families. Right, Donna?"

"We could give ourselves a modest fee." Donna nods. "How much do you think is fair?"

"That depends." Christy slides her sunglasses down. "Just

how much are we talkin'?"

"Lynnette acts like it's seven figures." I shrug. "But I don't know. It could be much less."

"How 'bout one-eighth," says Donna. "We can do what we want with our shares. Donate. Keep. Whatever."

Christy cuts in. "A quarter, because it should really be half, but we're being charitable." She pouts.

It's hard to look serious on an inflatable pink chair, but I try. "What if half goes to the survivors' families, a quarter to the town, an eighth to us, and an eighth towards studying gun violence?"

Christy tears her sunglasses off and dramatically tosses them on the grass. "I will not have my money go towards helping people take away guns. Our country was founded on guns."

"Our country was founded on White supremacy and genocide," says Donna.

I snap three times.

Christy gives a look of shock and disbelief. "If not for guns, how'd we win all the wars?"

Carefully avoiding her last question, I say, "There's a reason we're the only first-world country with this amount of gun deaths. Do you really want these shootings to go on taking lives anywhere, anytime?"

Christy sighs. "We've got a people problem, not a gun problem."

"I'm with Christy on not taking away guns." Donna turns towards me. " 'Cause you know it'd become race exclusionary."

"All right." I shrug. "We'll agree to disagree about guns. What do you suggest we do about the money?"

Donna adjusts the laptop screen. "Let's give the survivors' families half and Bixby a quarter."

Christy sighs. "Yeah, okay. If we can split the other quarter."

Another car drives by and honks. Christy perks up and waves.

"We should be careful they don't dig too deep into everyone's lives," I warn. "They can get to know the victims without pulling up dirt."

"And on the flip side," Donna adds, "they shouldn't glorify anyone, either. Now don't get me wrong . . . They should all be alive. But death has a funny way of sainting the undeserved."

"I don't want them to make us look like hicks." Christy retrieves her sunglasses and cool demeanor. "I want them to know we're no different from the city folk."

I look at her earnestly. "But you *are* different, in many ways."

"Well, we should be careful of who they interview. We don't want just anyone representing us. In small towns like ours, they always find the ones with bad teeth who don't know how to speak a full sentence."

I throw my head back to laugh, and the chair nearly topples. "I don't think we can control that."

Donna's mouth flattens into a line. "It should be mindful enough not to deify the shooter in the eyes of those like him." We nod as she types.

"It should steer away from the gore," I add. "No crime scene photos or graphic reenactments."

"But it should capture the terror," says Christy, shivering. "I want people to know what we lived through."

"I want the world to see how the town responded to me— despite being one of you. They should know about the calls, death threats, and vandalism." Donna continues typing.

"Just as long as they don't think we're all racist," says Christy.

"Oh, don't you worry," replies Donna. "That's all Black folks ever think about when we're sharing how we've been hurt by injustice."

Christy smiles, perhaps missing Donna's sarcasm.

"We should be aware that they might try to cause friction between us for drama's sake," Donna continues. "Let's not fall for it, ladies."

"Hmm. Is this, like, practical?" asks Christy. "I mean—it sounds good and all. But I thought the whole point of books and movies is to make them interesting."

Stifling a laugh, I tell her, "You've got a point."

"We can ask for certain things in our contract," explains Donna. "We'll choose our top non-negotiables once we finish this list. Maybe get them to agree that the final product meets our approval."

I feel a tinge of hope witnessing the three of us, as different as can be, working together for the greater good. Sitting in the deflating chair, I smile to myself. Maybe things will be okay.

THE TALK

Not wanting to face the tension with my mother, I stay in bed like a mopey teen. My head spins with worry about the shooter and the book. It's hard to feel there will ever be closure. While I'm successfully distracting myself from the more present fear, I'm foiled by two taps on the door.

"Knock knock. It's Mom."

I push back a snide remark. "Hey," I say, settling for something neutral.

She peers in. "I thought we should talk. Is now a good time?"

Propping myself up with pillows and making a show of it, I say, "I don't know. Got a pretty full schedule here."

She sits two-thirds of the way down the bed, her feet and eyes on the floor as if she's searching for something misplaced. "I'm sorry for the way things went yesterday. I wasn't at my best." She rubs the comforter between her index finger and thumb. "Can we try again?"

"Yeah. I'm sorry for some of my word choices, too. It's just . . . painful sometimes."

She always puts on her motherly mask for me, but at this moment, it slips. "I've been thinking about what you said—and you're right. I haven't been able to see things from your point of view. I never realized it'd be so . . ." She waves both arms in the air as if drowning. "Complicated, being a mother to a foreign child."

"And that's your privilege, bringing me to live in your world."

She nods, keeping her head down. "I see that now. But

they said all you'd need was love. It'd be enough. Nothing else mattered."

"Well, they didn't know shit. Love is important," I say, crossing my legs to sit up. "I know I'm one of the luckier ones. But love's not enough. Love doesn't erase our pasts, who we are, and that we don't belong—no matter how much it tries." I pause for a moment, feeling my nerves revving inside my chest. "You can love us all you want, but no amount of love will make us White. Your cloak might protect us a bit when we're young and when we're by your side. But once we're out in the world without you . . ." I fling my arm to the side. "Our cover's blown."

"The first time I saw that, I cried. You came home telling me about what some kid said. That's when I realized I wasn't prepared. Had I been your birth mom, I might've known what to say, 'cause maybe it'd have happened to me. I wondered what the heck I got us all into."

"I don't recall you ever trying to make it any better."

"I didn't know how." She gives an exaggerated shrug. "There was no manual on how to deal with those things."

"That's probably 'cause we shouldn't have been products."

"Well, I didn't mean . . ."

"I know you didn't. It's baked into you, and it's not all your fault. The adoption industry sucks. They say whatever they think folks want to hear—like love is all you need. That's why I hate that Beatles song."

"I was afraid to ask any questions. Didn't want them to think I was ill-equipped. Thought they might change their minds."

"Sadly, they rarely prioritize the kids. You know—the ones they're supposedly saving." I roll my eyes.

"Hmm." She stares at the floral wallpaper. She'd insisted on it when I was twelve, despite my hard lobby for turquoise.

"Instead, they protect their transaction," I continue. "You

know—all my life, I've felt like an exotic plant expected to thrive in incompatible soil. Everyone would stare, waiting for me to bloom into something else. When I couldn't, I blamed myself."

She drops her head. "That must've been hard."

I stare, blankly, at nothing. "Did you ever regret adopting me?" I nervously find her eyes.

"No." She looks up at me. Her hand reaches halfway for mine but falls limp to the bed. "But I won't lie. We adopted you for us. I wanted a child so bad . . . And we heard all these wonderful stories."

My heart races as I build up the courage to ask, "Why'd you choose Korea?"

"I knew a woman," she says without hesitation. "She adopted a local American girl. We went to her birthday parties. She was part of the family—as if from the start. You wouldn't even know she was adopted if you weren't told." She shakes her head. "At around five years old, her birth mother came looking for her. She sued them to get her back. She didn't win, but it put them through an ordeal. They took off into hiding. No one knows where they are now. I didn't want to go through what she did. Korean adoptions were popular then. We heard about it at church, and so we chose that. The idea that we'd get a child no one would come looking for while doing God's work seemed like a win-win."

"That's so messed up." I sigh. "For so many reasons."

Her back stiffens. "I hope you never know how it feels to want a child and to have your body betray you. To feel like less of a woman, a failure to yourself and your . . . partner. Only then will you know just how far you might go and how little space you might have to consider anything beyond that."

"I appreciate your honesty. And I'm sorry for your pain. But you know—being too wrapped up in my own suffering to consider how I might cause others to suffer? I hope that's not who I'll be." Her eyes are welling up, and I realize I'm not as cold as I may sometimes seem. "Look . . . There's no undoing the past. All in all, you've given me a pretty good life. You've always tried to make me feel loved. But what I need, in order to feel that love now, is for you to want to know me. The real me. Okay, there are limits, but you know what I mean. I want to feel you respect what life was like for me growing up in the middle of—" I stop myself from saying "nowhere." "Bixby," I finish. "And what it's like for me now."

Her brow furrows as she nods. "But what if I try and I can't?"

"Then at least you'd have tried. And that'd mean the world to me." My stubborn eyes begin to well, too. An invasive buzzing interrupts. I reach for my phone, and without looking, send it to voicemail. "I'm so tired of feeling the real me is too hard for you to look at."

"You were never hard to look at. You've always been beautiful," she implores.

"I'm lucky to have a mom who thinks that. But you think it because you're biased. And to be honest, it doesn't mean a whole lot until you really see me."

"I do see you, Lucy. You're no different from anyone else here."

My eyes lift to meet hers, full of regret. "Well, if you think that, you really don't see me. You want to know the hardest thing, though? It's that my whole experience of being raised without any others like me made it so I couldn't see me, either. It made me think of myself, Korea, and Asia as *less than*."

She clutches her chest and pauses a moment to soak in my words. "I guess you're right. A part of me sees you as White. There's nothing wrong with my eyes. I know how you look. I just never think of you as Asian . . . because you're my daughter—and, I don't know—it feels wrong to notice, when to me you're so much more than that."

"When people say they don't see race or color, they don't realize it's erasure. And it casts others into a role they never meant to play. We don't all have to be the same to be loved. It's okay to see and accept how we differ. And you know, for me, it's more than just race."

There's a quick change in her expression. She fidgets with her hands. I consider whether I got that from her through learned behavior. Or maybe I mimicked it on purpose, wanting to connect to her through inherited traits, the way other kids did with their parents. "I'm sorry you had to keep it all to yourself for so long," she says. She scoots up the bed to rub my knee. "I didn't realize I made it so uncomfortable for you to come out."

"All that talk about boys and the man I would marry . . . You and Dad had a clear picture of what you wanted from me. I know you didn't do it on purpose, but it made an impact."

Her eyes meet mine. "Is that why you married Kevin?"

"He wasn't your fault." I toss a hand in the air. "I was just so anxious to feel normal; I mistook it for love. I was still working through what it meant to like girls . . . and guys. A lot of queers think people like me are in denial. They don't believe we're legit."

"People didn't talk about things the way they do now."

Leaning forward, I tell her, "And that's why I correct Dad when he uses outdated language and says offensive shit. I'm not trying to give him a hard time. I just don't want to carry on the old way. It prevents people like me from moving ahead. It might be uncomfortable for you, but we've been uncomfortable forever. It's time the rest of you catch up and consider those who've been suffering for your comfort."

Mom lifts her legs up onto the bed and crosses them, swiveling her whole body towards me. "I guess you're right." She sits quietly for a minute, then says, "I'll try to be more mindful. But you know, it won't be easy."

"You're allowed to be human. Just don't be so defensive." Tears well in my eyes, and I fight them back so hard that it pains me. "I want to be allowed to be who I am without having any part of it erased. Spending my life trying to be a straight White girl . . . nearly broke me."

Her hand covers mine. "And I don't want that. You deserve to feel good about who you are." She pulls me in for a hug. My brain tells my body to burst the dam. I want to cry like the child who's been waiting her whole life for the safety of her mother, but still, I cannot. As much as I love her, she's not the mother I need to cry for.

My phone buzzes again, and we let it ring out.

"I'm sorry, Lucy. I'm sorry for every way that I've failed you."

"You haven't—"

"I have," she insists. "And I'll try to do better. But your father . . ." Her face contorts as she searches for the right words. I want to cry, but I laugh, and she laughs along with me. And oh, does it feel good to laugh.

My phone buzzes again. We loosen our embrace, Mom's sticky tears clinging to my hair as we pull apart.

I take the phone in my hands. "It's Donna. Let me see what's so urgent." I accept the call and say, "Hey. What's up?"

"Lucy. It's Jacob. Donna's in jail."

THINGS ARE NOT OKAY

I call Christy five times, but she doesn't pick up. When I realize I still have her childhood number memorized, I dial it.

"Hey, Louise. It's Lucy. Christy's not with you, is she?"

"If you knew that, why did you call here to ask?"

I bite my lip at her predictable nature. "Is she teaching a class?"

"Not till this evening."

"Shit."

"What's the matter?"

Not wanting to hear her gloat about what's happening with Donna, I lie. "Nothing. It's no big deal. I'll leave a message on her cell." I hang up and jump into Dad's car.

When I pull up at Christy's, her blue VW Bug is in the driveway. Approaching the house, I tune my ears to her voice. She's in there—perhaps with a friend. I knock on the door and ring the bell twice. Losing patience, I ring it twice more.

"Jesus H. Christ," she grumbles. I hear her footsteps drawing nearer. She flings the door open with exasperation. "I told you—" She halts as if she were expecting someone else. Her face is dialed up to eleven. Navy liner. Giant lashes. Diagonal streaks of peach. Highlighter and petal-pink gloss. She glares at me as I stand there, dumbstruck. Finally, as if about to combust, she says, "Lucy! What is it?"

Don't mention her face. Don't mention her face. "Were you expecting someone else?"

"No . . ."

I shift my weight to the left. "I've . . ." *Don't mention her face, damn it!* "I've been trying to reach you for hours."

"Well, come in." She holds the door open for me to walk through. "I was filming a video out back. I was in the flow of things. Do you know what that's like? You're doing your thing and it just comes to you. Like, you don't have to think. You just know what to do. Sometimes I feel it during yoga, but this is different."

"Yeah." I try to avert my eyes and look at random things in the room, but they land on that painting of Jesus.

She sits on the couch and taps the cushion for me to join her. "Now, don't get me wrong. It's terrible, what happened. All those people dying. But it's bringing something out in me." She grins shyly, as if to conceal pride. "I'm finding my voice."

I take a seat in the corner of the couch, shifting my body diagonally towards her. "Christy," I say, heating up. "Donna's in jail."

Her face contorts. Her powdered brows bounce. "No. That can't be!"

"Jacob called from her phone. She must've left it at home before supposedly turning herself in."

"That doesn't make sense," she spits, head shaking.

I quickly inhale. "Obviously someone's setting her up. She couldn't have confessed to anything real. I bet the cops dragged her in and made up this story, expecting everyone to believe it."

"The cops wouldn't do that."

My patience is slipping. "I know you want to believe the cops are all good, that they protect and serve everyone—but they aren't, and they don't. This kind of shit happens to Black folks all the time."

"But not here in Bixby."

"Yes, right here in Bixby. Snap out of it, Christy. Your denial helps no one."

"Should we go to the station? Should we tell them they've made a mistake?"

Astonished, I throw my hands in the air. "What good do you think that'll do?"

Christy shrugs. "Maybe if we tell them she was with us, they'll let her go?"

"Didn't we already do that?" I sigh. "She's in jail for killing fifty-six people. They say she confessed. They won't hear us repeat what we already said and release her." I huff, overwhelmed, averting my eyes from the area of the room with the Jesus painting. Inhale. Exhale. "But maybe you're onto something. Maybe you can use your prominence around here somehow . . ."

"My vlog!" A spark twinkles in her eyes. "I'll scrap what I was doing and make a video about her. I'll tell the world who she is and explain that she couldn't have done it. Maybe you can help?"

"Yes. Do that, Christy. But they don't want my face on your channel. I'll do what I can on my own. Use your Whiteness and popularity to her advantage. That's what allies do." A surge of energy rushes through me. "You can do this." And to seal the deal, I add, "Maybe this is your calling."

"Maybe it is," she wonders. "I always knew my life had greater purpose."

I bite my tongue and smile encouragingly.

INTERLUDES

On this beautiful day, no kids are outside. Hardly any adults are out walking or driving. This town may not change much, but it's been scared right into its shell. I feel it through the tires on the empty pavement. I sense it in my bones.

A call's incoming from Tae-Suk. I hit speaker. "Hey, Tae."

"Hey hey. How are things going out there?"

I sigh. "It's a mess. Donna's in jail."

"No shit . . ."

"Total shit." I stop at one of the few traffic lights in town and put on my blinker, its measured ticks echoing through the line.

"What do you think will happen?"

"Fucked if I know. How are things there?"

"Eh, all right. Are you staying long? No rush. Just wondering if we should contract some things out."

"You probably should." The light turns, and I make a right through the center of town. "I'd say I could work remotely, but now that Donna's locked up, I won't have the focus."

"No worries. Carin said to take as much time as you need. How are you holding up?"

"I shouldn't complain, considering what Donna and the families of the dead are going through. But I'm ready for it to be over. I spent half my life waiting to leave. And now here I am, sucked right back in."

"Do what you've gotta do."

Pulling into the driveway, I say, "All right. I've gotta run."

"A'ight. Let me know when you have a better idea of your

timing. And you know . . ." He pauses. "You can call anytime. You're my friend. Hit me up."

"Thanks. That means a lot."

When we disconnect, I relish the feeling of being reconnected to my life in San Francisco. I miss who I am there. I miss Alexis, my job, and my friends. What if they realize how well they can get on without me?

> Me: Hey babes.
>
> Alexis: Hey. Where you been?
>
> Me: Sorry. So much is happening here. I can hardly keep up, myself.
>
> Alexis: What's going on?
>
> Me: Mom and I had a really good talk. It might be a turning point.
>
> Alexis: That's great!
>
> Me: But while we were talking, Donna supposedly turned herself in??? No clue why. I don't trust it.
>
> Alexis: Shit . . .
>
> Me: Someone's gotta be setting her up.
>
> Alexis: Fuck that town.
>
> Me: Christy's going to use her vlog to try to change people's hearts.
>
> Alexis: Sounds like a decent way to help.
>
> Me: Yeah . . . I don't know what to do.
>
> Alexis: You'll think of something.
>
> Me: How are you?
>
> Alexis: Fine. Just missing you.
>
> Me: I miss you, too. Sorry I haven't been keeping in touch. My distance is due to the goings on here, not a reflection of how I feel about you.
>
> Alexis: Since we're talking about feelings, I should confess. I'm not totally over what might've happened with Lynnette.
>
> Me: What can I do to make things better?

Alexis: I 99.9999% trust you. It's just going to take time. Don't force me through it.

Me: Fair enough. I'm sorry again, for my recklessness.

Alexis: And I'm sorry things are still such a mess out there. Hope this shit clears up for Donna.

Me: You and me both. <3 you.

Alexis: <3 you.

MADDENING

No matter how many ways I try to wrap my head around Donna's confession, I know it's false. It came out of nowhere. She couldn't have walked into the BPD and turned herself in without any warning. Yet, sitting with Mom after dinner, what do I see on TV but her doing just that.

"It's not her," I blurt. "They hired someone to pretend to be her. Notice how you only see her from the back?" Another angle catches her profile. My heart sinks; I'm unable to further deny it.

"They could've forced her to walk in like that," offers Mom. "Instead of being handcuffed."

I picture Jalen and Jamal's little faces watching her on TV. Maybe Mom's right. They bargained with Donna, knowing she'd do anything to protect her boys from that image.

From my old bedroom, I call Donna's cell phone. When Jacob answers, I ask, "How are you holding up?"

He sighs. "I keep praying the Lord will shed light onto this soon enough, since Donna and the cops can't seem to."

"Have you talked to her?"

"Briefly, but she's not making sense. She ignored almost all of my questions. Kept repeating that it was the right thing to do. I've tried to decode that a hundred ways." Jacob exhales heavily.

"This is going to be expensive," I tell him. "Has anyone been in touch with her parents?"

"I'm her husband. I'll take care of it."

Instead of telling him that now is no time for pride, I suggest,

"What about Black Lives Matter or the NAACP? Maybe they can help somehow . . ."

"Are you kidding?" He sneers. "One sniff of either of those groups and they'll be all the more eager to convict."

"Shit. You're probably right."

"We'll find a way. The Lord provides for His faithful children."

"It's just . . . maddening." I fidget with my hand, pressing fingers to thumbs. "Sometimes I think I'll explode. I can only imagine what it's like for you."

"Well, don't be angry on our behalf."

"I'm not angry *for* you." I'm thrown by his statement. "As the only other Person of Color in town, I'm angry *with* you."

"Color? Huh. What color? I know you mean well, but I don't know how else to say this except: You ain't Black."

I close my eyes and take a deep breath, holding it a few seconds before slowly exhaling. "Of course I'm not Black. But as a Person of Color, I'm angry that this White town was out to pin it on her from the start."

"This White town. Have you looked at your family?"

"You say that as if it were my choice. Sure, in some ways, being raised here by White parents provided more safety than Asian parents might've. But I lost my Korean family, my lineage, language, and culture."

"I'm supposed to feel bad for the White privilege you had, now?"

I slap my thigh. "Would you give Jalen or Jamal to White people? Do you think they'd be better-off?"

He sighs. "I'm just saying: You're not one of us. These people don't see you as one of us, either. No matter how much color you think you might have, you're home, and Donna's in jail."

"I think about that every day!"

"Yeah, but you haven't lived it. But don't listen to me, right?

I'm just a Black man foolish enough to have come here."

"I want to listen to you."

"No, you don't," he says with a huff. "My wife's in jail for committing a crime she was a victim of. But you want me to listen to how hard your life is."

I toss the phone across the room, nostalgic for the old land-lines you could slam for dramatic effect. My whole body shakes. I don't know how the conversation took such a bad turn.

Jacob's voice echoes in my head. *You're not one of us.*

GUESS WHAT? YOU'RE RACIST

I'm still shaking from the conversation with Jacob when my phone bleeps from across the room. I reluctantly retrieve it. It's YouTube notifying me of new content on Christy's channel. She didn't waste any time.

Seated on what must be her back steps, Christy positions the camera so it peers up from thirty degrees, making her look larger than life. Her canary-yellow dress is adorned with white lace and white fabric buttons. Either she took some of that makeup off or she knew what she was doing with it. She sits there in silence for maybe a minute, gazing out past the lens. When she looks down, her clear blue eyes meet the camera.

"So, you've probably heard about Donna by now. You might've seen her on the news, walking into the Bixby PD? If your first instinct was to think, 'I knew it'—then, guess what? You're racist."

She leans back, lifting her chin. "You might think Bixby's full of hicks who hate Black people. Well, that's not true. Besides—Donna's not like the others you hear about on the news. She's a mother of two beautiful boys. She's married to their father." Christy holds up a photo of Donna and her family that was taken on the Fourth of July. "She's a patriot. Her husband serves the Lord. She's never been on welfare. In fact, her family was the richest in town. They donated money each year, helping Bixby become what we are today." She brings the blurry photo close to the lens, and it sharpens on the Devines for a few beats before she pulls the photo away.

"I grew up with Donna. She, Lucy, and me were best friends. Does that surprise you? Then, guess what? You're racist. I don't see color. I see people. I see a loving mom who's gentle and kind. As we sat on the floor in that art supply closet, waiting for the bullets to stop, she prayed with me. My mind was scattered—but Donna? She never lost focus. She had faith that the Lord would watch over us, and He did. That's who Donna is. Not some poor, violent Black girl from the city."

I smack my hand to my face.

"And thank God. My childhood wouldn't have been the same without her or Lucy. I'm grateful our town was blessed with their presence. Otherwise, it'd have been me in that closet alone. I'd have had a breakdown, for sure."

She pauses, turning her head to the right, resting her chin on a fist. Her head stays still as her eyes shift around.

"Think of what you saw again on the news. Was it a Black girl turning herself in? Or was it a woman, a human named Donna—a mother, daughter, wife, friend, and believer? Now, I know blue lives matter. The cops put their lives on the line to protect and to serve. I'm not saying they're setting her up, but something's not right. Maybe, the loyal woman she is, she decided the only way to let us move on was to incriminate herself? Maybe the PTSD is taking a toll? You know—she's had to hire security around the clock to protect her family from death threats and vandals. Did you know that? Are you okay with it? If you are, then guess what? You're racist. Because you might see a Black woman, but I see Donna, my lifelong friend. And Donna didn't have nothin' to do with the tragedy that took fifty-six lives on July second."

Her body relaxes back into its starting position. Eyes brimming with confidence, she delivers one final blow: "Think on that." She tilts her head sassily before the picture goes black.

I bang the heel of my palm against my forehead before releasing a loud grunt of anguish.

If Christy's the best we can hope for, we're fucked.

SHIT WHITE PEOPLE SAY

I lie the wrong way on the bed, legs against the wall and one hand on a phone. "They say she confessed—but to what? Clearly, she wasn't the one with the gun. I want details. If they're going to say she hired someone, who is he? Where is he?"

"They're scrambling to create those details now." Alexis clicks her tongue. "The lies will spill out soon enough."

"And the world will believe them." Reaching for a hamstring to pull forward, I tell her, "There's a clip of her so-called confession. Fox will air it at nine."

"I'm sorry, babe. It's not fair."

Reaching for the other leg, I mumble, "No, it ain't."

"Maybe I should organize something up here. Start a movement."

"Hmm. Great idea, but it should probably be led by Black folks."

"I'll get the convo started, see if it goes anywhere." Alexis moans. "Woman, I miss the fuck out of you. No pressure, though. I respect what you're doing."

"I don't even know what I'm doing anymore."

"You're being there for your friend, standing by."

"It's not enough." I roll back and flip onto my stomach.

"Do you think . . ." My muscles tense from her tone, and I pause. "Do you think Donna would be as upset as you are, had things been reversed?"

"You mean if I were in jail and she were out here?"

"Yeah."

"That's not even a legitimate question."

"Why not?"

"Because." I sigh. "Aside from racist immigration policies, Asian Americans aren't locked up en masse. Bixby's not out to deport me."

"I just wonder if she'd be as loyal to you."

"What does it matter?" I sit up, cross-legged, face flushed with annoyance. "What's right is right."

"Never mind," she says, defeated. "It was just a dumb question."

"I'm going to have to do this with you now, aren't I?" I moan. "You did this the day we got shut out of Master Pizza, after I was hounded by the press. You were questioning how well I know Donna, acting like maybe the town had a point. You said something with Donna was off."

"I didn't know much about her then."

"That shouldn't matter. Look . . . I was too tired to get into it that day. But it bothered me then, and it bothers me now."

"Hey," she sings. "I didn't mean to upset you."

"But you did. Don't you realize your questioning is in line with the shit White people say?"

"No," she says nervously. "I don't."

"That's what kills me." I sigh. "There's always this air of disbelief, questions of doubt. Who cares if Donna would go to bat for me—or whatever Devil's Advocacy you want to entertain. I'm not the one they suspected. I'm not the one who's in jail. For reasons I think you know."

"All right. I see what you're saying. I don't doubt Donna's innocence now."

"Your first instinct was to doubt." I tap my fingers on my collarbone. "And you're still set on her being questionable somehow. White folks love to pose unrealistic 'parallels' to minimize the realities of Black and Brown folks."

"Last I checked, I'm not White."

"You sure?"

"Hey." Her voice rises. "Are you trying to push me away? Is that the stage we're at now?"

"Of course you're not White. My retort was too harsh, but don't turn this around." My shoulders tense up. "I know this is hard to hear, but I need you to hear it. Okay? When I told my dad you weren't White, he nearly shit. Because the world perceives you as White, that's got to influence how you see the world. I grew up with this kind of thinking and don't want to be around it now. Just . . . examine your instincts."

"All right." She lets out a measured exhalation. "I'll consider your words."

"Thank you. Love you."

"Love you. Good night."

THE RIGHT THING TO DO

There's a knock at the door. I twitch from my sleep, forgetting where I am before my eyes reach the grounding landmarks of the room. I call out, "Just a minute." Reality flows like sand through the maze in my mind.

"I'm making pizza downstairs," Mom says through the door, bribing me. "It'll be ready in ten minutes. And there might be a bottle of Chardonnay."

I hate Chardonnay. Wearily, I say, "Be right down."

The mirror shatters as I'm washing up. A voice shrieks. I jump back three feet, heart racing, to find the mirror intact. I tousle my hair with my hands and head downstairs as if life is normal.

I pull one of the IPAs I bought earlier out of the fridge, unable to handle another of Dad's Bud Lights. I follow my nose to the oven, turn on its light, and peer in. "Smells delicious."

With an awkward but ambitious smile, Mom announces, "It's my Asian, Gay-Loving Pizza."

She's overcompensating, but I'm touched by her efforts. "My favorite kind!"

Mom outdoes herself. The crust is thin and solid but puffed around the edge. Omitting the sauce, she goes extra on fresh mozzarella. Paper-thin portabella slices are sprinkled with parmesan and drizzled with white truffle oil.

"This is amazing."

She looks pleased. Swirling wine in her glass, she asks, "Should I open my shop and ban homophobes and racists?"

"Yes," I implore between bites. "Just don't do it in Bixby. You'll go out of business."

Finishing her plate, she heads to the living room and turns on the TV. "It's on soon," she calls. "Don't worry about cleaning up. We'll do it later."

My nerves have me shaking. I grab another beer on my way to the couch. "So, what do you think about Donna?"

She settles in on the other end, adjusting the padded stool beneath her feet. Crossing her ankles, she shrugs. "She's always seemed like such a nice girl. But I guess I can't say that she's ever seemed happy."

"This town never treated her well."

"It hasn't," she says, pausing to sip wine. "Don't know why the Carters ever chose Bixby, to be honest. I have nothing against them, of course. They're pleasant and generous folks. It's just strange that they'd want to be the only Black folks for miles."

"You know, some might ask the same of you—why you brought me here."

Her head turns, and she looks piqued. "Well, it's not the same thing. Where else were we supposed to live? In Korea? Your dad and I don't speak Korean. We've been here for generations."

"I didn't speak English. I had generational roots in Korea. I'm just saying that maybe it's time you examine these things. Like why it's more understandable for White people to bring a child of color here than it is for a whole Black family to move in."

She picks up the remote and says, "Huh. I suppose you're right."

When Donna's face appears in the corner of the screen, Mom turns up the volume. An older White man sits at a desk, blathering on about Bixby. I tune him out, waiting for Donna's square to fill the whole screen. She's in the interrogation room at the Bixby PD. I recognize the dull walls and harsh lighting.

She says, "I, Donna Devine, am turning myself in because it's the right thing to do." A male voice off-screen asks what she's turning herself in for. "The shooting at Bixby High on July second, in the year of our Lord two thousand sixteen." The voice asks about her involvement. She responds, "No comment." He asks something unintelligible, and she repeats, "Because it's the right thing to do." Another pause. "No comment." She repeats, "It's the right thing to do."

The picture flips back to the newsman. "Well, there you have it." He prattles on, and Mom turns down the volume.

"That's no confession," I say.

Mom picks up her wine and asks, "You don't think?"

"Listen to what she's not saying. Why do you think, if she turned herself in, she wouldn't explain how the bullets were going off behind us? And when we were locked in the closet?" I nod quickly. "Someone's put her up to it."

"The cops?"

My shoulders bounce. "Probably."

She shakes her head. "It's hard to believe we could live in that world."

I study her face with as much compassion as possible—because she's my mother, because she wants to learn. But I don't mince my words. "Whether or not that's what's going on in this case, we've been living in that world all along. It's time to wake up. This *is* the real world."

SHE AIN'T SHIT

As I pull up outside Christy's house, Sophie dances and waves. It takes me back to when we were young, and Christy would lead us through her routines. She was always front and center, with Donna and I flanking her sides.

"It's just Lucy." Christy motions for her daughter to stop. Apparently, they only perform for their fans.

Louise—clutching a can of Bud Light—starts in as I walk up the lawn. "Why'd you get my baby involved in this mess? She don't need any trouble." Christy averts her eyes while Louise carries on. "She was doin' just fine as it were. That video lost her thousands of fans."

Christy turns her back to me. I answer Louise. "It's what friends do. We support one another through thick and thin. Donna's innocent. Seeing her on TV last night confirmed it. She's been set up."

Louise shakes her blond head of hair. "I don't know what you saw, but the rest of us heard her confess, clear as day. That girl made her bed. No reason for Christy to jump into it." She snorts. "Or maybe you'd like to see that."

"Louise?" My face scrunches. "I've tried to be kind. But if you can't treat me with respect, you don't deserve mine."

"Ooh!" She hugs herself and feigns a chill.

"Donna's innocent. And Christy and I will stand by her."

Louise glares at Christy, nodding with glee. "Tell her, baby."

"I'm sorry, Lucy. I know you mean well, but you don't live here. I got my big break, and I'm not gonna blow it. Donna made her decision. I don't understand, but she did what she did. I can't help anymore."

"What are you saying?"

"My people are pissed."

"Donna and I are your people."

"Ha!" Louise howls with laughter. "That's a good one."

"We are," I tell her, unsure who I'm trying to convince at this point. "Those people are strangers. Why do you care more about them than us?"

"Donna's in jail," Christy says with a huff. "And soon you'll be back in San Fran. These people might not be my friends, but they care about me. They respect me."

My eyes bulge. "They care about you? How? All you are to them is a talking head. What can they give you?"

"My own show." The corners of her mouth rise—like a child caught in the act. "All I had to do was take down that video and quit publicly supporting Donna."

"You're selling out your friend for fame?" I ask, sounding more shocked than I feel.

"It's not that simple." She sighs. "I've been thinking. That book deal? I'm out. I'd have to compromise up the wazoo. On my show, I can say whatever I want. Just me. From the heart."

"It doesn't sound like you'll have free rein if you have to renounce Donna." I search for some sign that the woman I want to believe exists is in there. "You're better than this. I know it."

Louise pipes back up. "Maybe you ain't such a great judge of character? Ever think of that, Miss Know-It-All?"

I don't touch her unintended jab at her daughter. I stay focused on Christy. "What about all that talk of how much you owe me for saving your life? I don't want anything but for you to reconsider. Donna needs our support. You're making a mistake."

"Don't fall for it, baby." Louise laughs. "Soon we'll learn she was in on it, too."

"Mom? Hush!" Christy paces around, picking up Sophie's toys. "You did save my life. I'll never forget it. But this doesn't have anything to do with you and me. It's not even about Donna. You've got your great life out west. And Donna's got plenty of money."

"What good is money if she's locked up for life? If her kids are without their mother?" I beg, trying to appeal to both her childhood and motherhood. "The world is listening to you. With fame comes responsibility. No one will be loved for everything they say and do. But it's important to have some conviction."

"The conviction is coming!" shouts Louise. "For Donna."

Sophie runs in circles holding a Barbie doll in the air, shouting, "The con-fiction is coming!"

Christy's mouth eases into a semi-smile. "I've gotta consider my little girl. I want her to have options."

"She's a beautiful, blond White girl," I say flippantly. "She'll have plenty of options."

Christy's fired up. "So was I—and my mother! What'd that get us? Huh? I'm so sick of this White privilege nonsense."

"Um, you live in the exact replica of the house you used to dream of when we were kids. You're married to a burly, powerful man who loves the shit out of you. You've got the daughter you've always wanted. And now you're going to host a show on TV! That's what it got you. What more do you want?"

"Nothing!" She lowers her voice and says, "This is everything I've ever wanted. Am I supposed to be sorry for that? All for what—White guilt? It's a one-time deal. How can you ask me to turn it down?"

"Because Donna needs our help," I say earnestly. "And I thought friendship meant something to you."

"Look around," she demands. "Go ahead. Take a look. Do you see any friends here? Yeah, you can talk about what my looks got me. It never favored me with friends, though. All those jealous bitches only cared about gossip."

"You think you lack friends because they were jealous?" I tilt my head to the sky. "You lack friends 'cause you slept with their men or they're dead!"

"I thought it was love!" she hollers stubbornly.

Sliding my sunglasses down, I let my eyes pierce through her lies.

"So what?" Christy shrugs. "I did them a favor. They learned some hard truths."

I turn back towards the car, feeling defeated.

"You're just gonna walk out on me?" Christy screams as she follows. "And you lecture me about friendship?"

"Just let her go, baby," says Louise. "You've got bigger fish to fry. She ain't shit."

VALIDATION

I don't pay attention to where I'm driving, but I eventually end up at the pond. It's serene, shaded by bushes and trees, with wildflowers and tall grass. Leaning against the hood of Dad's sedan, I'm transported back twenty-something years.

* * *

Donna and I were tossing stones. She'd needed to vent after another blowout with her mom. We never had to say where. We'd call and hang up after one ring. When that happened twice, we knew where to go if we could. Like the closet at school, it was our spot for a little refuge.

"They treat her like some kind of slave," Donna said with a huff, heaving a rock overhead, not even trying to make it skip. It landed in the water with a *thwump*. "You've seen her. She's old and fragile. She used to just do the yard. Now they've got her doing everything. But she says they take care of her. She's thankful for the work." *Thwump. Thwump.*

Mrs. Davis did seem worn, but she always looked pleased to be there. "You don't think?" I asked, tossing my stone like a frisbee.

Donna shook her head. "Her life would be a whole lot easier with a car, but she can't afford one on what we pay her. To commute from the city, she takes a bus to the train to another bus, and Mom grabs her from there. It takes her two hours each way! I asked why they can't just buy her a car or pay her more.

But she says she doesn't want her to feel like charity."

"You don't think it'd make her uncomfortable?"

"Of course not. Mrs. Davis doesn't have much pride—'cept for in her work. She keeps the yard pristine and does all the odd jobs. I've never heard a complaint. But I know she struggles." Donna searched the ground for more stones. "They have no trouble donating huge sums of money elsewhere. But they get credit for that. I told Mom that's the difference."

"What'd she say to that?"

"She sent me to my room."

Searching the ground for more stones, I asked, "Will you be in trouble if she finds out you left?"

Donna shrugged. "More White folks are coming for dinner tonight. They'll pretend like everything's fine. But if I have to hear one more 'With my eyes closed, I'd think she were White . . .' "

I laughed. "People always say I sound White, too—as if it's some kind of achievement."

"Like we're all supposed to sound some certain way."

Donna sat on the boulder and folded herself to her knees. "Everyone thinks my folks are so great. They're celebrated for being rich despite being Black. People miss the whole picture. You know? I'm still the only Black girl for miles."

"I know," I moaned. "People tell me to be thankful for being adopted all the time. As if that's all that matters."

"Sometimes I just want to be a regular Black girl with a regular life. I'm not trying to complain, but sometimes I just want to be normal."

"I get it." I twisted a blade of grass between my fingers. "I can't even picture 'normal'. Guess I'd be on the other side of the world, speaking another language."

"You'd be with your real parents."

I couldn't look at her when I groaned. "Nah. They threw me away."

"How do you know?"

"I heard my dad say it." My eyes met hers. "He didn't know I was there."

"Or maybe he did."

I thought for a moment. "He's not that mean . . . or clever."

"Well, maybe he don't know jack?"

"It doesn't matter." I shrugged. "I'm here now."

She jumped up and yelled, "Go!" This was our thing. My heart raced as I pumped my legs to catch up to her. We ran alongside one another, hopping rocks and branches and weaving through trees. I can't even recall how it started, but it gave us what we needed. We got to be two regular kids in a place that transcended all the bullshit that Bixby thrust upon us.

"Now I feel kind of bad," Donna confessed, out of breath, sitting back on our rock. "There I was complaining about my folks, not realizing you've got it worse."

"How do you mean?" My brows lifted.

"My parents are rich and out of touch, but I'm still their daughter." She nodded. "You were taken from your country. Your folks were probably poor and you might never know 'em."

I peered over at her, sitting quietly, soaking in her words. I told her, "I don't have it worse. But thanks." That was the first time I'd ever felt seen—like I had some kind of right to my sadness.

A huge grin spread across her face as she said, "S-I-S-S."

"Sis?"

"Sisters in Shit Situations."

I giggled. "I love it. We should get jackets made."

THE RIDE

Strolling aimlessly through the countryside, wondering what I'm still doing in Bixby, I see a truck drive by and slow down. When I register that it's a brown pickup with a blue door, my heart stops. It backs up and idles beside me.

"Stomping through the old haunts?" asks Kevin, squinting from the sun.

I nod, caught off guard by his presence.

"Hop in. Let's go for a ride."

"Nah," I say, kicking dirt around the gutter like a child.

"Why not? Got somewhere else to be?" He bites on a cigarette.

"No . . . I just need some space . . . to clear my head."

"C'maaan." He smiles, reminding me how charming he could be. "It'll be good to catch up. Besides—I want to talk about something important."

"Like what?"

"Hop in and find out."

Inside I'm shaking, but my body moves on its own. As I'm opening the passenger door, I want to force myself to turn around and leave, but I can't.

He sticks the cigarette behind his ear. "You movin' back?"

My eyes fixate on the beige farm landscape ahead. "That'll never happen."

"Never say never."

I roll my eyes to the left, peering at him suspiciously, but I don't say a word.

"Heard about Donna."

"Oh yeah?" My heart races. "What have you heard?"

"That she turned herself in. Didn't you hear?"

"Of course." I sigh, annoyed that he doesn't have more. "It's all lies. Someone's setting her up."

To my surprise, he nods in his usual way, bobbing his head slightly left and right. "Probably."

"Glad to hear you agree. Not many do." I size him up on the sly, seeing him in daylight for the first time in years. He's wearing the local male uniform: loose-fitting jeans, an unfashionable t-shirt, and sneakers. Thin lines have gathered between his brows, but his soft brown eyes are still giant puddles. "Got the day off?"

"I finished up early."

"You still in construction?"

"I manage sites now."

"Yeah? Good for you."

His eyes dart to me. "Is it such a surprise?"

"No," I say apologetically. "I figured you'd do well." But when I say it, it sounds like a lie.

An uncomfortable silence washes over us. Then he asks, "So, who you think done it?"

I shrug. "No idea. You?"

He tilts his head. "Hard to say."

"You live here. You know this town."

"Your guess is as good as mine." When I glance at him, I see the corners of his mouth start to rise.

My finger takes aim at his face. "There it is."

"There's what?"

"That smirk." I twist a few degrees to the left in my seat. "Some things never change."

"That's true." The truck turns left, kicking pebbles up onto the pavement. "But there are still all kinds of surprises."

"Such as?"

His smirk grows. "You being back here, for one. Thought the last time would've kept you gone for good."

I ruminate on his words but act unaffected. "I had to see Donna and Christy."

"Christy," he says wantonly. "How is she?"

I don't succeed at concealing my bitterness when I tell him, "Better than ever."

He turns his head to study me. "You've never been the jealous type."

"It's not jealousy; it's disappointment."

He scratches his head. "I wouldn't think that your friend doin' well would be so disappointing."

I fight back the words on the tip of my tongue and settle for saying, "It's a long story."

"Well, she didn't disappoint Bixby. She's still here, makin' us proud."

"She turned against Donna."

"Naw. I watched her vid—"

"She took it down. She got an offer to do her own show. On TV. If she stops supporting Donna."

"All right." His head swivels towards me. "Can't say I blame her. All of Bixby spent her whole life tellin' her she was special. Sure she's been waitin' for outside recognition."

"I'm sure she has been, too. But I thought she was better than that."

"And that's your problem, Lucy." He smirks again. "You're always wanting to believe people are different. You're too stubborn to see what's in front of your face."

Something in his voice sends chills up my spine. I cross my arms to conceal my shiver. "What are you trying to say?"

Kevin bounces his shoulders and tilts his head, but he keeps quiet.

"You know, Christy's mom said the same thing the other day—that I'm not a good judge of people."

He changes the subject. "How's this new life workin' out? Heard you've got a hot girlfriend."

"I like my job. I love where I live. And yeah—Alexis is great."

The truck jerks to the right as he bangs a turn without any slowdown or warning. Hanging on to the roof handle so I don't fall onto him, I picture myself dead in a ditch. He pulls to the side and slams on the breaks. My eyes scan around the shaded area that I'm sure I'll end up in.

I manage to ask, "How 'bout you? Do you have anyone?" Just act normal, Lucy.

"Something's been bugging me fierce." He scrunches his face, squeezing his eyes shut. His hands are in fists. I contemplate jumping out. "Why'd you marry me?"

"Why'd I . . . marry you?" I echo his words to give myself a chance to take them in. "It seemed like the right thing to do." I remember Donna repeating those words on TV the other night. I add, "We were close. I thought it was right."

"But you knew you liked girls."

"You said you knew, too," I remind him. "So, what does it matter? We tried."

"You made a fool of me." The strain in his voice is unnerving. "Girls around here are afraid to date me. Everyone jokes that I'll turn 'em lezzy. You don't know what it's like."

"Guess I don't." I'm suddenly more angry than frightened. "I only spent my whole childhood being teased. You were there."

"It's worse as a man."

"Really? You think it's harder to get teased as a grown-ass man than as a young Asian girl in an all-White town?" I know I

196

shouldn't challenge him now, but I can't help myself. "Straight White men have it hardest. I know." I roll my eyes so hard they ache.

He pounds his palm on the wheel. I jump. His body's shaking. "This is what I hate about you! You think you're so smart—that your pain's all that matters. You never saw me as anything but a way to kill time. Say it!"

My body shakes involuntarily from his anger. I want to slip out of the car, but I'm frozen. My mouth, then my whole body, forget how to move.

"You know what?" He glares at me with eyes of fire. "I wish I could've finished what I started."

As I sit in his chill, he turns the ignition, swings the truck around, and drives us back the way we came. I nearly choke on my heart beating up in my throat.

Calmly, as if none of that happened, he asks, "Where'd you park?"

"At the pond," I whisper.

"What's that?"

"The pond," I repeat, louder.

When I climb out of the truck, I don't look back. I nearly thank him for the ride, out of habit, but I catch myself before spitting it out. I feel his eyes on me as I slide into the front seat of Dad's car. I'm wondering if Kevin will pull out a gun.

He drives away.

I sit there shaking.

IT WAS HIM

Mom's not home when I return. I storm through the living room and kitchen, open the sliding glass door, and plop myself down on the lounger. I pull out my vape pen and take a long drag. The smoke works its way to my lungs.

> Me: It was him. Kevin. My ex.
> Alexis: What about him?
> Me: The shooter.
> Alexis: I'm calling.

I answer the phone. "He's violent and believes Donna's innocent."

"Hold up." Alexis's voice is steady and strong when she asks, "Did you see him again?"

"Yeah. I was walking around the countryside, and he picked me up. He made it sound like he had something important to tell me. I thought it might have been about Donna. Anyway, it started out fine. Then he lost it. He was shaking. I was shaking. Holy fuck. I'm still shaking . . ."

"He just happened to pick you up? That's sketch. He was following you."

"Maybe." I slip my pen back in my pocket and pull my sunglasses down from my head. "I must've been in denial about him."

"You think he's capable of the shooting?"

"I didn't think so, but . . ." After a deep breath, I tell her about the night that happened before the divorce. "I was foolish to dismiss it."

She clicks her tongue a few times. "It's not your fault. Trauma can do fucked-up things. You were trying to cope."

"Yeah. I know . . ."

"But also, you have a habit of dismissing people's mistreatment—and straight-up abusing—of you. Especially folks from that town."

"It's in my blood, being forced to diminish so much for so long here."

"Yep. I get it." She sighs. "But recognize it's A Thing."

"All right. I'm working on it."

She clears her throat and speaks assertively. "So, we don't know if it was Kevin, but you should go to the cops. Tell 'em whatever you think might be helpful. Let them investigate."

"They won't. They think Donna did it. They'll send me away, and it'll get back to him, firing him up more. You know how small this town is. He's got friends here."

"Yeah," she agrees. "Or maybe this will spark someone else's suspicion of him, and you'll end up saving Donna. Go directly from the cops to the airport. He can't get you here. If he tries, he'll have to get through me."

"All right." I grunt. "It's worth a shot."

"By the way, I spread the word about a protest for Donna. My girl Tamika has taken it up. It's happening this weekend. If you're back, we can join them."

I sigh. "What would I do without you?"

"You don't have to worry about that," she says.

DISBELIEF

Déjà vu. The bare gray walls suck my energy dry. Fluorescent lights dig into my pores. Detective Whitley sits across the table, tapping the top of his pen on his knee.

"I hear what you're saying, Ms. Byrne, and I'm sorry for what you've been through. But I don't see how it all connects."

I fight back a groan. "You don't think he's worth looking into?"

"Being violent with you once or twice doesn't mean he's got it in him to shoot up a reunion." His eyes are steel-gray and unflinching. "That's a big jump. Don't ya think?"

I fling my arms into the air furiously. I sit back and try to remain calm. "The men who've carried out mass shootings tend to have a history of domestic violence. Look it up."

Glaring at me as if amused, he says, "Pseudo-journalism ain't fact." He lifts the pen from his knee and clicks it open and closed a few times. "Besides, you have no records—no proof."

"I'm sitting here telling you now. Can't this go on the record as proof?"

"It will go on the record, but not as proof. You've got no police report from San Fran? No photos of wounds from the ropes on your skin?"

"It wasn't premeditated. He used random clothes from around the room."

"Well," he says, chuckling. "That's not so bad. You had me thinkin' it was serial-killer level."

The top half of my body shakes against the table as I lean

forward. "What does it matter what he tied me up with? The effect was the same. Had I not found my way out, I might've died."

And, with all seriousness, he says, "But you didn't, Ms. Byrne. You found your way out just fine."

"After hours of agony!"

He leans back. "How 'bout this?" Whitley holds the pen in his teeth a few beats before waving it around. "I'll put this here on the record. If we have any run-ins with him going forward, we'll give it a look."

"What if he's smart enough not to have any more run-ins? He gets away with it, then? Donna rots?"

"Ah." He sits back, amused. "That's what this is."

"No, it's—"

"Uh-huh." He looks at me as if he's pleased to crack open the truth. "Well, I'm afraid your friend Donna confessed. We've asked her to name the shooter several times, and each time she declined. There's not much we can do about that."

"Listen. It's not about Donna." I raise my voice out of desperation. "Don't you want this guy off the streets to keep him from causing more harm?"

He resumes tapping the pen on his leg, studying my face. I've always been intimidated by the unfounded confidence of White men, but I try not to show it. He says, "Look . . . I'm sure it's been hard. You've probably got PTSD. Your senses are heightened and shit."

I sigh, gazing down at the Formica table. A silhouette of my head and shoulders appears. I straighten my posture and keep my voice as calm as I can manage. "This has nothing to do with my PTSD. I just thought you might want to know what one of the men in your jurisdiction has done. If you want to let it slide? That's on you. I'm headed back to California. Knowing this town, word will get back to him, and that's not a risk I'm willing to take."

He nods and smugly says, "I'll see you out."

THE BIG PICTURE VIEW

At thirty-something-thousand feet, I contemplate the fuckery.

In Whitley's mind, I'm suggesting that Donna conspired with Kevin to shoot up the reunion. He won't hear that Donna's innocent. Even if she'd been involved, she'd never partner with Kevin.

Kevin would have acted on his own, of course. But he was one of the more popular kids. What could he have had against our class? I've been so out of touch with him and Bixby. It could've been anything.

And then a stray thought tugs at my nerves. He did it to get to me. He never thought I'd escape. Maybe that's what he meant by finishing what he'd started . . .

The flight attendant hands us water and tosses packs of mini pretzels onto our trays. The short break allows me to reexamine my thoughts. I scold myself for blowing things out of proportion.

Then I see Kevin in his truck, shaking and shouting. He's the right shape and size. He wasn't at the reunion—or so he says. And he's a White guy in Bixby who knows Donna didn't have anything to do with it.

But I still don't want to believe it. Could I have been married to a murderer? We spent six years together. I like to think I'm fairly aware of people, but maybe—as per Kevin and Louise—who I want to believe people are blinds me to the truth.

Maybe that's why I've been tolerating Christy. Because it's obvious she's a fame-seeking, self-serving racist. She befriended Donna and me when we were young because it brought her attention. But once she became the It Girl, she moved on. I'd chalked it up to teenage drama and given her the benefit of the doubt.

People act like focusing on the good in people will make you a virtuous person. But sometimes it makes you a fool.

Maybe Christy's a fool, too—and Mike wasn't with his military pals, but behind the mask and the gun? Maybe he was jealous of someone, given her flirtatious nature and promiscuous past.

Since I'm trudging through this muck, I might as well include Donna. As the only two kids of color surrounded by Whiteness, her friendship was a gift. But we've had so much distance. I didn't know who she was becoming in Chicago. And she didn't accept who I became in San Francisco. The fondness we share is for who we once were. Back then, we were both hiding in plain sight, trying our best to get by. Maybe I'm wrong about her. Maybe she turned herself in because she was involved, and being a God-fearing woman, she wants to absolve herself of her sins—or however that goes.

And what about me? Whitley sees a pathetic girl with PTSD, loyal to her friend, paranoid about her ex. Dad sees a girl who complicates her life by making the world uncomfortable. Mom's starting to see me for who I am—whoever that is. I don't know how Alexis views me, but I'm guessing it's as better than I am, since she's still with me. Carin sees a broken survivor unwilling to do the work. And Tae-Suk probably sees a sympathetic character he'll one day use as inspiration for a script. Or maybe that's unfair, and I'm overcompensating for past naiveté . . .

Who really knows anyone? We curate so much of what we reveal to each person. We let people think we are simple, believing it's all they can handle. We humans, with such capable minds, simplify ourselves and one another. Why do we do this?

Why must we employ such confinements? And yet we crave fictional stories with imaginative arcs and wild, unpredictable characters. Why is the wholeness of truth so overwhelming when it comes to real life?

People are afraid. We're afraid of each other and what we might learn of ourselves. So we turn off the light and back out. We double down on what we want to believe, tightening our blinders. No wonder we're missing the big-picture view.

DUALITY

There she is, smiling among the stiff, suited chauffeurs with their expressionless faces and printed-out signs. She's draped in a sapphire sundress and wearing worn ankle boots, her dark, auburn-tinged hair hanging wild. Her sign reads: HOT BABY BYRNE. It's written in flaming red and gold glitter on black poster board.

"How'd you know my flight info?"

She pulls me close and smacks her lips against mine. "I called your mom."

"This poster . . ." I clasp the edges, face full of awe and amusement.

"It's a little extra." She shrugs. "But we were making signs for the protest. Thought it might put a smile on your face after such a shit week."

I throw my arm around her and squeeze, our compressed hips maneuvering into a clumsy gait. "It's great to be back here with you." Glancing around SFO, I see other queer couples embrace without fear or concern. There are Asians and Blacks and people in hijabs. As my muscles relax, I realize how tense I have been. "I never want to go back," I say.

"You have a choice." She stops walking. My eyes meet hers. "You can always say no."

"Yeah, well, that doesn't always feel right."

"I know." She sighs as we move on. She flicks her sunglasses down from the crown of her head. "Life can be a real kick in the cunt."

"If Donna gets out, I'll go back. We need to talk, and she'll never come out to The Land of the Gays."

"She really hates us that much—queer folk?"

"I don't think it's hate." I shrug. "I think it has more to do with her religion."

"Pfft." Alexis throws my suitcase in the back of her car and slams the door. "This is what I was saying about you giving folks too much credit." I realize she's right.

Heading up the peninsula, I take in the familiar clusters of pastel houses built into the ash-blond hills.

Alexis asks, "Mind if I stay over? Or do you need some alone time?"

"Stay." Then I hear myself say, "Maybe it's time you move in?"

Her mouth goes round like a chorus singer's. "Are—are you sure? Why the quick change of heart?"

We'd broached the subject before the reunion, but I wasn't ready. I didn't want to "U-Haul" it, as lesbians joke. On some level, it could be that at a time when so much is unstable, I'm clinging to her. But I tell her, "I think a part of me was afraid, since I committed to Kevin before knowing who I was. Seeing him the other day . . ." I shiver. "It reinforced how much I've changed. My intolerance of their intolerance is proof of my growth."

"You tolerated it because you had no choice. Back then, it was survival. Having no choice is soul-destroying. That's why I want you to realize now that you do—have a choice. Maybe not with everything, but always with me."

"Always with you," I echo. "That sounds pretty nice."

She places her hand atop mine. "I'm proud of your commitment to growth. It's what I need in a woman."

I temper my grin, since I'm never fully able to accept feeling love. There's something in me that both shies away from and desperately craves it. Perhaps it's because I'm scared I might lose it. And maybe that's why I'm not hard on Donna for her homophobia. I'm afraid to lose her again, too.

SISTERHOOD

It's a beautiful day in San Francisco. The sun beats down from a cloudless sky as we settle into our summer—which is most people's autumn. It's just a few of us at Civic Center, holding signs the group made last weekend.

THE BLACK GIRL HAS A NAME
DONNA'S INNOCENT!
FREE DONNA DEVINE
S.O.S. SAVE OUR SISTER
WE SEE YOU, DONNA!
BLACK LIVES MATTER
STOP POLICE CORRUPTION
DON'T FALL FOR THE SETUP

I take a moment to myself and think, *It feels good to be doing something, even if it's too small to make waves.* And then they arrive from all angles, gathering with signs and devotion.

One of the women from our circle, Tamika, climbs onto a box. She lifts the megaphone to her lips. She's fierce and unapologetic. Her chest heaves as she bellows, "Black lives matter! Black lives matter!" The crowd moves in and chants along, fists in the air.

I join them. "Black! Lives! Matter! Black! Lives! Matter!"

Somewhere in the crowd, someone bangs a drum.

Boom! Boom! Boom!

Boom! Boom! Boom!

The low frequencies rattle my lungs.

We shout, "Donna's life matters! Donna's life matters!"

Two vans pull up at the outskirts of the crowd. Huge cameras and boom stands with big fuzzy mikes come forward to capture our fury.

"Stop! Police! Corruption! Stop! Police! Corruption!"

I've never felt comfortable following another's lead, but this feels right. It occurs to me now that in all my life, I've never had a leader of color. Every teacher and boss has always been White. I tuck that acknowledgment into a file in my brain.

Through the megaphone, Tamika commands, "Let us acknowledge we're on stolen ground and take a moment to honor the rightful owners of the land: The Ohlone Tribe." We stand unified in silence. "Thank you for being here and showing we will not sit comfortably while one of our sisters is set up and locked up! No! We will rise up and make as much noise as it takes until Donna is free!" The drums roll. "Set! Her! Free! Don-na Devine! Set! Her! Free! Don-na Devine!"

As we chant, clap, and stomp, the news cameras capture it all. The crowd's faces are angry. Some are streaked with tears. Some radiate strength and a deep sense of purpose. I feel them all at once. For the first time, I understand Sisterhood.

I reach for Alexis's hand and squeeze. She peers over at me, mouth furiously in sync with Tamika's. We holler, "Save our sister!"

Wet semicircles form on the fabric under Alexis's arms and between her breasts. Her face contorts as she gives everything to her words. I feel the cool beads of sweat roll down my forehead, stinging my eyes. Our hands are sticky, and my feet are sore as we march down Market Street.

I've never felt so in love, so alive and connected—yet so removed from the cause I'm fighting for. As my body is charged from the buzz of these women, something inside feels hollow.

REVELATION

A lavender eye pillow presses gently down on my eyes—just enough to feel soothing. As I'm lost in momentary bliss, the still water moves. Foam tickles its way up my neck and chin. I toss the pillow to the side and see Alexis shin-deep in suds.

She taps me with her foot. "Lift your legs."

As I scooch up, she lowers herself down, cross-legged, perpendicular. She takes my feet in her hands and starts massaging them one at a time. The water's high now, rolling over the side just a little.

"Heaven," I whisper, my eyes going weak.

"We went viral." She presses a thumb to an arch. "Twitter. Snapchat. Insta. Facebook. Journalists and everyday people."

While I felt the high before, I'm now feeling the comedown. A vision of Donna sitting on a filthy mattress in a jail cell flashes before me. Sometimes all these things do is temporarily boost morale. I force a weary smile so I don't appear ungrateful.

The hot steam imparts a dewy sheen to Alexis's skin. Her eyes—like chameleons—appear deep like mocha in this lighting. Her hair's piled in a messy bun. I say, "Thanks for helping make it happen."

She pinches my shins and calves, working through the tension in my legs. "I didn't have to do much. Tamika and her crew did all the work."

"But you planted the seed. Don't sell yourself short."

When she smiles, her whole face blooms. "All right. I'll take it."

I reach for her knee. "I've never felt so close to anyone before—like I really have nothing to hide."

"I know you. I see you."

My throat tightens. "Well, there are some things you don't know." And now that I've said it, my heart races. I realize there's no turning back.

"I doubt it will scare me away." But I feel the uncertainty, the hesitation, as her fingers ease up.

"It has nothing to do with you . . . But not sharing feels dishonest."

Votive candles flicker on the countertop, multiplied by the mirror. My limbs and my mind feel calm, but there's a herd of horses trampling my heart.

She squeezes my thigh. "It's okay. I'm ready for whatever it is."

I take a deep breath. "When I was young, I overheard my parents talking about me. My mother was freaking out because I wanted to know where I came from." I let my words cling to the humidity that surrounds us. "And that's when I heard my father say it—that the woman I was born from threw me away like trash."

"I'm sorry you had to hear that." Her face tightens as her voice softens. "That would have a big effect on a child."

I nod and fidget with my fingers. "For a really long time, I believed it. Mom didn't protest. Because I was so young, I took it literally. That image stayed . . . It haunted me. It put me off my Korean family—and Korea—altogether. Dad made it sound like throwing me away was a normal, thoughtless Korean act. I was ashamed of myself and the people who would've been mine."

You know when you hear someone's story and want to cry, but you don't want to cry harder than the one who was hurt because you don't want your pain to override theirs? I witness Alexis wrestle with this. Tears well in eyes that keep flinching to hold them.

"Things started to change when I came here for school. Asian people were everywhere. At first, they scared me. I didn't want to hear how whitewashed and un-Asian I was. Some take pride in their lack of culture, as if it makes them more American." I shrug. "But I didn't want to be a Banana or Twinkie. I met another adopted Korean, and she told me about our online community. I was pretty much a fly on the wall, watching others give words to things I never knew how to say. It was life-changing."

"That's really cool."

Our eyes briefly meet, but I need to avert them if I'm to go on. "As I hovered in those groups, my own story was developing, but I told no one. My American file was bare, appealing more to adopters than the truth. But I tracked down my file from the agency in Korea. I was expecting to find what everyone else finds: that, due to poverty, I was left somewhere to be found; that I had a young, unwed mother; or that my records were destroyed in some mysterious flood or fire." I swallow hard, not inhaling until I can safely breathe without bursting into tears. "But they said that my mother was murdered. And I was there, but he spared or didn't see me. I was lucky."

Lucky Lucy, I think again.

At this point, Alexis breaks. Her arms reach out, and I lean forward to meet her. We hold each other. Her tears drip down, and the bubbles make way for them, spreading out around their drops. "It's okay to cry," she whispers. "Just let it all out."

I push back a few inches so we can rest our foreheads against each other, our fingers entangled. "But don't you see? I can't." My lips fumble as if trying to shake the words out. "Had I cried,

I would've died, too. Now my body won't let me."

I want to tell her how badly the guilt has corroded my insides. Because, had I cried, maybe someone would've come to help. Had I cried, knowing she was a mother might've sparked just enough in his heart to stop him; to save her, save us. But what I've already shared is enough—too much. And I'm sorry for making the woman I love break down like this.

When she catches her breath, her rich, deep eyes search mine for something she hadn't known to look for till now. "Do you remember anything?"

I fixate on the little round holes her tears cleared in the bubbles. "I was two and a half. It's hard to know what's a memory and what my imagination filled in throughout the years. But sometimes I can see her feet pushing these blue quilted slippers across the floor. I hear her singing a sweet melody. And then screams. I see a set of stunned eyes meet mine; two hands carry me off to a room full of babies and toddlers crying out for their moms. But maybe none of it's real. I might never know."

I no longer feel the heat of the water on my skin. It's either cooled down or I've gone numb. I pinch my thigh and continue. "After learning that, other things started to make sense. Why I'm always on guard. Why, wherever I am, I always know the exits and worst places to be. This is why I survived the shooting. My body's been preparing for some kind of attack my entire life. In my dreams, I've escaped death thousands of times. It sharpened my instincts."

The muscles in her face give in. I hardly recognize her. "What a shocking revelation . . ."

"So, when Christy kept calling me a hero, I couldn't accept it." I nod. "The only reason I knew what to do was because I failed my own mother."

She jumps in. "You didn't—"

"I know." I hold up a hand. "I was a toddler. But sewn into the fabric of my being, no matter what my mind knows, I feel that I failed."

Her hand clasps my upper arm and squeezes. She gently shakes her head before pressing it to mine. "I don't know how you've carried this all on your own. It's too much. But you've got me now. Okay? Let me help you hold it."

She cradles my head against her shoulder. I beg for the dam to break—for the chance to release all the pain that I've carried for decades, for the chance to feel vulnerability and love—but it holds strong.

DENIAL

When I return to work, people look at me with either pity or fear. Some look away, unsure of what to say. Using my phone as a prop, I scroll through endless nothing as I walk the halls.

Carin doesn't knock. She takes a few shallow steps, exaggerating a quizzical look.

"Sorry I didn't call first." I roll my chair back from the desk. "Didn't know I was coming home until Thursday night. Hope I didn't throw things off."

"It's all right. I've got work for you." She examines my face with hesitation. "I know you wanted to keep it a secret, but there are videos circulating, and you're in some of them. A lot of people know now—that you were there."

I knew this, of course, but hearing her words drives it home. "Yeah, I figured."

"Listen . . . I'm sorry about your friend. I'm sure it must be upsetting." Her body stiffens. "I just . . . don't get why it's become a race thing." She waves her head around at its supposed ridiculousness.

I pull my head back in horror. "What?" I manage to ask meagerly. It's that moment that always seems to hit when you least expect it.

Carin tucks a few chestnut strands of hair behind her ear. Her voice softens. "Don't you think this kind of stuff only makes it worse for true racial injustice?" Dumbfounded, I struggle with words for too long. She employs a patronizing tone. "I understand. Sometimes Ashwin will jump to conclusions before he thinks better of it. I'm sure it's not easy feeling the world's judging you for your color or foreignness—even when it's not."

I shake my head. "Carin . . . You . . ." I pause and sigh. "That's not how it is."

She nods sympathetically, as if she's in on something I'm not. "I see it all the time. People rush to throw race into the mix when they're grasping at straws."

"Do you know how many Black people lived in Bixby when I was a kid?" When she doesn't answer, I tell her, "Three. Donna and her parents. Guess how many live there now." She looks at me as if suddenly fatigued. "Two. Donna and her husband. She had to send her kids off to his sister because it wasn't safe."

She shakes her head. "What's the point?"

"You have no idea what it's like where I'm from. Half of Bixby is ready to lynch her. Plenty tried when she was a kid. Since the shooting, she's received death threats and had racial slurs painted on her property. She's had to hire security."

"So, based on the unfortunate acts of some misguided kids, your whole town is racist since it's mostly White?"

"That's not what I'm saying." If I let them, my eyes would roll out of my head.

"I have an Asian husband. I understand racially charged incidents fairly well. The slurs sound racist. Sure. But the rest is just frustrated people upset that she wasn't brought in soon enough."

My right hand flies from my lap to my mouth. I hold it there, afraid of what might come pouring out. Dropping it to my lap, I exhale. "Don't you think I'd have a better idea of racism and the people who live there than you would?"

"So, my thoughts are invalid?" Her voice erupts like I just waged a war. "What is it with you people? I've got news for you: Good White folks exist! You say you want equality, but you keep pushing White people out. How is that equal? You don't want to hear us. I swear—people who consider themselves 'of color' are more racist than Whites."

I'm so overwhelmed that it's hard to choose which snippet deserves first response. Her words slither around my brain and squeeze. "You think you're one of the good ones? Can't you even hear what you're saying is racist?"

"Oh, that's great. The woman married to an Indian man is a racist." She rolls her eyes.

"Hate to break it to ya, but being married to a Person of Color's not some magic power that makes you not racist."

She crosses her arms. "And neither is being a Person of Color."

"Well, with that I agree. But don't Whitesplain racism to me."

"Whitesplain?" She scoffs. "Wow. You have no respect for me, do you? This isn't the Lucy I know. This isn't the Lucy I went to bat for. This isn't the Lucy who listens with compassion and helps junior staff develop a better eye and technique!"

"That's absurd!" I throw my arms in the air and drop them heavily. "When you offend a Person of Color, you shouldn't expect them to make you feel good. Why should we be at our best when you're at your worst? That's White supremacy for ya."

Her jaw drops. "N-now I'm a White supremacist? This is getting way out of hand. You're way out of line."

I drop my chin down and peer up at her, shaking my head. "The saddest thing is, your obsession with being considered One of the Good Ones is what keeps you from actually being one."

"What's that supposed to mean? Enough of the riddles. Just say what you mean."

"If you'd actually consider what I've said and apologize— rather than jump in with defensiveness—you'd show you're not racist. Instead, your ego wins."

"Don't twist things around!" She stomps. "You're the one being racist here. I won't have you manipulate me into thinking otherwise."

"Tell me: How am I being racist?" I tilt my head, inspecting her carefully.

"You're saying that just 'cause the cops and the people in your old town are White, they locked up the Black girl."

"She's a woman, and her name is Donna." I shake my head. "And that's way too simplistic. You're obviously missing the point. It's like you're purposely trying to misunderstand because you're afraid of the truth."

"I reject that." She paces the room, huffing. In a minute, she softens again. "Look . . . I care about you. It's hard watching you struggle. I've tried being supportive. I've given you time off and the name of a wonderful therapist. But instead of taking care of yourself, you're using your energy to fight against your own interests."

"You're just upset I haven't followed your advice—which was overstepping, but I was too nice to say. I answer to you when it comes to work, but that's where it ends." I shake my hair out. "And don't try to act like you know my interests. I'm interested in justice, and Donna's not guilty. She's being set up. In the meantime, the shooter is free."

Carin shakes her head. "Denial will just hold you back. Confront the truth now, or you'll make it harder for yourself. My husband—"

"Forget about your husband!" I say, louder than I prefer to speak. "Just because you're with an Indian man doesn't mean you understand race like I do. You're not woke by proxy because you're married to a Brown man."

"Ashwin doesn't appreciate being called Brown," she fumes.

"Well, maybe that's part of the problem," I snap.

"He's a—"

"Human?" I ask with a smirk. "Does he think because race is a social construct, it doesn't have real effects? Is the best way to solve racism to stop talking about it?"

There's a complex look in her eyes. It's a mix of resentment, surprise, and agreement. "Ashwin knows that being Indian is only part of who he is. He doesn't use it to deflect from when he's done wrong."

"Well, isn't he just the model minority?" I sigh. "Why are you taking this so personally? Why does it matter so much to you?"

She leans on the arm of a chair. "My brother's the kindest, most big-hearted person I know. He's also White. And a cop. I suppose that means nothing to you. But I've sat with him too many times . . . I've seen him shake with fear—for his life and his family's. It's not just one way, you know. A lot of Black people want all cops dead—including the Black ones. Black lives matter, but blue lives matter, too."

I reach for the orange putty that's shaped like a cat. I dig my fingers in, stretching it every which way. "You know, the police force began with slave patrol. White supremacy is woven into its fabric. No. It *is* its fabric."

"Maybe that's true. But no one likes being talked down to, you know."

"Here you go again, asking me to prioritize your feelings when you're the one who caused the offense."

Her arms fan out to her sides. "I'm just saying: Trying to make us feel dumb doesn't help sway us to your side."

I smirk. "But I thought you were already on our side? You're One of the Good Ones. Right?"

"I'm voting for Hillary! Okay? I voted for Obama twice!" she shouts hysterically. "I'm not one of those racists you think we all are! Sure! Black folks were mistreated—a long time ago and sometimes still today. But White folks shouldn't pay for the sins of our ancestors! This is not *Game of Thrones*!"

"If you're so Not Racist," I say, leaning forward, "then why are you certain of Donna's guilt without knowing a damn thing about her?"

"Because she confessed! They wouldn't hold her there just 'cause she's Black! My brother's a cop. I know how it works."

"You know the law 'cause your brother's a cop. You're not racist 'cause your husband is Brown." I glance up at the ceiling, blowing a stray hair from my face. "Got it."

Her voice rises an octave. "You people—"

I stand up. "Are sick of your shit."

Walking out of my office, I fold my rage into cohesive speaking points and head down to Human Resources. I walk through the maze of gray cubicles and knock on the door of the head of the department. With unmaskable pity, she says, "Lucy. How are you? Come in. Take a seat. Do you need more time off?"

I shake my head. "I'm here to file a complaint."

GOODBYE, LYNNETTE

I see her pale pink hair from two blocks away. She sits on my front steps, looking bored, an elbow resting on a thigh and her chin on the heel of a hand.

As I approach, I tell myself not to get riled. There's been enough fuckery today. I call out, "Please don't come to my home without asking first."

Lynnette's face lights up. "Lucy, my dear! It's so good to see you. It's been hella long. Did you forget about me?"

"Believe it or not, there are other things going on in my life."

She tilts her head back and cackles. "You should be a waitress at a diner. You're a hoot! They'd get a kick out of you." Her hand pats the spot beside her.

I remain standing a few feet away. "It's not happening. Christy bailed and Donna's in jail. Besides, the story's not over yet."

"And nobody cares but you." She smiles like a salesperson. "Once you sign, you'll get an advance and the chance to decide where the story ends. Don't you want the dough?"

"I don't think so, Lynnette. It's more trouble than it's worth."

"What if I told you it's seven figures?" I pause for a moment and shrug. As if reading my mind, she says, "I'm sure you could think of some good ways to spend it. Set up a program for the families. Pay your friend's lawyer. Start a new business. Hell, you could do all of those things. You don't have to pick one."

"Do you need the fifteen percent that badly?" I size up her desperation. "Did you blow through your own loot already?"

She slumps down, back rounding over her knees. "I'm just

trying to help. I wish you would listen."

"If I listen to you, then what? We're best friends?"

When she peers up at me, I see it in her eyes. The mask slips. She responds with a shrug. "Is that so wrong? I've got plenty of dough but no friends. My childhood fucked me up."

I sit down beside her, studying her face. "I know, and I'm sorry. It sucks. My childhood fucked me up, too. But we're adults now. We can't go on hurting people and blaming our wounds."

"But what if this is the best I can do?" Her face begs for pity. "I've read every self-help book there is. I've been in so many programs. What more can I do?"

My mind starts wondering what I can say to help ease her pain. Then I hear myself say, "I feel sorry for what you've been through, Lynnette, but it's not my problem to solve. Do you know you're the second White woman who's been trying to tell me what to do with this trauma? I'm tired. I need space to deal and heal on my own."

"See, this is what I need—a friend who can tell me hard truths. Someone to guide me."

I rest my forearms on my thighs. "Well, I'm not your woman. I can't do this for a stranger who's trying to exploit me for personal gain."

"It's not like that," she pleads. "Come on . . . No one knows survivors like other survivors."

With a tilt of my head, I insist, "It is *so* like that. I really wonder sometimes if people like you truly believe you're trying to help. Or, somewhere at the core, do you know you're manipulative and why?"

Her head hangs down low. "We can never be friends?"

"You want some hard truths?" I sit back and give it to her straight. "You knew when you saw me that I was a target. You thought you could get something from me. That's not the start of a healthy friendship."

She sighs. "I just wanted to be part of something bigger than me."

"You haven't had enough?" I stand up and stretch, wondering how much of what she's shared resembles the truth. "Careful what you wish for. When something big comes along and defines you, you lose the chance to just be yourself—which is all I ever wanted." I head up the stairs. "I don't know why you all can't leave me alone."

"Lucy?" she calls. I pray she'll just let me go. I turn around with an impatient look that weighs down half my face. She shrugs. "I lied. I sold my story, but not for as much as I said. And I never had your deal on the table. They said if you were in, they'd figure it out. It would've been huge, but it wasn't secured."

She wants to arrest me with this radical honesty and keep the convo going. But I nod and unlock the front door. I don't bother turning around when I say, "Goodbye, Lynnette."

A SMALL SPARK OF HOPE

A note on the coffee table reads: Had to go back to work for a few hours. Parent/teacher thing. There's pizza in the oven.

I throw a couple of slices on a plate, grab a beer from the fridge, and let myself sink into the couch. It's one of those over-sized couches that's not very stylish or supportive, but it feels how I used to imagine clouds feel. Now that Alexis is here, we'll probably replace it with something sleeker. She has a better eye for style.

My father's words pop into my mind. *You kids don't seem to care about hanging on to much.*

One: His generation wants to cling to ideas, rules, and values that prevent social progress. Two: This pizza is good, but it's not as delicious as Mom's Asian, Gay-Loving Pizza.

My phone buzzes.

> Christy: I'm probably the last person U want 2 hear from but UR ex Kevin was brought in by the cops. Thought U might want 2 know.
>
> Me: Thanks for telling me. Any word on what for?
>
> Christy: Not yet. Mike's talking 2 his friend at the station.
>
> Me: Can you let me know when you get some deets?
>
> Christy: Sure. It's kind of weird, right?
>
> Me: . . . Yeah.

This could amount to nothing, but my body is buzzing with a mixture of fear, relief, and excitement. This could be it. They might have found something that ties him to the shooting, and

Donna might finally go free.

Unable to contain myself, I call Donna's phone. Jacob answers. "Hey, Lucy."

"Hey. Sorry about our last conversation."

"I appreciate that."

"How are you holding up?"

"You know, I'm so mad at myself for agreeing to come to this town, putting my family in danger. This is every Black man's nightmare." He sighs.

"It's not your fault."

"Well . . ." I can practically hear him shrug. "Anyway, thanks for your apology. I might've gone a little hard on you, too."

"Don't worry about it. My timing was shit. I shouldn't have pushed myself to the front like that. Sometimes I'm too defensive when I feel rejected. But I was out of line. I never should've gone there. Not then."

"Be as it may, you did get me thinking. I shouldn't have said you had White privilege. I never realized what adopted people might have lost—especially when adopted to another race. Maybe the pastor in me only focused on the good. Now I see it ain't all sunshine and roses."

"No." I laugh. "Most certainly not. Thanks for hearing me despite my terrible timing. It says a lot about you. And hey—I might have some good news."

"I'm listening."

"I got word that my ex-husband was detained. Before I left Bixby, I told the cops I suspected him for the shooting."

He takes a moment to let the information sink in. "And they've got him in custody?"

"That's what I heard—from Christy, via Mike. He's got a friend who works for the BPD."

"And you think it's because they connected him to the crime?"

"I don't know, but it would seem likely. I mean, they didn't want to do anything on the day that I told them. But maybe they had second thoughts. I don't want to get your hopes up . . . But, fingers crossed, this is it."

"I've been praying every day."

Despite how I feel about such things, I tell him, "I'm sure that's helping, too. How's she holding up?"

I hear his footsteps across the wood floor as he paces. "They won't let me see her, but our lawyer says she's doing all right."

"I'm rooting for her."

"I know you are, Lucy. She knows it, too."

"Thanks. Let me know if you hear any news, and I'll do the same."

"God bless."

A visual of Kevin behind bars fades into view. I shiver from the coldness of his face. But then I see Donna stepping out of her cell a free woman.

I want to shout from the deepest part of my soul. My body moves to the pulse of redemption, its rhythmic persistence connecting me to what's always been beating inside: a small spark of hope for an improbable homecoming.

WHITE WOMEN

Tae-Suk hurdles over the chair and lands on it, just as Tae-Suk as ever. There's a sneaky look of amusement on his face as he asks, "Did you get Carin fired?"

"She was fired?" My heart jumps at this unexpected news.

"That's what people say." He scratches his head and then fingers his hair with his signature move that always results in a perfect wave. "Word is, you had something to do with it. It was the final nail, though—so they say."

"Here it is," I say, finding an email from HR in my inbox. "I wasn't trying to get her fired. Just schooled."

"What happened?"

"She showed her true colors." I shrug. "Said I'm racist for supporting my friend instead of blindly believing the cops. All because her brother's a White cop and that video of me chanting 'Black lives matter' struck a nerve."

He laughs but then sharpens his eyes. "You know, there've been other times she's said things . . . But you know how it goes. She's my boss. Her boss is White. Didn't seem worth the trouble."

"What kinds of things did she say?"

"Borderline stuff. Equating racism to feminism. Talking about the PC Police. Little things here and there that made me wonder where she really stands. She tries to come off like she's so liberal, but she's got some pretty messed-up ideas in her head."

"That's White Feminism for ya."

"I've never heard that." He laughs. "But man, does it fit!"

"I think I mistook her control freakishness for support. She was so keen on helping. I thought she connected to me through her trauma and wanted to use what she'd been through for good."

"Her trauma?" His eyes search mine. "What trauma?"

"She confided in me after the shooting," I say, thinking he feels left out.

"How long ago did it happen?"

"Five years, she said."

"I was working for her then." His eyes bulge. "Man! I feel kind of bad for not knowing . . ."

I furrow my brow, confused. "I'm honestly surprised you didn't know."

He fans out his arms. "How was I supposed to?"

"It was a huge deal. It put Ashwin in a wheelchair."

"No, it didn't," he scoffs. "He's been in that chair since he was a kid."

"You're joking . . ."

He cocks his head. "Why would I joke about that? What'd she tell you?"

"A train wreck in India." His eyes are wide. Chills rush up my arms. I hug them to my chest. "Could that not have happened?"

He shrugs. "I don't know." He looks out beyond me to the city before his eyes reconnect with mine. "Train wreck or not, she told me he was born with a condition I forget the name of. It's not like I asked, but she offered it up."

"Motherfucker."

"Nah, that's *her* condition."

"She went on about PTSD and how I needed to work through it. She was an expert because of their experience. Why would anyone lie about something so big?"

Tae-Suk shakes his head. "Some White women, man . . ."

"Did you ever meet Ashwin?" He nods. "What's he like?" I ask.

"He's all right, but he's not what I was expecting."

I lean back, confused. "What were you expecting?"

He shrugs and flutters his eyelids. "She always mentioned he was Asian in certain contexts, right? Even how she'd say his name. Ashwin this. Ashwin that. It's like being with a man named Ashwin made her interesting. So I wasn't expecting him to look so White."

Doubly confused, I ask, "He looks White?"

"He's biracial, but I wouldn't have known he was Indian if not for her constant reminder."

I slowly release my fury through a toneless whistle. "As if co-opting my trauma wasn't bad enough, she exploits her husband's ethnicity to make herself seem progressive while invalidating our truth?" Closing my eyes, I shake my head.

Some White women, indeed.

HE WAS NEVER VIOLENT WITH ME

Christy texts me a link to a news article from the city nearest Bixby. I click and immediately recognize Kevin's high school picture. He's smiling coyly, showing those giant puppy dog eyes. The headline reads:

BIXBY BOY PLEADS GUILTY TO RAPE.

First thought: *He's nearing forty.* Second: *Why'd they use such an old, flattering photo?*

I'm not surprised by the rape, but I'm horrified. Reading on, I learn that he followed a woman home from a queer club in the city. He pretended to be visiting another tenant in her building, and she held the door for him. As her keys twisted to unlock her apartment, he shoved her inside and down to the floor. He fled. She called the cops, who urged her to go to the hospital. When her friend arrived to take her, they noticed his wallet on the floor. The cops picked him up the next morning.

Once again, I teeter at the intersection of guilt and gratitude. It could've been me. Did our drive that day push him to the edge? If he regretted not being more violent the night he tied me up, did he regret it that day, too? He had me so close and could've easily overpowered me, but something stopped him. Why didn't it stop him from hurting this woman? Why must she suffer for what he imagines are my sins?

I call Detective Whitley. "I heard about Kevin."

"Yeah, we got him."

"Did you search his house?"

"Nah. We've got what we need. He's pleading guilty."

"You don't want to check his place for guns or anything tying him to the shooting?" I ask incredulously. "This is proof that he's violent—just like I said."

"It's proof that he likes violent sex." There's cruelty in his voice. "But that's a whole nother thing from a shooting, Ms. Byrne."

"Rape isn't sex! It's violence and power!" I shout.

"If you say so."

Stifling my rage, I ask, "So, what happens now?"

I can almost hear his shrug. "It's a private matter. And as far as I know, he's no longer your husband, so you'll just have to wait like everyone else to find out."

Once again, I wish I could slam the phone without breaking it. I take my index finger and stab the button from so high in the air that I miss twice.

> Me: That poor woman.
>
> Christy: He was never violent with me. Was he w/U?
>
> Me: Yes. When would he have been violent with you?
>
> Christy: We had a fling in between UR divorce and my marriage.

I start typing "It figures" and backspace without sending. The only thing that surprises me here is that it wasn't while he and I were together.

> Me: Well, I believe her.
>
> Christy: I believe her 2. The cops wouldn't arrest him otherwise. He's always been a good Bixby boy.
>
> Me: Unlike Donna.
>
> Christy: ??? Donna's not a boy.
>
> Me: You know what I mean.
>
> Christy: Donna confessed.
>
> Me: If she really confessed, don't you think she'd have given more

detail? Don't you think we'd have known, sitting with her all those times in between?

Christy: I didn't say she was guilty.

Me: Well, if she confessed and wasn't guilty, what does that mean? She was coerced or framed. Say whatever you need to say on your show, but don't bullshit me.

Christy: I'm not going through this again. Just thought Ud want to know what was happening with Kevin, like I promised.

Me: Thanks for doing the least.

MEMORY LANE

"How'd you all become friends, anyway?"

We're in bed, sipping sparkling rosé—Alexis's favorite. I slide a paperclip over the top of a page and put down my book. "We met in preschool. Bixby Country Day. It's not like out here, with waiting lists and choices. We just had one. Christy's mother wouldn't have been able to afford it, but she worked in the office, so she got in free."

"I hate how classist education is," gripes Alexis.

I nod. "Donna and I were always playing. We didn't have the language for it yet, but we must've gravitated towards one another, being the onlies of our kind. One day, Christy joined us. We were doing some handclapping game that she wanted to learn. She kept joining us after that."

Alexis tosses her tablet aside and lifts her knees. "Maybe because you two were different, she thought you were special. I see it in my classroom sometimes. When someone stands out, they're a novelty at first."

"We were friends through half of tenth grade." Recollecting, I add, "But things started falling apart in the sixth, when Christy's looks were starting to blossom. Donna was getting bullied. Christy could've stopped it, but she never interfered. She wasn't willing to risk her popularity. Sound familiar? Donna and I sensed it. But you know . . . We were kids."

Alexis sits up on her pillow and plays with my hair. Her warm hands feel so nurturing. She asks, "So, how'd it all fall apart?"

I take a sip of wine and rest my glass on the nightstand. "We were planning a surprise for her birthday. Christy caught us whispering at my locker. She thought we were talking about her behind her back—and I guess we were, but it was for the party. We knew her popular friends were planning some other thing, but we wanted to do something special. Looking back, we were grasping at straws, trying to keep it going, not knowing it was all a lost cause. We were meeting down in that closet less and less . . ."

Alexis massages my head. "What were you going to do?"

I swivel to face her. "Donna's dad bought a fancy karaoke machine—before anyone imagined you could have one at home like that. So we planned a karaoke night with all of Christy's favorite songs. We were going to get costumes, deck the place out . . ."

"Fun!"

"We thought so." I shrug. "But it never happened. Christy corralled a bunch of kids to trash our houses. Eggs. TP. Silly String. We knew it was her, but she denied it. Had they only done Donna's, she could've gotten away with it. But because they did mine, it was too much of a coincidence. My parents refused to believe she had anything to do with it, of course. They loved her. Thought she could do no wrong. I think they always saw her as the daughter they might've had."

Alexis lifts her glass and says, "I saw that, too—on the Fourth. Both of your parents were gaga for her and her kid."

"She's everything I'm not: straight, girly, White, blond. She's a mom, and she never left Bixby. Oh—and she married an army man! Anyway, that was the end of it. A year or so later, she half apologized for jumping to conclusions, but she never confessed or apologized for the vandalism. Since she turned on us over such a small thing, and never fully came clean, all trust was gone."

"She strikes me as someone who's deeply conflicted."

"Really?" I scoot back to sit level with her. "I always saw her as someone who knew exactly what she wanted and was determined to get it. Men, her daughter, that house, the show . . ."

"On the surface," she says, nodding. "Sure. Looking back, she was almost too normal right after the shooting—that night at her house. But at the barbecue at your place? There was something uneasy, something searching and scared. I think she tries hard to come off a certain way."

I wonder if not having a father figure might have influenced how she is with men—needing desire to validate her worth. Then I realize how much time I've spent trying to understand those who refuse to understand me.

I shake out my hair and lift Alexis's shirt up over her head. "I'm so tired of memory lane," I whisper. "Let's go somewhere else . . ."

THE MINDFUCKEN

On the way down to Montara Mountain the next morning, I give Alexis the side-eye from the passenger seat. "Hmm. You have a Korean-made car, a Korean-made phone, and a Korean-made girlfriend. I'm starting to have my suspicions."

"Yeah—when I saw you, I thought hey, that girl would go great with my Kia."

I laugh. "That's cool. I'm just with you for your White-passing privilege."

"You know how I hate looking White. It erases my ancestry and how I feel inside," she moans.

"It was a joke in the same spirit as yours. Look—I'm not trying to erase your background. I know what it means to you, and I'm sorry it hurt you." I put my hand on her leg. "But people who can't hide their color are oppressed and killed over it. Your discomfort of being White-passing doesn't compare to how it protects you."

She takes a minute before she responds. "If I could, I'd look more Brown. It sucks feeling excluded from my people."

"I understand the not fitting in." I sigh. "That's pretty much been my whole life. Now, don't get me wrong, because I love being Asian. But, had I grown up in Bixby not looking so Asian, my childhood would've been a hell of a lot easier. If Donna were White-passing, do you think she'd be in jail?"

"Well, it's hard to know . . ."

"Not this again."

"What?"

I sigh. "White people always act like there's no way to tell when there are plenty of stats that support it."

"Why are you calling me White again after I specifically said that it hurts me?"

"I'm not calling you White. I'm calling out your behavior."

"Girl . . . I lead my school in diversity training. I've got three different discriminated groups in my DNA."

I huff, shaking my head. "And that doesn't mean you don't also have internalized bias or White-passing privilege. When you say you wish you looked Brown, it trivializes the pain and suffering of people who do. It re-centers you."

She inhales and exhales slowly. "I don't mean to do that."

"Okay. But you know it's not about your intent."

The car slows as we ascend the curvy roads. "I've been thinking a lot since our last talk. I'm sorry for what I said about Donna that day. I see how it sounded like I was taking the side of the oppressors," says Alexis.

"That's because you were."

She holds up a hand. "At the time, I thought I was just offering another perspective."

"You were offering the White perspective."

"I know. I was wrong. That's what I'm trying to say." She huffs, parking the car. She gets out and stretches in silence. A few minutes later, she pulls me near. "Hey. I appreciate you talking to me about this stuff. I'd hate it if you felt that you couldn't."

I attempt a half smile. "Thanks for hearing me out."

She kisses my temple. "I'm trying."

"I know. And that's why I bother."

Climbing the Brooks Falls Loop, we work out our residual aggression. The ground has a purple hue from the minty-green trees, ashy shrubs, and grass. Hawks, vultures, and an eagle soar above. We stop to admire them here and there. And when we make it to where the falls would be, the drought is so severe they aren't running.

"It's still beautiful," offers Alexis.

She carries on, but I'm lost in my thoughts about Donna and how much hinges on the Bixby PD getting things right. The rally drew more attention to the situation, but, as I'd feared, it didn't make change. I picture Donna behind bars. I picture our old classmates' graves. It's hard to reconcile how I'm out here among all this beauty while they can't be.

"Hello? You in there?" Alexis waves her arms. I snap back to the moment. She asks, "Where'd you go?"

"Just thinking of Bixby."

"Maybe it's time we get you hooked up with someone."

"I don't want to talk about it." I sigh. "Especially to a stranger."

"Yeah, I know, but don't tuck it away."

"I just want to be past it."

"I wish it were so easy." Alexis stops and takes in the view. "There've been times I've wanted so badly to be beyond my own pain that I've faked it—till I was so good at faking it, I even fooled myself for a while. It's a mindfuck. Actually, it's like a turducken."

"A turducken?"

"Yeah!" She laughs. "Never thought of it like that until now—but it's so what it is! You take one piece of your suffering and bury it in the carcass of something else so you can't see it. Then you stuff another piece of your pain inside that one. Pretty soon, you have no idea what you've created. It's one big, ugly beast that you cut up and serve yourself daily."

"A mindfucken!"

"Yes!" she cries. "A mindfucken!"

I press my lips to Alexis's. The birds sing. The wind blows

through the trees and the grass. It's like a cheesy romance novel. And then an unnatural sound steals us from the moment. I pull out my phone. "Didn't think I'd have service out here. Should I take it?"

Alexis shrugs. "It already killed the vibe."

It's the Bixby area code. "Hello?"

"Lucy Byrne?"

"Yeah . . . Uh-huh. Oh . . . Hmm . . . Well, I suppose. Okay. Yep. Bye."

I slide the phone back into my pocket and stand in silence. My eyes trace where the cove of houses meets the shore and where the ocean fades into the sky.

Alexis asks, "Well?"

I swivel and steady my balance. "Bixby PD wants me back for questioning."

"When?"

"Soon as I can get there."

"Why?"

"They've got new evidence to go over. Maybe it has to do with Kevin. Whatever it is, they need me there for it."

"Shit. You just got back."

We begin our decline in silence, holding in most of our thoughts.

"Are you scared?" Alexis asks.

"Of what?"

"The possibilities?"

"What can they do?"

"I don't know. Look what happened to Donna."

I stop and face her. "They don't see us as the same. You know that."

She chews the inside of a cheek. "Well, it feels like I'm letting you walk into battle alone."

"Listen." My face stiffens. I focus my eyes so she registers my serious intent. "I don't want to hear anything against this, but if it's not looking good for Donna, I'm going to find a way to get locked up with her."

"What?" Her eyes open wide as she stumbles back a few steps. "Why?"

"To get a better understanding of what happened. So I'll know how to help when I'm out."

"I'm not supposed to protest this?"

My head slowly shakes from one side to the other. Our eyes are locked.

"What'll happen if they don't put you in the same room? It'll all be for nothing. It'll stay on your record."

I shift my weight to one hip. "I just have to do this. Okay?"

Her face looks frantic. "How?"

"I'll figure something out. Just . . . Don't come looking for me till I call you. Okay?"

"Well . . ." I can see it's taking all of her restraint to stay calm. "Okay. But as soon as you're ready, I'll be there with—"

"Bells on?"

"Fuck the bells. A badass attorney."

DADDY ISSUES

The Bixby house is empty when I arrive. Mom left a floral-patterned balloon floating above the banister. I give it a one-sided fist bump out of empathy—since we're both tied to this place.

Collapsing on the sofa, I text Alexis that I've arrived as another text comes in.

> Christy: We need 2 talk. Call me when UR free.

I start to reply, but my phone shuts down.

Dad walks in and asks, "How was the flight?"

With a half nod that barely acknowledges his presence, I mutter, "Fine. Can I borrow your phone?"

"Sure." He removes it from his back pocket and tosses it over.

I open the text app and groan. "Fuck." I realize I need my phone for Christy's number. I tilt my head back out of frustration before glancing down, eyes landing on a message from Christy Fox. I think surely it must be a different Christy Fox. Then I admit my utter denial.

Dad grabs a Bud Light from the fridge and heads out to the grill. I hold my breath and click on the last text.

> Christy: Running late. C U soon.

Scrolling back, I see:

> Dad: Don't get the wrong idea here but wondering if you could meet at our old rendezvous.

"What the ever-living fuck?" I say out loud.

I make a move for the front door and open it up to my mother. Her face is beaming with joy. "Honey! I'm so glad you're home!" She squeezes me tightly. "Wish it were under better circumstances, of course."

I manage to say, "Thanks, Mom."

"I'll make something to eat."

Heading upstairs, I say, "Gotta plug in my phone."

I drop Dad's phone on the desk, plug mine into the charger by the bed, and collapse. Unable to fully grasp what I've stumbled upon, I put a pillow over my face and groan.

What the hell? An affair? Christy and Dad? Does Mom know? She can't . . .

After taking my agony out on the pillow again, I let go and feel the weight of it resting on my face. It slows down my breathing.

There's a knock on the door followed by Dad asking, "Do you still have my phone?" There's something in his voice. He's nervous. Perhaps he's realizing his mistake.

I point towards the desk, not bothering to remove the pillow. "Jet lag?"

"Yeah," I lie, my reply muffled.

The door closes and he's gone.

My phone powers up.

> Me: In Bixby. Busy now?
>
> Christy: Nope. Mike's out with Sophie. Want 2 come by?
>
> Me: When?
>
> Christy: Give me 15.
>
> Me: See you then.

I splash cold water on my face and pat it dry. Finger-combing my hair, I study my reflection. "You ready for this?"

Running downstairs, I round the corner and march towards Mom, who is meticulously laying out vegetables and hummus.

"Can I take the car?"

She looks disappointed. "You don't want to stay and catch up?"

"I promise we'll do that later. I've gotta talk to someone."

"Everything all right?"

"I don't know," I reply honestly.

"Well . . . Okay. Go do what you need."

Perhaps out of pity, I pull her near and peck her cheek. "Thanks, Mom. You're the best. I'll be back."

Her face is aglow as she calls out, "Okay. Be safe."

When I pull up in front of Christy's, I don't stop to question what I'll say or do. My body was always preparing for a near-death experience—but never for the moment I'd learn my father was having an affair with my childhood friend.

As I'm stepping out of the car, a taxi starts up across the road. It looks like that guy—Oscar—who picked me up from the bus. I lift a hand to wave, but he drives off.

Christy opens the door looking apprehensive, but she speaks in her usual cheery tone. "Come in! I made some sangria."

"Hey." I follow her into the kitchen. "Did you see the guy in the cab?"

"No. Why?"

"It's weird, seeing people from our class. I keep forgetting some survived by staying home."

"Yeah." She pours two tall glasses of sangria and embellishes them with festive straws. "How was the flight?"

"Fine. Listen, Christy. My phone died, and I had to borrow my dad's. I saw your name in there. What's that about?"

Her smile fades, and she pauses uncertainly. "I, um . . . We . . . He . . ."

My lips wrap around the straw, my eyes fixed on hers. Across the kitchen island, she pulls out a stool but evades eye contact.

"He wanted to talk about the shooting. He was worried about you."

"Why would he talk to you about it?"

"Well, I was there with you . . ."

"Why wouldn't he just call me?"

Christy sips her sangria, peering into the glass as if its contents hold the answers. "He doesn't know how to talk to you."

"That's crazy." I huff. "I'm so easy to talk to." Christy raises a brow, and I give her that one. "Well, why would he feel more comfortable talking to you?"

"I don't know . . ." Her eyes shift to the other side of the room.

I say, "Your old rendezvous?" Her right eye starts to twitch. "Tell me about that." I watch as she nervously stirs her straw through the ice and fruit. "Talk to me," I insist.

"I'm trying to find the right words."

"Try harder."

"Okay. I'll just spit it out. Years ago, we had a fling." She looks bored with the topic already.

"How many years ago?"

"I don't know . . . Before Mike."

"How long did it last?"

"It was nothing. Just here and there for a couple of years."

"A couple of years?" I raise my voice. "Why him? Did you come on to him—just like you've come on to every man who was ever happy with someone else?"

"I resent that!"

I point a finger straight at her and say, "You resemble that."

"I've always liked him." Her confidence returns. "I used to catch him looking at me all the time when we were hangin' around your house. I always wished he were mine. When I was old enough, we had a little fling. So what? It's not a big deal. It's in the past." I press my lips tightly, afraid of what might come out. Christy adds, "I'm sorry you had to find out."

"That's what you're sorry for? That I know? You're not sorry for fucking my dad?"

"It's complicated. I don't expect you to understand. He's a good man."

"I thought he was."

"He is. But he's not perfect. No one is."

"Spare me."

"You know, he could've died fighting for your people. Don't you think that messed him up some? Doesn't he get a right to be human?"

"I'm fucking Korean! And no—his service in the Vietnam war doesn't give him a pass to fuck my friends and cheat on my mom!"

"Hate your father if that's what you want." She looks faint for a moment. "But he loves you—and your mother."

"Is that what he said while you were sucking his dick?"

"No, it's what he said the other day! We just talked this time. You don't have to believe me, but it's the God's honest truth. Henry—"

"Henry!"

Her eyes roll. "Your father's a good man. But he's human. And I suppose you want to let this one thing define him. Don't forget how lucky you are to have a dad. You have someone to call 'not good enough' when some of us would've been happy with him, warts and all."

I watch her play with her drink as I fill up with contempt. I try empathizing. "I'm sorry you grew up without a father. I lost a mother and father, too."

"See?" Christy shouts. "You're so ungrateful! Do you hear yourself? How is he a bad father? How does having an affair

take away from any of the things he's given you all your life?"
She goes to the fridge and pours us both more sangria.

"Thanks," I say, caught off guard by the normalcy. I take
another sip. "I'm not saying his affair makes him a bad father.
I'm saying that what he did—with you—disgusts me. And what
he did to my mom disgusts me." My mouth goes sour. "And
what you did disgusts me, too."

"Well, I guess it's your right to be so disgusted. But you're one
to talk . . ."

"What?"

"It's a little rich for you to be judging other people's sex lives.
Don't you think?"

My jaw drops. I don't fire back as soon as I'd like, my brain
stammering from her words. "Because I'm queer, I have no
moral compass?"

Christy smugly responds, "What's right to you isn't right to
many—including God. So if you want to act righteous, don't be
surprised when I call you a hypocrite."

"Nice. You fuck my father and use my sexual orientation to
make me the bad guy."

"Do you have to keep saying that? I mean, it was more than
just sex."

"Which is it? More than sex or just a little fling?"

"I cared for him!" She slams her fist on the counter. "And as
a matter of fact, I still do!"

"And what about my mom? How can you look her in the eye
and smile like you didn't betray her, too?"

"She had nothing to do with it."

"You're used to it." I tilt my head. "That's what it is. I could
give two shits about you sleeping around. It's just that somehow
they're never single! Didn't Mike have a wife when you met
him? Was it a box you checked on your dating profile?" My

fingers gallop into the air as I mime typing. "Must . . . be . . . married. I need . . . a challenge."

"Get out of my house!"

The stool squeaks against the linoleum as I jump from my seat. "Gladly." Catching myself as I walk out of the kitchen, I pause and say, "You know . . ."

"What?" snaps Christy, narrowing her eyes.

I shake my head in defeat. "Forget it."

"Go on. You were going to say you wish you'd left me to die!" Her face is red, and her chest is heaving.

"No," I say, blinking while shaking my head. "That's not what I was going to say."

"Yes, you were!"

"I was going to say that I wish things didn't have to get so ugly."

She yells with full force, voice breaking and trembling from the volume. "Liar! I don't trust you! And neither do the cops!"

I sigh, pretending not to be shook by the sheer force of her. "Whatever. Call me if you want to talk later."

As I'm climbing into my car, I realize I never asked what she wanted to talk about in the first place.

THE WORDS OF A WHITE GIRL

Sitting under the fluorescent lights of the BPD's interrogation room, I see an old-school camcorder on a tripod glaring at me, mirroring my entire Bixby experience. Despite my exhaustion, a small speck of hope tickles my chest—hope that Donna will soon be free, and we can finally begin to put this all behind us.

An officer I've never met enters the room with a sneer. He hits record.

I ask, "Is this about Kevin?"

He backs up against the wall and cocks his head. "Kevin? No. We want to talk some more about the shooting."

"Yeah. I told Whitley it could've been him. Thought that's why I was here—that maybe you found something at his house?"

He slides onto the chair across from me and leans on the table. "This has nothing to do with your ex. You're here because Mrs. Tilden had a recollection. Both you and Mrs. Devine were together 'fore the shooting broke out—up at the buffet. Thought we'd never find out, didn't you?"

My face twists into a scowl. I'm not ready to believe my ears. "Christy said that? I doubt it. I just saw her last night, and she said nothing of it."

He tightens his smirk a few notches, looking me up and down. "Uh-huh. She sure did."

Tilting my head to the ceiling, I try to remember being with Donna at the buffet table, but such a memory doesn't exist. "I don't think that's true."

"Well, it's not in your best interest. Is it?" He places his hands on his hips—like he's about to square dance.

"When did Christy say that?"

"Last week."

"Huh . . ." This must be what she wanted to talk about before I cornered her about Dad. As bad as she is, I can't imagine she'd willingly implicate us. "I don't remember seeing Donna at all—until we both saw her running ahead."

His face is disbelieving. "You and Donna thought you'd get away with it, so long as you had a star witness. Christy was ideal." He fans his hands in front of his face. "The most popular girl in town. Somehow still the prettiest. And you come out the hero who saved her."

"That's crazy." I employ my best chuckle. "Cops turning witnesses on each other is a cheap TV plot. It's not working on me."

"Look here. The Black girl's already being held. All we want from you is to know who pulled the trigger. So go on. Tell me his name."

"You think Donna and I conspired with someone to shoot up the class?" My head jerks. "Why would we do that?"

" 'Cause you're a couple of racists out for revenge."

"That's right. We're the racists." I roll my eyes. "We're the ones with all the power here."

He grins and shakes his head. "I thought you Orientals were supposed to be smart?"

I lean back in my chair. "You don't even care that we didn't do it."

"Your poor parents. They did everything for you. Didn't they? And then you go and shame them like this."

I tilt my head back. "Where's your proof?"

"Your star witness."

"Really?" I press my fingernails into my thumbs. "All you

need are the words of a White girl?"

"People like you disgust me," he spits.

"Asian people? Or queers?"

"I don't care if you're yellow, purple, or green. You're a disgrace to our country. You've had your time. We've given you the benefit of the doubt. And now look—you had to go and prove us right. We've got plenty of starving White kids right here at home. But instead, we end up with more of you. That's what's wrong with this country."

"You're what's wrong with this country. Fragile White men who can't handle the thought of losing a little power. So what do you do? You put on a badge and arrest as many Black folks as you can before they encroach on your precious privilege. That makes you feel powerful again. Good for you, right? You're the disgrace."

He leans over and slaps me so hard that the chair topples over. My head hits the floor. From the corner of my eye, I see blood. I won't lie. I'm scared. See, White people want Asians to believe we're like them—until the first chance they get to justify treating us how they really see us.

My fear metabolizes into anger. All the tension inside me explodes. I know what I have to do. Jumping up, I go at him full force. A few blows connect with his jaw before his arms wrap around me, rendering me defenseless.

Detective Whitley rushes in and separates us. "What the hell's going on? What happened to her face?" To my surprise and to his credit, he looks concerned.

Bad Cop kicks a chair across the room. "She was mouthing off."

"You're two and a half times her size. What did you think she would do?" Whitley fixes my chair and helps me back onto it. "You okay?"

"This racist prick is a monster," I grumble.

"You're the racist monster! My cousin died because of you!"

Whitley shoves him away. "I'll take it from here!"

From the hall, Bad Cop shouts, "Dumb gook faggot!"

"You're just proving my point, asshole!" I call out.

As if disappointed, Whitley says, "You've left me no choice now. I'm going to have to arrest you for assaulting an officer." He shakes his head. "Why have you gotta make things so hard for yourself?"

"You sound like my father." I huff. "You know we didn't do it. You saw us right after it happened. We sat in this room. Don't you think you'd have known if we had been guilty? Don't you trust your own judgment?"

"It's our job to find the shooter, and we think you know who it is. You could've just answered our questions and been on your way. It's not like we were gonna lock you up—until you crossed the line."

"Where's Kevin? Is he still in the building? You're not going to put me anywhere near him . . ."

"He's been transferred to a prison."

My heart lifts an inch from relief.

LISTEN NOW

Donna's sitting upright on a cot, back straight and both feet on the floor. Her eyes follow me as I'm escorted two cells down from her. As I'm shoved inside, I think about how despite what I'm being jailed for, they never bothered with handcuffs.

I stand with my hands clasped around the bars. I move my head side to side, angling for a clear view. "Donna," I say. She looks away and prays like the Devil's fast on her tail. During her pause, I try again. "Talk to me. I know you're not guilty."

But she keeps her head bowed and frantically whispers, "I owe the Lord a morning song of gratitude and praise, for the kind mercy He has shown in lengthening out my days . . ."

I lift my eyes to the security guard on the other side of the room. He nods. "It's all she's been doing since she arrived. Never saw such a strong display of faith. Got me thinkin' maybe she didn't do it." He looks as if he's just said something profound— as if her duty to his God counteracts what he thinks of her Blackness and guilt.

I think back to that time in kindergarten when Brett called her the N-word. The rest of the class howled, not yet understanding what it meant but appealing to his tone. And in middle school when Kate accused her of stealing her hairbrush and using it on her "nappy cooties." And Judd—the one kid brave enough to admit to his crush on Donna—had his locker decorated with Donna's face pasted over clippings from a Black pornographic magazine.

And then it occurs to me: The people of Bixby believe

Donna's guilty because they know they did all they could to drive her to it.

Donna knocks me out of my zone by speaking something other than prayer. "Lucy." I look around and notice the guard has left. "I'm tired of being the White man's scapegoat." Her eyes are wide open and honestly a little frightening.

"Thank God," I say, relieved by her presence. "Let's do something."

"You think if it were that easy, I wouldn't have tried?"

I open my mouth to tell her why I'm here, but she sings to herself. "He kept me safe another night. I see another day. Now may His Spirit, as the light, direct me in His way . . ."

Frustrated by her sudden departure, my eyes scan the room. There's not a guard in sight. I retreat to my cot, concerned about her state of mind. She's been here alone for too long. How will she hold up when she gets to court?

I say, "Donna, if it weren't for you, I don't think I'd have survived growing up in this town. I'm going to do everything I can to help you out. But I'll need your help."

She pauses a few beats, and my heart and hope perch on her silence. And then she carries on singing.

I shake my head and say, "Shit. Maybe my dad did it to protect my mom from finding out what he did." I don't really believe it, but I need to hear myself wonder.

Without asking why I'd propose such a thing, Donna says, "It wasn't him."

"How do you know?"

"Because I saw him—the killer."

I'LL TELL YOU

Bad Cop guides Donna's parents into the room, saying, "This is a rare exception. If it were up to me, you wouldn't get special treatment. We all know what you gave the town was for show and tax breaks; it wasn't from the good in your hearts. But lucky for you, I'm not calling the shots. Be quick. You've got ten minutes." Dr. Carter nods. Bad Cop turns and leaves.

Donna rises, approaching the bars. "Daddy!" He wraps his hands around hers and kisses her forehead.

Mrs. Carter reaches in to rest her hand on Donna's shoulder. "Sorry, baby. We did all we could."

"What do you mean, you did all you could?" Donna shakes her head.

"They're charging you with murder and conspiracy. The best you can do is cooperate. Tell them all you know."

Donna pulls away and sits back on her cot. "They don't wanna hear it." She rests her head in her hands, then looks up. "And apparently, you don't either. It's the same old dance. I'm being brought down by White folks, and here you are, telling me to comply."

"It's not like that, Donna," says Dr. Carter.

"Oh no? 'Cause it feels it to me! Once again, you're taking their side."

He stifles a shout. "We're not taking their side. We're trying to help you survive."

She shakes her head. "My survival was always on me. It was never on the White kids causing me trouble."

"Be careful now," Dr. Carter says lowly. "That's why they claim you did it."

Donna looks to the ceiling and sighs.

Mrs. Carter jumps in. "Everything we did was for you. And we did it so well that you can't see how good you had it. We grew up in poverty and violence. Forget about teasing and pranks. People were dying. We brought you here for a better chance."

"Well, how'd that work out?" Donna snickers. "Be honest. You didn't move here for me. You moved for a fancy job, and you liked how those White folks made you feel important. You probably hoped somehow I'd turn White, too."

"Do you know how hard your daddy worked to be a top surgeon at that hospital? Why do you think there were always White folks at the table? Because White folks were the only ones at the top—especially back then, when you were a child. We never wanted you to be White. We only wanted you to be safe and have the opportunity of White folks."

"And you thought being the only Black girl in town would allow that?" Donna asks, face twisted with skepticism.

"Were we perfect? No. We made some mistakes." Dr. Carter sighs. "But we tried our best to protect you and teach you to fend for yourself. If that made you feel unloved, I'm deeply sorry. More than you know. But I'll tell you: Everything we did, we did out of love."

Donna sits quietly for half a minute. "So, now what? Your money's not good enough, and I'm still not White enough. And believe it or not, I'm innocent."

"We believe you." Mrs. Carter inches closer to the bars, her watery eyes peering in to see Donna more clearly. "We've always believed you. I'm sorry I never said that enough. Now, come here before we have to go."

Donna walks to her parents and rests her head against the

bars. The three of them hold on to each other in silent prayer for the final minute.

* * *

I give Donna a few hours to herself after her folks leave. While I'm sure it meant a lot to finally have that conversation, it also means a lot to find out they can't help. Any bit of hope that someone can save her is gone.

Finally, I gently ask, "Donna, are you ready to tell me who it was?" She opens her mouth, and it hangs there a moment, on the edge of a much-needed truth. She reverts to prayer. "The Lord—"

And I snap. "To hell with the Lord! Did He protect our class-mates? Is that what you think they died from—a lack of faith? No. They died from a man. And you saw him. So tell me. Tell someone! Those people shouldn't die in vain and neither should you! Look, they're not going to keep me much longer." She sits quietly for almost too long. About to break, I urge, "Donna! S-I-S-S. Remember? Come on, now. We're in this together."

Her face eases into a smirk. And then, in a soft but serious voice, she says, "Okay. Hush now. I'll tell you."

TWO FOR ONE

Chills rush up my spine as I tell her, "He drove me home in his cab. I almost thought, but . . . He seemed so calm . . . Holy shit! He was with the survivors' families protesting outside the station!" My heart pounds from the brazen behavior. "Christy . . . Does she know?"

"I don't think so." Donna tilts her head thoughtfully. "If she thought it was him, she'd have done something to protect her daughter."

I can't seem to stop shaking my head. "So, how'd it go down?"

Donna takes a deep breath. "I was picking stuff up for dinner. He was up the aisle with a shopping basket. There was something in his walk. Couldn't say what it was, but when I saw him, my body went cold. Then I looked down at the black jeans tucked into his boots, and suddenly I was transported back to that night. I was coming from the bathroom when I saw a man leaving the boys' lavatory with a rifle. For a second, I slipped back into the girls' room, frozen in fear. But then I came to grips and started walking in the other direction. And as soon as the shooting began, I ran. I even told the cops later that night. But somehow, between then and that moment in the aisle, it slipped my mind. Seeing him there made it all come flooding back."

"I would've freaked the fuck out."

"I did." She shivers. "I dropped the sparkling cider I was holding, and he turned around. He took a good look at my face—which was probably stricken with fear. I rushed out of there, searching my bag for my phone, but I'd left it at home.

Hopped into my car—before I could lock the doors, he was right there beside me in the passenger seat."

"Holy shit."

"He pulled out a handgun and pointed it at me. I thought for sure I was done. I started saying my prayers, but then he rambled on about how hurt *he* was—by Christy. Imagine! Relying on the emotional labor of a woman while terrorizing her . . ." She shakes her head. "She was all he ever wanted. Once he had her, it was a dream come true, but then she acted like it was nothing. He whined and moaned this to me. He thought they might go to the reunion together, but then she patched things back up with Mike. So he thought he'd get her—and Mike with his defenses down—along with anyone else who got in his way. But you know, Mike wasn't there. And Christy got away. Said he didn't expect to kill so many. He was caught up in the adrenaline of it all. Said it was too easy. And then he went crazy—you know the way some White folks do? Said maybe the fact that she lived was fate, that they still had a chance after all." She rolls her eyes and sighs.

I rub my eyes. The room spins. "So how did this lead to your supposed confession?"

"He ordered me to drive to the Bixby PD. With the gun pointed at me, I did what he said. Then he told me to march in there and turn myself in. Said he knew the town wanted me for it, and he couldn't trust me, so it was a preemptive strike. If I ran, he'd shoot me and head to my house to shoot Jacob and the boys." She starts tearing up. "I thanked the Lord that we'd already sent the boys away, but I couldn't bear to think of him killing my Jacob! Jacob never wanted to come here, but he did it for me."

My eyes are welling up, too. "I'm so sorry, Donna. That's terrifying."

She wipes her face with her hands. "So, I did what he said. In that few hundred feet, I was so scared I couldn't think straight. I thought of telling the truth—that he was out in my car—but was afraid if I did, he'd still make it to my house and kill Jacob before they caught up with him. So I stood there like a zombie and lied. Then I started praying—'cause I knew if I said too much, it'd put Jacob in danger."

"There's got to be something we can do . . ." I'm pacing my cell, feeling helpless and enraged. "He can't get away with this."

"But he will. Till he meets his Maker."

I remember how the cops wouldn't investigate Kevin when I asked. Donna's right. If she tells them about Oscar, nothing good will come of it. They'll think we conspired again. "You can't go down for this. We can't let him win."

"Well, have you got any bright ideas?"

Our eyes connect and hold in a way that I've only ever allowed with Alexis. I think out loud, shaking my head. "We need to find a way to work around their system, 'cause fuck knows it's not designed for us to work within it. Damn Christy . . . She never considers how her actions impact anyone . . ."

Donna perks up. "I've got it! We'll sound the alarm . . . with a threat against Christy! Nothing makes folks run faster than the chance to save a pretty White girl."

"Yes! We'll make it look like the threat's from him! And that's how they'll catch him—by thinking they've cracked it themselves. I'll use my call to get Alexis's help."

Donna's chest rises high. She holds her breath, contemplating our plan, and slowly exhales through puckered lips. She twists her head around a few times, cracks her neck, and says, " 'Kay. Let's do this thing."

HOW IT'S DONE

"Finally! What's going on? You okay?"

Through the phone, I tell Alexis, "The rock. It was aiming for one bird, but she flew away."

"Come again?"

"The great bird of Bixby. Town treasure."

"Okay . . ."

"The rock that caused all that damage was meant for her. But she flew away."

"Keep going."

"We know who threw it, and we need your help."

"How so?"

"Send a pebble to the bird so we can trace the arc of its path. You follow?"

"Keep talking."

"The bird flapped its feathers in a sacred dance and then flew away. If we throw a few pebbles from his direction, someone might see the path. They'll go there and find all the rocks."

"Do you have a name?"

I think for a moment. "He's a real grouch. Green with envy."

"Is he, like, total trash?"

"Pure trash. And also, his dad was the only friend of Tom Hanks on that island. He wasn't real, but they sure had a ball."

"Was he a nosy neighbor, peering over the fence—in a hat?"

"I love you." I sigh with relief. "Can you call Jacob and my folks? Tell them not to worry."

"I got you. And, Lucy? I miss you."

"I miss you so much."

We go a few days with no contact or news. I start worrying that it's too complicated, that I'll have to wait till I'm released— because surely they can't hold me much longer. Donna and I don't talk much. I pace around, practicing breathing techniques to calm my nerves. Donna resumes her prayers. I see how it soothes her. For the first time, I find myself wishing I could release my anxiety by trusting in some higher power.

* * *

When he's found, he is dead. Oscar J. Wilson made it to the Pacific Northwest. His body lay in a parking lot with a gun and a whimpering dog by its side, chin on chest. Had he kept his mouth shut, he'd still be alive. But he had to brag about an affair with Christy Fox Tilden when her show aired in a bar. Another punter wouldn't believe him, and that set him off, says the barman. When it escalated, they took it outside. And, well, Oscar lost.

When they come to release us, it's easy to act surprised. Despite what we set into motion, anything could've happened.

"It's a miracle," declares Donna.

I stand beside her without protest. She squeezes me so tightly I can hardly breathe.

JOINED FORCES

As I open the front door of the lavender cape, Mom launches towards me from the couch. "I went down to that station three times and demanded to see you! You'd think being a lifetime resident would've counted for something." She holds me at arm's length and nods regretfully. Her eyes water as her thumb gently grazes the wound on my cheek. "I guess you were right. My Whiteness and status don't protect you." Her shoulder nearly knocks out my teeth as she throws her arms around me. "I'm so glad you're home."

Over on the couch, Dad swivels his head towards me. "Good to see you outta there."

I tilt my head in his direction, unable to give any better.

Alexis flew in last night. We sit on my old bed with our knees and fingertips touching. "Tell me how it went down," I beg, gazing into her eyes as if magic lives there.

"Remember Tamika?"

"From the rally?"

She nods. "At first, I was going to fly here—break into his house and use his landline, since Bixby still uses those things. But Tamika found his number within minutes. She knows how to bounce a call from a different number, so we bounced it from Oscar's cell phone. She's skilled like that."

"Were you there when she made the call?"

"We made three." Warm vibrations tingle across my hands as she speaks. "The first was a warm-up. We didn't want to mention anything about Oscar or the shooting, just in case it prevented Christy from calling the cops."

"That's so smart."

Her face practically sparkles as she wiggles her head around a little. "The next call was short and equally vague. We wanted to make sure she was taking it seriously—that odds were good it was being traced. The third time, Tamika went strong."

"What about her voice?"

"She used a vocoder. Anyway, here's what she said." Alexis scrunches her neck and speaks in a deep tone. "I thought we had something. I felt like the luckiest man alive. Then you tossed me aside. Fifty-six are on you."

Chills rush up my forearms. "Tamika wasn't afraid to get caught?"

Alexis shrugs and shakes her head. "She lives for this stuff."

I think for a moment. "I wonder what would've happened if he'd died before you made the calls? We're lucky the timing worked out."

"We were just in time." She nods. "They found a sketchbook with the reunion invitation and a few drawings of plans. Just sitting in his bag. Like, he didn't even burn it."

"I should've connected the dots." I sigh. "That day I confronted Christy about her affair with my dad, Oscar was outside her house."

"He was?"

"I didn't make anything of it." My eyes slowly gravitate to the window. "He's a cab driver, after all. And she shrugged it off. But he must've been stalking her or something."

Alexis taps my hands. "I can't believe what you and Donna went through." She caresses my cheek.

"I don't know how Donna dealt. She was there for a long time, alone." I let my upper half flop down to the bed. "Would you lie here with me? I never thought I'd appreciate being back in this bed so much."

Squirming down beside me, she slides her hand over my stomach. Although she's four inches taller, she rests her head on my chest. "We're quite the team," I tell her. "I loved knowing I could count on you to pick up on my clues when I called you that day."

"I won't lie. I was worried." She peers up at me. "We should make Hasbro a 'Thank you for helping us break through the racist incarceration system' card. Hallmark sure hasn't got one."

I laugh. "Yeah, we should write it in code."

"Maybe a series of stick figure drawings with lots of frantic arrows and circles."

"Guess this, motherfuckers!"

We laugh.

As I'm lost in deep thought, she taps my chest. "Why the serious face all of a sudden?"

I want to brush it off with another joke, but I tell her, "I fucking love you. And I'm so glad it's over. This part, at least."

THE GOOD GUYS

Oscar's face is plastered across every publication and news channel. Most photos are of his younger years, his reddish-brown shag framing pale blue eyes. They take me back to our high school days. He was a mediocre athlete whose teammates kept him around for his unpredictable humor and inappropriate drawings. He was the guy at the party who, desperate for attention, would always go too far. When he wasn't center stage, there was an awkwardness that kept him from really connecting. Looking back, it was probably inferiority or resentment because his teammates got all the girls.

Article after exposé asks how a good man could go to such lengths. A national publication buys the rights to his sketchbook, with plans for a psychological analysis. Some argue it glorifies a killer, while others claim it's the insight we need.

Putting down the paper, I huff. "Here's your insight: Men feel entitled to women—and when they don't get what they want, they get violent."

Dad cracks open a Bud Light. "That's not fair to the good guys."

"When you 'Not All Men,' you deny the problem and become part of it."

He shakes his head and takes a swig.

Sure, I could've approached it more gently, but I'm still bitter about his cheating on Mom—who chimes in to say, "Even so, that's no way to talk to your father."

I hear the words "I wouldn't be so quick to defend him if I

were you" spill out of my mouth before I can stop them. Dad shoots me a quizzical look laced with fear.

Mom catches her mouth agape and asks, "What's that supposed to mean?"

"Never mind." I resist the urge, realizing it's not my place. "I shouldn't have said that."

I expect we'll go on in our typical way, holding everything in while building further resentment. But Dad surprises me when he laments, "Maybe if I were a better example of a man, you'd have never gone gay."

Mom gasps. "Henry!"

"No, Dad. I'm not queer because of you. I'm who I was always going to be. You can bring a baby into your home, but you can't expect her to be what you want, no matter what you do. I'm my own person. I'm queer and I'm Asian—like it or not."

"I've never had a problem with you being Asian. I risked my life for many of you, in case you forgot."

I shake my head in disgust.

Mom says, "You're fine the way you are, honey. Tell her, Henry."

"Of course she's fine." He pouts. "I don't have a problem with her. She's got the problem with me. It's like she wishes we never adopted her. If only she knew what little she's worth over there . . ."

"Bullshit."

Mom jumps in. "Lucy—"

But I cut her off. "My mother never threw me away. You shouldn't talk about things you know nothing about. We were rarely discarded because we weren't loved. And I have a problem with you because you act like who I am is an insult to the world."

He shrugs. "You just take it that way." He chugs from his can and goes to the fridge for another. "What am I supposed to do? I'm not allowed to be who I am around you, either."

"There's a difference between not being able to be who you are and not getting away with saying ignorant things you actually believe." I grab one of his watery beers from the fridge. "Our pain's not the same. Mine's from your inability to accept what I am. Yours is from me not hiding it."

"I tell you your girlfriend fits in here, and you find a way to spin it that I'm wrong. I've never talked about PTSD to anyone but my brothers in combat, but I tried with you. It's just not good enough. I know I've failed you as a father. Isn't that what you want to hear?"

I take a few sips before declaring, "You don't get points for claiming your failure resulted in my being queer. Being queer's not a defect. If you want to talk about your failure—it's in not understanding that."

"Maybe so." He puts down his empty can and bounces his shoulders. "You act like I don't think you're good enough for me, but the truth is, you've got it reversed."

"Maybe so," I echo. And because it's been gnawing away at the back of my brain for some time, I spout, "For all I know, you're voting for Trump."

He crumples the can in his hand and retorts, "So what if I am?"

"He's against immigrants, and your daughter is one. He aligns himself with White supremacists. He mocks the disabled. And you're okay with these things?"

Dad shrugs. "I trust him more than I trust all the rest."

"He's a hateful pig and a liar!"

"What do you want me to say? Not everyone's perfect like you."

I storm up the stairs to my old room. My body's shaking from all of that tension. I suddenly wish I'd grabbed another beer, but I refuse to go back down for it.

REASON

A victim's family member creates a website to share photos and in-depth stories of the dead. It becomes an outlet for their families, helping them remember the victim as more than just a tragic one fifty-sixth.

I receive emails from countless media outlets and agents looking to represent my story. One asks: Now that the shooter's dead, are you at peace?

I don't reply, but the answer is no. My body was in a constant agitated state from early childhood trauma. The shooting amplified it. Every sound that can be remotely confused with terror, gunshots, or breaking glass flings my heart across the room. I'm hypervigilant. You wouldn't know it by looking at me—and in a way, that makes it worse. Repressing it for the appearance of normalcy increases its power over me.

While I'm glad we know who it was and why, peace doesn't come from those answers. People search us for hope, but if hope's what they want, they should look for ways to teach men to control themselves. They should make it harder for the Oscars of the world to have access to guns.

Against my better judgment, I watch a clip of Christy's latest show. She plays up that she was the original target—omitting the fact that she slept with him, of course.

"Some whack-job with a schoolboy crush came gunning for me, and I lived." Her posture and delivery are strong as she waits for the crowd to finish cheering. "But people want to make this a race thing—just because they locked up Donna, who happens to be Black." She cocks her head and pauses for boos. "I'm looking forward to Trump. He's the breath of fresh air we need. It's time to shake things up. And I don't know if I should say this, but screw it. If it's okay to be pro-Black, why's it so wrong to be pro-White?" The crowd goes wild. "I'm pro-everyone! But these folks try to shame us and call us racists. They're the ones who focus on race in every little thing that happens around the world. Am I right?" More applause. "So, the killer—Oscar J. Wilson—was White. But all of his victims were White. They can't claim racism on this one—not when the only two alumni who weren't White survived. I'm the one who was targeted. But he missed. Now, I've got a beautiful little girl who just happens to be White. You better believe I'll do everything I can to protect her, because White lives matter, too. We shouldn't be ashamed to say it." The camera pans to a standing ovation.

* * *

I ring her bell. When she opens the door, Christy throws her arms around me and plants a big kiss on my cheek. Her warmth weakens my resolve.

"Come in! I'm so glad to see you! I'll mix us a spritzer. I've gotta go easy on the sangria because the sugar's unforgiving— especially on-screen." She pats her nonexistent tummy. "A woman's worth is tied to her desirability. I'm not fond of it, but it's just the plain truth."

I thank her for the drink and pull up a stool at the kitchen island. "You never seemed to struggle with those games."

She giggles. "It's sink or swim, baby, and I've fought too long and too hard to drown now. Have you seen the show? We've come a long way from my YouTube days. I've got a girl to do hair and another for makeup. They buy and press all my clothes.

It's a dream come true."

"I don't think it's for me."

"Psh!" She slaps my arm. "It's for everyone." She passes me a glass, and I suck down half of it in one gulp.

"You know I was in jail, right?" I refuse to let her carry on as if everyone's been out here having a great time.

Her face morphs with exaggerated sadness. "Yes, that was awful! I'm just glad the cops were on top of things once Oscar started threatening me. I hate to think what would've happened otherwise."

"Yeah." I nod quickly. She doesn't know that I know about her and Oscar, and it's not my priority. "Donna and I had lots of time to consider what might've happened. Can we talk about that? Like . . . I don't know . . . your involvement?"

Christy puts down her glass. She throws her hands to her face, Home Alone style, and squeals, "Oh my gosh, I nearly forgot about that. I swear—I didn't mean for it to go as it did. I never said you did nothin'. I agreed that their story was possible, but I never said you were up at that table together. I just said you could've been. I tried saying they had it all wrong. They wouldn't listen. But I knew the truth would come out in the end. And look here—it did."

"But it might not have. You were willing to put our lives in their hands, and they wanted us for it. You knew what they thought, and you just let it go. We were locked up while you were out here getting standing ovations. That didn't feel wrong?"

She gets up to fix us more drinks. "Can't say I'm happy with how it went down, but you and Donna are free now. The cops did their jobs. It's all good, right?" She nods like a bobblehead doll.

I take my glass without any thanks and shrug nonchalantly. "Is further traumatization good? Donna was held at gunpoint.

She thought she might spend the rest of her life behind bars. But no harm, no foul?"

"Well, it hasn't been a cakewalk for me, neither. I was targeted by a killer. I feared for my life and Sophie's."

Something in me snaps. "Your uncontrollable vaj has caused death and injustice, and all you can think of is yourself?"

She stands up, holding on to the counter, looking dizzy from how I know what I know. "You're . . . victim-blaming."

"I'm not blaming you for the deaths. That's on Oscar. I'm blaming you for not giving a fuck about who you fuck and its ramifications."

"How was I to know he'd go postal? And, you know—you love to slut-shame me, but it wasn't all my doing! Oscar came to me! Your dad came to me! I never twisted anyone's arm! So why do I get all of the blame?"

And I realize she's right. All these men flock to her like she's some sort of White-gold prize. I concede. "Look. I honestly don't care how many men you've been with. Of course they share the responsibility. What bothers me is that you never consider the fallout."

"Just because I don't say it doesn't mean I don't feel it." Christy sits back down and guzzles the rest of her drink. "I feel awful about all of those people dying over something so stupid. Every morning, I ask myself why God chose me over them. I'm not glad they all died, but now I've got this show where I have a chance to make an impact. I've got lots to say, and I'm just getting started. Did you know I had an abortion when I was young? It's haunted me every day since. I want to help change the law so other girls don't make the same mistake. Maybe those fifty-six lives Oscar took will be saved in some other way? I have to believe that everything happens for a reason."

I rise, and before I can stop myself, I say, "Then I hope you understand the reason for this." I toss the contents of my glass in her face. She's dripping with spritzer—face twisted in shock—and for once, she is speechless.

TRANSCENDENCE

I'm trying and failing to skip bloated stones when Donna pulls up with Alexis. I empty the handful of pebbles into the pond before taking a seat on our old rock. "Thanks for meeting me here."

"It took a minute. I was at your house looking for you when I got the two single rings." Donna rubs my back. "You okay?"

"I just came from Christy's."

"Wish you'd told me before. I'd have come along to give her a piece of my mind."

"I watched an infuriating clip and just hopped in the car, fueled by rage. I didn't even wait for Alexis to get out of the shower." My eyes fixate on the inverted reflection of the sky and the trees. Alexis rests her head on my shoulder. I point to the pond. "That's pretty much it right there."

"What?" Alexis asks.

"Life in Bixby: Where reality's nothing but ripples in some twisted inversion."

"True enough." Donna slaps her palms on her thighs. "Jacob and I are getting out of here soon. Can't wait to be back with my boys."

"Who bought the house?" I ask.

"Some local's relative. Or so they say. I wouldn't be surprised if the town pitched in to buy it, just to see the back of me."

I turn my head to get a look at her face. It's softer than it was in jail, but she looks as worn as I do. "Have you got a new place?"

"Not yet, but we'll rent someplace near Jacob's church." She raises her brows and asks, "How are things with your folks?"

"Things with Mom are great, but it's a lost cause with Dad. How are things with yours?"

"Much better now that the air was cleared." She nods. "Didn't realize I was carrying so much resentment till I was in jail. But the fact that they showed up and said what they said? It gave me a better understanding of them. And maybe them of me."

"Glad things feel better."

Donna smiles, nudging my side. "So, go on—tell us what happened with Christy."

My mouth twitches. All the frustration I've been holding in must hit a nerve as it bounces around inside. I break into a fit of laughter, unable to get the words out. Just when I think I've cooled down, the expressions on their faces make it repeat. I can't look at them. When I finally get my bearings, I squeak, "She was awful. Her absolute worst. I said her uncontrollable vaj has caused too much trouble and threw a drink in her face."

Alexis yelps. "You what?"

"Yes, girl. Yes!" Donna throws herself back, bending over the rock. She's a quarter of the way upside down and sounds like she did when we were here as kids.

"She was so offensive! I lost my mind!"

Alexis grins. "Sounds like you found it."

Once the laughs settle down, I tell them, "She was a big part of my childhood, though. You know? I was fond of our times together. I wanted to believe she was different. I spent so much time trying to focus on where she and I intersect that I let it override the rest. I thought I'd been tolerant, but maybe all I did was enable her."

"Same!" Donna's face is serious now. "All that 'You're one

of us' talk. Pfft!" She shakes her head. "She always said she considered us White and took offense when we didn't like it. I'm tired of giving passes to people who tokenize me—as if the rest of us are so bad. But the sad thing is, for too long I complied. I got upset with my parents for catering to White folk—but with her, I kind of did the same thing."

"Sometimes it felt good to pretend." I nod. "When you're a kid and you feel so alone, the lie can be soothing. And then you've been doing it so long, it's just second nature. But no matter how much we played along, it didn't stop any of this from happening, did it?"

"Nope. In the long run, it never pays. And you know, come to think of it, I owe you an apology."

"For what?" I lie back with her on the rock. Alexis joins us.

"I've been unfair to you about being gay—and unfair to gay folks in general. I should've never turned my back on you when you came out to me in that email all those years ago. I figured I'd never see you again, since I hadn't for years."

My chest aches from her words. "I appreciate you saying so now."

Alexis's hand finds mine and gives it a squeeze. I swivel my head towards her, and we kiss.

Under her breath, Donna says, "Still don't like PDAs." We all snicker. Donna carries on. "The other night, as I sat in a moment with God, I knew he was telling me that you and your community deserve my compassion. No one should be hated or mistreated for being themselves. My God would never cosign that."

"It means a lot that you accept that we are who we are." I tap her hand and quickly remove it so she doesn't get the wrong idea. Being pan, I'm always nervous that people will misinterpret my affection.

Donna shields her eyes from the sun, peering over at me. "I struggle each day to hold on to my faith. If it were easy, I suppose it wouldn't mean much to have it. But Lucy—you act more godly than many who act out in His name."

The three of us lie, laughing and sharing, gazing up at the sky through the trees, until our backs ache. We're transported again to somewhere that transcends all the bullshit thrust upon us—if only for one afternoon.

TOO MANY STORMS

It was bound to happen sooner or later. Statistics show that the US averages more than one mass shooting a day—so an emotional planner like me should be prepared. But I'm not.

Tae-Suk and I are having an after-work drink when it's announced on TV. Someone asks the bartender to turn off the music. We watch in silence as another White man's face is framed on-screen adjacent to footage of chaos. Survivors are shocked and crying, but that doesn't stop cameras from being shoved in their faces. I slide off the barstool and wordlessly tap Tae-Suk on the shoulder before walking out.

It's not long before we learn that twenty-two died and forty-three are injured. The touring Latinx band escapes unharmed. Since the list of victims' names and faces is long, the name and face of the shooter stand out. On his social media accounts, he bragged about "cleaning house." He wrote: It's not enough to build the wall. We need to exterminate them from our country.

The shooter was gunned down by police. He had a record for beating his ex and affiliations with White supremacist organizations. Despite that, one media outlet circulates a photo of him with a kitten from twelve years ago.

I want to pick something up and throw it, but I don't want to perpetuate violence and destruction. I find a cardio kickboxing workout to channel my rage. It's not enough. I have so much to say but lack articulation. So I punch and roundhouse my way through the week, avoiding nonwork conversation. I bike through the city at night, when there are fewer cars and people.

Sometimes I go to Ocean Beach when it's empty and scream into the waves, letting their power swallow mine.

One night, when I think she is sleeping, Alexis follows me. She walks up behind me and places her hand on my shoulder. I donkey kick her in the stomach, realizing too late.

"I'm sorry!" I shout over the roar of the riled Pacific, dropping down to my knees. I pat her back as she folds forward on the sand. "I'm so sorry . . ." I whisper, collapsing alongside her.

She holds up a hand. "You've got to do something." Her skin glows in the moonlight. "I don't know how to help."

"I don't think anyone can," I confess, sifting sand through my fingers. "We're all fucked."

With a look of total sincerity, she says, "We're on the verge of electing our first woman president."

"You have too much faith in this country." I peer at her sadly. "She's not going to win. The flaws of women and men still aren't weighed as equal. And you were raised in one of the most progressive parts of the country. You don't see who I see; you don't hear who I hear."

"Maybe not. But I know things are changing for the better. It's just going to take time."

"But we don't all have time!" My fists pound the sand. "Wake up. Everyone's been falling for the same shit for too long: guns aren't a problem; feminists are more dangerous than toxic masculinity; Obama's election means we're post-race." I roll my eyes up and groan.

"You can't lose hope." She places her hand on my forearm.

"How can I not when the same shit repeats day after day, year after year? They want you to think we're making progress so you stay complacent in your comfort of believing so." I toss sand in the air like confetti. "How can I have hope when in 2016, Black and Brown folks are still being locked up unfairly?

Not everyone gets out in time—or with anything left to live for. They're eaten up by the system. Their families collapse. And how can I have hope when guns are a freedom worth more than life itself? It doesn't matter how White or how young. They don't see that they're hurting themselves; they're killing themselves."

"More people are speaking out every day against gun violence and racism."

"But not enough." I feel the weight of the sky on my shoulders. "Not enough with the power to make any difference."

"That's why we need you in the fight. We need everyone."

"I'm tired of fighting. I hate to say it, but it's the damn truth."

"You're depressed—and rightfully so." She rubs my back. "I'm worried about you. I'd never have followed you out here otherwise. I'm not some kind of stalker. Look at me." I turn my head towards her. "Are you in danger of ending your life?" she asks.

I scoff. "I'm in danger of someone else ending it. We all are."

She brushes the back of her hand across my cheek. "Would you tell me if you were?"

"I'm not suicidal." I shake her off. "I'm overwhelmed. Just the fact that we've been entertaining this pathetic man for the highest office says something. You know? He's gotten this far, despite all he's said and done. People are okay with it. There's no shrink who can make all of that disappear. If there is, call them in." I throw a hand up and let it drop to the sand. "Let 'em save us all."

She looks out at the ocean for a moment. Gesturing at the horizon, she says, "My elisi used to tell me, 'Alexis, you cannot control the Storm Out There. You can only control the Storm In Here.' " She points to her sternum, turning towards me. "She said, 'It's up to you to learn how.' "

"I have too many storms," I moan. "They're all crashing

together."

"So, what will you do? Let 'em overtake you? That doesn't sound like the Lucy I know."

I consider her words, glaring down at my feet. "Maybe the Lucy you knew wasn't real. Maybe she's who I felt I needed to be to survive, but I can't keep up the act."

"Or maybe she was real, but it's time for the next Lucy to fade in and take over?"

"What—I'm supposed to be, like, my own superhero? I just fly in and rescue myself? Nah . . . I can't."

"Bullshit. You're the strongest person I know. Look at what you've lived through already. You didn't come all this way to give up. You're just getting started."

I smile a little and moan, "Don't say that. I'm so fucking tired . . ."

"I know." She pats my thigh. "Let's go home and get some rest."

MEANING

After some Internet sleuthing, I find Donna's novel. Her main character, Chantel, is a Black woman in her twenties, living in a town like Bixby. The story is set in modern times, and she uses apps to tap into a dating pool beyond her small town, sending her on dating adventures. Donna's style is snappy and sincere, speaking to readers like we're best friends. I imagine it gives her a sense of purpose to write these books for young Black women.

I've never had a purpose beyond my survival. Sure, I've had hobbies and a pretty cool job. But I yearn for an articulated purpose—something to give my life meaning.

As if reading my mind, Tae-Suk slaps me on the shoulder. " 'Sup, Lucy? Still living the dream?"

"Hmm." We walk through the halls, side by side. "Maybe it's time to find something bigger."

"Beyond being death-defying and ruling at word games?"

I shrug. "I don't know, but you said it yourself: This can't be all there is to it."

"That was rude. I was trying to make a point and it flopped. Life can be whatever you want it to be. That's what I meant."

"I don't know. Maybe you were right. After surviving so much, I should make my life worth it."

He ruffles my hair with his hand. "After surviving so much, you don't have to do shit. Just be you."

I bump him with my hip. "Well, maybe I've got to figure out who that is."

* * *

I've been fantasizing about my Korean father. He tells me he's sorry that he couldn't raise me.

Sometimes he's a landscape painter. He holds out his hand, walking me through the countryside to an idyllic location. He sets up his easel, and I wander around taking pictures.

Sometimes he's a poet. Since I can't read Korean, I listen to the rhythm of his lines, his heart beating measures into my soul. When he tries to explain it, sometimes we laugh at his mistranslations.

When he speaks of my Korean mother, his voice goes soft.

My mother was an English teacher. Had she lived, and had I still been adopted, we could communicate now without assistance. "No," he says. "She was a singer." She sang ballads to me all day long, and that's why they make me so emotional now.

When I ask why she was killed, he tells me, "It was just random violence."

Random violence means no one is safe. Anyone who feels safe is naive—sheltered enough to live in peace.

Random violence stole my mother and my chance to live as a whole Korean with my family. Does that mean I don't love my American parents? Of course not. If I didn't, I wouldn't feel the pain caused by my father or the guilt towards my mother. But my love for them can't erase what I've lost.

While Alexis is sleeping, I pull up my adoption files on my computer. I read through them again, not realizing I'm holding my breath until my mouth pops. I write my adoption agency:

Dear Sally,

It's been several years since I received my file. I thought what I'd learned was enough, but I guess I just needed more time. I would like my father's contact info if you have it.

Sincerely,

Lucy Byrne

I climb back into bed next to the woman I love—a woman I wouldn't know without my adoption. I fall asleep dizzying myself with cruel Would You Rathers for adopted people. Would I rather my Korean mother be alive, or would I rather be here with the love of my life? Would I rather be raised as a burden on my grieving father, or would I rather be isolated from my people?

When I wake, I'm not expecting a response yet, but one's there waiting. It reads:

Dear Lucy,

I'm sorry to pass on the bad news. Your aboji died in 2012. He took his own life. In 2010, he left a letter in case you came looking. If you'd like, we can forward it on.

We have the contact info of his sister, the one who brought you to us. Please let us know if you'd like her information.

Blessings,

Sally Kim

Alexis comes out of the shower to find me stunned speechless. "What's wrong?" She wraps her damp arms around me. I hold out my phone to let her read it. "Oh no . . . My poor Lucy . . ."

And I wonder which came first: Poor Lucy or Lucky Lucy? It seems life's been a cycle of them chasing each other.

I finally break down. My head spins. At moments, I wake from the crying only to wonder what I'm crying for. Then it comes rushing back.

I cry for my mother. I cry for my father. I cry for the scared little toddler I was.

I cry for my American mother and how she only wanted a child of her own, not knowing that babies aren't interchangeable.

I cry for my American father and how I sometimes wish I didn't care for him at all.

I cry for the woman that Kevin raped in my place.

And I cry for the fifty-six people that Oscar gunned down. I cry for their loved ones, too.

I cry for this world that feels so hopeless.

I cry for myself and the things I've survived.

In brief moments, I'm numb. I think to myself, *This is who I am now.*

As if reading my mind, Alexis puts a bowl of soup on a tray, not bothering to wrangle me out of bed. "This doesn't change a thing. You know that. Right?" When I don't say a word, she continues. "It was true yesterday and the day before that. You're still the same woman that I know and love. It means nothing— except that you know."

But I worry I'm vulnerable, like my Korean mother, and too overwhelmed, like my Korean father.

USE EVERYTHING

When Christy's text lights up my screen, I huck the phone across the room.

The physical distance allows me to wonder more about what went on with her and Dad. Was she his only affair? Were all of his hauls truly for work? How could he be so careless? It's easy to be appalled by him lately, but he's not wholly bad. And neither is Christy. She's a good mom, and in shallow moments, she's fun to be around. That's what messes with me.

Alexis finds my phone on the floor and places it on my nightstand with no questions asked. Hours later, I give in and look.

> Christy: I hate how we left things. Can U talk?
>
> Christy: I was thinking . . . maybe U could come on the show? U could share how U feel about everything. Could be a learning opp 4 me and my audience.
>
> Christy: So it's over? Almost 4 decades of friendship? Just like that?
>
> Christy: It's because I'm White, isn't it? I don't think about how we're different but U seem obsessed with it. Come on my show. Help us understand.

I sit on the window ledge, inhaling from the vaporizer pen. I exhale out the window. The phone rings.

"Christy, I don't want to talk."

"Right now? Or ever?"

"Ever again."

She sighs. "So, we had a fight. Friends do that, right? We've known each other since we were three or four. Come on. Don't be like this."

"You know, Christy, it's my fault for not being like this all along. I've put up with your racist, disloyal ass for too long. I must've been out of my mind."

"Racist?" She coughs up a snicker. "I'm, like, the least racist person I know!"

"Well, that's fucking scary."

"How am I racist? I was friends with you and Donna when no one else was."

"We were friends till you saw us holding you back. You never stood up for Donna. You know, your support could have shaped her childhood. It wouldn't have been half as bad."

"What do you think? I'm some kind of magician? I never had that kind of power."

"You did and you knew it. But you chose not to use it. Instead, you protected yourself. And you know—I saw that clip where you said I look prettier now and less Asian. My mind is still spinning from how I could look less Asian and why you think that's better."

"I just meant you look less stereotypically Asian. Your hair was long and straight. It was gorgeous but—"

"You're not doing yourself any favors."

"Damn it, Lucy! Not everything's meant to be racist!"

"You mean: You don't realize when you're being racist."

"How is it racist to say you look prettier now? Why can't you just take the compliment?"

"Because it's not a fucking compliment to look less like my race! Ugh! This is why I can't with you."

"Look." Christy sighs. "I don't always say the right thing, but you assume that I have bad intentions."

"I don't care about your intentions. When you center your intentions, you put yourself over the feelings of the person you hurt. I'd prefer you to be more concerned about the effect your words have on me. But you can't. You don't care."

"Hmm. This is why you need to come on my show."

"Are you high? I'm not coming on your show. You want to exploit me. Gang up with your minions and tear me apart on TV."

"See? Again with the negative assumptions. That's a hard way to live . . . I just want to help you make yourself heard. Maybe we can learn something from you."

"I'm not interested. And neither is your audience."

"How do you know?"

I laugh. "You're delusional if you think they are."

"I'm trying to do good here."

"If you want to do good, I support that. You don't need me for it." I take another drag from my pen, staring out the window, feeling thankful I am where I am.

"Hey. I want to ask you something." I don't answer. "Hello? You still there? I hear you breathing."

"What?"

"Did you mean to save me?" There's nervous desperation in her voice. "Or was I just the closest in range?"

I gaze up at the birds on the electrical wire. "What does it matter?"

"I just need to know."

"I meant to help you. I didn't know if we'd make it. But it was instinctive. If you recall, there wasn't much time to think." There's a pause on the line. "Is that it?"

"Why me? We hadn't spoken in years."

"I don't know. I saw you and I did what I did." I imagine she wants me to tell her she's special, but I ask, "What's this about?"

After a short pause, she asks, "Do you regret it?"

I take a deep breath, sending the inhalation down to shake

up the truth. "I don't regret it. No. I don't wish you were dead. I wish death on no one."

"So it's got nothing to do with me. I could've been anyone."

I roll my eyes, feeling the heat rush to my head. "I said I don't wish you were dead. I don't want you to die, Christy. For fuck's sake."

"Then why don't you want to be my friend anymore? What have I done that's really so bad? I'm making the best of a bad situation. You could too, if you weren't so darn proud."

"This. This is another reason why I can't be your friend. You blame anyone not doing as well as you for being where they are. Yet at the same time, you need to believe you're more deserving. You don't get it—and you don't want to, so you never will. "

"You love playing the victim." She chuckles. "Do you think I'd have my own show if I did that?"

"Are you not always denying White privilege because you grew up in a trailer? And without a father? How is that better than when I share my struggles?"

"Lucy." She sighs. "Everyone has struggles. But the ones who consider themselves 'of color' somehow think that theirs are worth more than ours. You think it's up to us to solve all your problems. You've gotta use everything—"

I stab at the End Call button. I land it on the first try.

TRIGGERS

I click on the link, expecting to see Christy's face. But to my surprise, it's a familiar pink-haired woman I'd hoped I'd seen the last of.

The talk show host is a Jackie Kennedy type. She asks, "So, how did this all come about?"

Lynnette's face is aglow. "Well, what can I say, Marsha? I'm a lucky girl. I hooked up with a stranger one night. She looked troubled—and well, I won't lie. Trouble's my biggest addiction." She winks and the audience laughs. "Thought I recognized her, but I couldn't pinpoint from where until we were half in the bag."

"It must've been interesting, realizing you were drinking with one of the three survivors of The Reunion Massacre."

"That's right. Tried to get her to tell me, you know? It's much better if it's out in the open. But she wouldn't talk. So I told her my story, which I highly recommend." She holds up a book and puts on a salesy grin. "Sadly, I wasn't able to encourage her to take ownership of hers. I thought it'd be healing and empowering. But you know—I'm not polished. Just look at me here!" She comically slaps her thigh. "I don't always go about things the best way."

"When did you get the idea to write the book for her?"

"Well, I first encouraged her to write it. But that wasn't going to happen, so I talked to my publisher about my situation—my proximity—and she agreed that I had a story. That's when we came up with the idea together." She fans her hands out. "*Triggers* will be out November 2017. Just in time for holiday gifts."

"And it's written from the perspective of Lucy Byrne?"

"I don't know what you're talking about. My character is Lindsy Burns." When she winks again, the crowd snickers, and she eats it up. "It's fiction, based on true events. I'd give some of the money to Lucy—I mean, Lindsy—but she was adamantly against it, so . . . ." She shrugs. "Some folks don't like money. Go figure."

I've seen enough.

> Me: Yep. That's Lynnette . . . in all her glory.
>
> Donna: You going to do anything about it?
>
> Me: Nah. It's out of my hands. She's exploitative and offensive. I don't want to think of or see her again.
>
> Donna: Well, you're going to have to once the book's out.
>
> Me: I'll worry about it then.
>
> Donna: So, speaking of triggers . . . I have a personal question. You don't have to answer if you don't want.
>
> Me: Ask away.
>
> Donna: Are you still experiencing PTSD?
>
> Me: Less often but yeah.
>
> Donna: I had a bad panic attack last weekend.
>
> Me: Sorry to hear. You okay?
>
> Donna: Yeah. Took the boys to the city to see a Black woman's photo exhibit. I want to expose them to what I wasn't exposed to. As we were heading out, I heard some loud bangs.
>
> Me: Oh no . . .
>
> Donna: Pulled the boys to the floor. SMH. Come to find—a delivery man just dropped a few boxes. O.O They echoed through the lobby.
>
> Me: Ugh. That sucks.

Donna: Everyone stared. Some pointed me out, recognizing my face. The ride home was not fun. I was so mad at myself.

Me: It's not your fault. It's normal. <3

Donna: Anyway, we found a place to rent while we get a feel for the neighborhoods in the city. I want my boys to have friends of color.

Me: Of course. I wouldn't wish a childhood of racial isolation on anyone.

Donna: And these boys . . . Obama didn't live up to all I'd hoped, but my boys have only known a president who looked like them. When Trump gets in, they're going to need to be around their people all the more. How am I going to explain how we went from Obama to that???

Me: Shit. I hadn't thought of how confusing it'd be for the kids.

Donna: I'm hoping the city will help ease our nerves.

Me: I don't want to be discouraging, but out here in SF I still get triggered << even by that fucking word.

Donna: I know. > < It's apt but cruel.

Me: Mine mostly show up in nightmares and visions. When it happens in public, I worry about offending other people.

Donna: Yeah, worrying how my reactions will affect my boys keeps me from processing what I should. From taking care of me.

Me: Nobody talks about this. It's too much pressure to be the perfect victim. So, thanks for reaching out and being honest.

Donna: Glad we have each other.

Me: <3 Hey—I'm enjoying your book!

Donna: That means a lot. :-)

Me: Five stars all the way!

Donna: Okay, gotta split! <3

Me: Talk soon. <3

VULNERABILITY

Breaking through the dam the other day gave me access to a new river. In my head, I still know everything I fear, but I feel it less in my body. It's only now that I realize how much pressure I've been under for so long.

When my mother calls, I tell her the truth about my Korean parents. Her voice cracks. "As much as I love you, Lucy, I'd rather she'd lived—even if it meant we'd never have met."

She's been making her way through a reading list I gave her, mostly comprised of transracial adoptee authors. "There's so much I didn't know. The corruption and layers of pain . . . It's hard to think it's more Christian to take a poor woman's child than to help keep her family together." Her acknowledgment feels like love.

"Anyway, I know I said I'd never be back," I tell her, "but I'll be in Bixby next month for a video project."

"Your job's filming something in Bixby?"

"It's not for my job. Donna and I are filming some of the families and friends of the dead."

"Are you making a documentary?"

"We don't know what it is yet. We'll see what kind of footage we get and take it from there. I want to amp other voices. Right now, there's just Christy. It might all go to hell. I don't know."

Later that night, Alexis asks, "Are you sure about this project? Thought you wanted to put it to bed? Won't it just keep you tied to that trauma and town?"

I sit down next to her, taking a swig of her wine. "I've been thinking about what your elisi said about the storms."

She nods with a look of confusion. "It kind of goes against what you're doing. No?"

I shake my head. "That's why I want to do it."

"I don't follow . . ."

"I want to try to make something of what I've been through. We've become so desensitized to these shootings. I want to show the ripple effect of each life. It won't change policy, but processing our pain and sharing it with the world might help some of us heal."

Alexis sits quietly for a moment. She nods with an easy smile. "That's beautiful, babe. One life really does have a ripple effect. You'll do an incredible job."

I put my hand on her cheek and kiss her left temple. "I couldn't do it without your support."

She takes a sip of wine and leans in aggressively. "Lucy, just give yourself credit for once. The call is coming from inside the house. It's been there all along. You just didn't know it."

"O . . . kay . . ." I say, pulling back with a shiver. "Only you could creep me out with a pep talk."

She flashes a smile and clicks her tongue. "I've got skills."

Moving in for a kiss, I say, "Yes, you do."

She pulls back. "Like, I can scare you with four words."

I smile devilishly, excited by her playfulness. "Try me."

"Let's. Get. A. Dog."

"What?" I jump to the corner of the couch. "Who *are* you?"

"You're allergic to cats." She shrugs and repositions herself, smoothing her skirt. "Imagine the messy, sloppy love of a dog. That in-your-face 'love me love me' love."

"Yeah, that's not working for me. Dogs are so needy," I say, feeling shook.

"They are. But you'll love it. You'll see."

"Oh, this is for me?" I smirk, inspecting her face, wondering where this is coming from.

"An emotional support dog. Yeah."

"I don't know . . ." My vision blurs as I stare down at nothing. "To be responsible for another life is too daunting. Too vulnerable. Too scary."

She smiles, knowing she'll get what she wants. "And that's why we should do it. You'll see what you're capable of."

I lean back and fold my legs below me. "Is this your Gateway to Kid talk?"

"Come again?" she asks, leaning back.

" 'Cause I remember you telling my dad that we can have kids, and I'm not into that for, well, reasons."

She twirls the stem of the glass between her fingers and says, "Go on." She lifts the wine to her lips.

I rest my elbow on the arm of the couch, leaning farther away. I was hoping to avoid this conversation forever, but it's time. "Well, you know how I feel about adoption."

She waves a hand around. "I'm with you on that. Adoption wiped out half the Cherokee side of my family tree."

"I also don't think it's right to create a child who won't know half their history. Donor babies have grown up now, and they're sharing similar feelings of loss as adoptees. The only ethical way is to use sperm from someone who'll remain in your life forever—which I can't even think of right now . . ."

"Okay." She nods. "We can talk more about it some other time, but it's not where I'm at now. I just want you to feel capable of loving when loss is inevitable."

"Why?" My heart thumps. "Is this your way of preparing to leave? Throw a dog at me and then run out the door?"

"No." She laughs. "Because loss is always inevitable when it comes to love. And you're still holding back, waiting for the next shoe to drop—as evidenced by your response. Loving an animal will open you up. It'll be good for you. Look, you've been through so much loss, and in such tragic ways. Loving with your whole heart—while you can—is vulnerable but worth it. You'll see."

SARANGHAE

When the email notification pops up on my phone, I'm sitting with Tae-Suk in the grass along Embarcadero. We're splitting a pizza again—well, he's devouring two-thirds of it. I must have a look on my face, because he asks, "What's up?"

"Sorry. I don't mean to be rude," I say, unlocking the phone to peek at the message. "It's from my adoption agency. It's a note from my father . . . Longer than I expected . . . and in Korean."

He holds out his greasy hand, retracts it to wipe it on the grass, then throws it back out. "I'll read it for you."

"Um." I hesitate. "My father's dead. I found out recently."

"Oh shit. I'm sorry." He takes back his hand and doesn't bother resuming his rampant face-shoveling.

"I guess nowadays people would say that he died from depression."

"Suicide's a real problem in Korea," he says quickly. "I'm sorry. I didn't mean to—"

"It's fine."

"So, the letter?"

"Guess he wrote it years ago. When I learned about my mother—who was murdered when I was young, by the way—"

He leans forward and loudly spits, "That doesn't get a 'by the way.'"

"I'm sorry I didn't share this with you. It's so private and well . . . hard to talk about."

"Shit, Lucy. I'm sorry."

"My dad died in 2012." I squint at the phone. "It says here that he brought this letter in March 2010, in case I came looking for him. Guess he waited a while, but I was too busy dealing with the grief over my mother. I didn't want to know more. I wasn't ready."

Tae-Suk puts the cover down on the pizza box and scoots beside me, our hips touching. He stretches an arm around my back. "Your lack of response didn't kill him. You know that. Right?"

I nod my head quickly. "Yeah. Thanks."

"Should I read it to you?"

"First in Korean. Then you can translate. But will you also write it down later so I can read it myself? I'm sorry. Is this asking too much?"

"No. Thanks for entrusting me with it." He takes the phone from my hand.

As he reads in Korean, the rhythm and tone of his voice are foreign yet familiar. I've never heard him speak Korean before. I want to cry without even knowing what he's saying, but I refrain.

"Now I'll translate. 'My dearest daughter, Moon Ji-Ae.' "

"Whoa. That's the first time I've heard my real name . . . Go on." I lie with my head in his lap, my eyes tracing the clouds.

He continues. "In-Sook and I named you for strength and love. In the few years we had known you, you quickly lived up to your name. Your mother, In-Sook, loved you very much. The two of you were my world, my everything. On the night I came home to the police scene, I lost all of us. I wasn't fit to be your father. When I looked at your face, I saw the ghost of your mother. My sister, Kyung-Hee, thought she'd do us a favor by taking you away. It was meant to be temporary, till I got my head straight. But it was harder without you near. Days later, when I went to retrieve you, they said it was too late. They'd sent you off to be taken care of, better than I could. It made me think they were right. What good was I to your mother, in the end? But I've not stopped loving you, Ji-Ae, and I've never stopped loving In-Sook. I hope you are dining off silver and gold, and getting the best education. I hope you don't hate me for the countless ways I've failed. I can still see the light in your eyes, and hear you calling me Dad. Remember us, too—your mother's soft voice singing "Saranghae". Remember the painting we made with your little finger shaping the birds in the sky. Sometimes it feels like a dream because it was long ago, in a better life. But if you close your eyes and remember those first two and a half years, I hope it leads you back home to me. And if not, I understand that I lost that right. Please forgive me, daughter, if you can. I was just trying to live. I'm not always as strong as I want to be. Your mother was the stronger of us, and her blood runs through you. If she were alive, she'd want you to be as free as the birds in our painting. I still have it with me. It waits for your return. I hope I will be here, too. In the meantime, please know you are so very loved. Your father, Moon Sung-Soo."

Tae-Suk places my phone on the grass and rubs the top of my head. He rains salty tears down on me. I sit up, stunned and unable to speak. I'm frozen in time, trying to soak in my father's words.

"You're not crying," he manages to say. "You can. It's okay."

My body aches from my muscles working overtime to keep it together. It was hard enough letting myself cry at home. There's no way I can do it out here in public, before returning to work. "I can't," I say. Once I start, I might never stop.

He releases a nervous laugh, squeezing my arm. "Well, I'll cry for you so you don't have to . . . until you can."

In my head, a voice keeps repeating, *Saranghae. Saranghae. Saranghae.*

THE STORM IN HERE

I want to tell you I'm healed, we have a woman president, and this country has made progress towards decreasing gun violence. But here we are.

It's six months after Trump's election, and the ratings on Christy's show have skyrocketed. She's morphed from the hot girl next door to some swanky supermodel in designer dresses. I don't bother with the clips anymore. She's stopped trying to drag me back in.

Donna and I didn't get the footage we set out for in Bixby. The people we'd hoped to do justice to couldn't get past my eyes or Donna's skin. So now a new film's in the works. It's a story of racial injustice—and why women of color must unite to dismantle patriarchal and White supremacist systems.

I gave in to Alexis, and we got a shelter dog. My love for her scares me to death. Each day, it's a struggle to file away the fact that someday, I'll lose her, too.

I haven't talked to my father since the election. Mom says he's excited by Trump's win. He and his comrades have been running down memory lane. I don't understand it, but somehow they have respect for the draft dodger. She still doesn't know about Dad's affair, but she's thinking of leaving him anyway.

"It's not just about what he did back then over there," she explains. "It's that he boasts of it now. Talking about all the women he had like that when he has an Asian daughter? It makes me sick. Said he might even have a little half-breed or two. His words. How dare he? His sperm count was low, by the way. I'm sorry. You don't need to know that."

"Do what's best for you, Mom," I tell her, holding back so much more. Part of me hopes there's still room for repair, and a part of me is already letting go.

The Storm Out There is brutal. I often feel like an oarless dinghy being slapped by rip currents, holding on to what I can and spitting out dirty water. As Alexis's elisi advised, I'm working on the Storm In Here. I've accepted that it will never be fully tamed but a lifelong balance.

My aunt, Kyung-Hee, and I have been communicating using Google Translate and Kakao. From what I can piece together, we share the same nemeses—Guilt and Grief.

The pilot's voice spills through the overhead speakers. He tells us it's twelve and a half hours to Incheon, and we can expect a pretty smooth flight.

Alexis turns her head, face blooming with that mischievous smile. "Like Swiss cheese, ripped jeans, and Jesus."

It takes me a minute. I answer, "Holy."

"Like a pig in . . ."

"Shit."

"In TLC, it's Left—"

"Eye!"

She laughs. "A fresh blank of bread!"

"Loaf?"

"And a female sheep."

I think for a moment and give her a kiss.

Tae-Suk pops his head up from the seat in front of Alexis. I paid for his trip in return for translation. He says, "No wonder you two always win. It's not a game to you; it's a way of life."

I've been told that I didn't sleep on my trip from Korea, and I can't sleep on my journey back, either. It's hard to believe that in twelve and a half hours, I'll meet someone related by blood—someone who knew me in a past life. I'm afraid of how she'll respond to my being with a woman, but I'm done with disguising myself for approval. From what I've read, much of Korea is still homophobic. I try to prepare for rejection, thankful to have Alexis and Tae-Suk by my side.

I'm still processing the fact that some of my visions were real. My father's painting. My mother's voice. I cover my head with the blanket and try to rest my eyes.

In my head, Omma's voice echoes, *Saranghae*.

The plane lands before I'm ready. Passengers stumble into the aisles. Someone drops their carry-on bag. "Mianhamnida," they say with a bow. I nod and rub my sore head.

When we pass through the gates, there's a sea of hopeful faces searching for their people. They close in on me. My heart's leaping out of my chest.

Shaking my head, I ask, "How will we find her?"

Alexis points. "Is that you on that poster?"

Sure enough, there's a woman holding a giant photo of my face from when I was about two years old. Another bounces a poster that reads: LUCY 지애 Ji-Ae. When they spot us, they wave frantically.

I glance at Alexis, wide-eyed. "This is it." My nerves flutter up in my chest and throat.

One of them shouts in Korean. Tae-Suk turns to me. "She wants to hug you. Is that okay?"

I nod, stepping forward. We embrace. Her warmth against me is both foreign and familiar. Her scent awakens my two-year-old self. I fall to pieces.

All the guilt and the fear that's usually present when I want to cry dissipates. Her tears or my tears pool in my ear. We're bawling so hard that we drop to our knees right there in the crowd, no fucks given. We stay like this for some time before pulling away to search each other's features. To my disappointment, we don't look alike. I was hoping for physical validation—some proof of belonging.

We both rise. My head's slightly spinning. Needing to get it out of the way, I wipe my eyes, turning to Tae-Suk. "Can you tell her that this is my girlfriend?"

When he does, she nods. She says something in Korean and taps the woman beside her. He says, "And this is her girlfriend, Jung-Soon."

"Romantically? Does she understand?" I ask.

He translates, and she wraps her arm around Jung-Soon, pecking her on the lips. My arm snakes around Alexis. Kyung-Hee releases her partner and bows deeply. "Uh suh oh seh yo!"

Tae-Suk looks to me. "She says, 'Welcome home.' "

Home. I let that word drop from my ears to my chest and expand to fill my whole being. So much has happened since I last stood on this land. I no longer know her. She no longer knows me. But her song flows through my veins, her scent clings to my skin, and there's a yearning for truce in the air.

Kyung-Hee weaves her arm through mine and tugs me along. Our collective pain converges, vibrating through my skin.

She speaks something quickly, and Tae-Suk translates, "It's too bad I couldn't have brought you home sooner. I'm sorry. I never should've sent you away."

And I tell her, "We can't change the past, Auntie. Sometimes our world crumbles. But look at us—standing. Two pieces that found our way home to each other."

She speaks, and Tae-Suk interprets, "Yes. Everyone was falling apart. But here we are, piecing what we can of them and ourselves back together."

ACKNOWLEDGMENTS

In December of 2016, I dragged myself out of bed and started writing this book. I put aside my first version of *Keurium* and went full tilt into the first draft of *Everyone Was Falling*. It was hard to believe that after a decades-long journey of freeing myself from a toxic narcissist, another was elected president. I needed a project to funnel the pain and gaslighting of living as a Person of Color in a time rife with friendly fire. This was it.

Until there's more varied representation of Own Voices stories that include adoptees and People of Color, society moves me to state that this is *one* adoption story, and *one* pansexual woman's story. Not everyone adopted feels the same as Lucy, or the same as I do. Donna isn't every Black woman raised in racial isolation, and—needless to say—Christy isn't every White woman.

I had the great pleasure of working with the skilled and astute Émelyne Museaux. Cautious of overstepping or misspeaking on behalf of my Black American characters, I knew I could trust Émmy. Her input was invaluable, and her ideas brought the story further to life. She even inspired the cover design! Check out her podcast, *The Good. The Bad. The Basic.*—and be on the lookout for her articles and YA novel.

My manuscripts are always safe in the hands and heart of Laura Major. Her love of literature shines through each step of the way, and her final touch was exactly what I needed before bringing this story out to the world. The importance of being a White woman able to appreciate this book's content can't be understated. Laura has many artistic talents, and I can't wait to read what she's writing.

Throughout the writing process, I consulted with Ave Giorgio, Minyoung Lee, and Eric Strickland on certain details of Korean culture and translations. Lisa Nanibush Urizandi was helpful with Indigenous cultural considerations. Much gratitude to all.

Leo White has given me support and space as I wrote deeper into my intersecting identities. It's incredibly freeing to have a partner who encourages me to be my full self without judgment, guilt, or emotional constrictions.

Several have offered refuge and support without realizing how much they were giving. I hold dear: late night drinks and discussions with Jennifer Russell and Darcie Takeuchi; long phone calls with Alice Austin; heart-to-hearts with Becky Bourdeau; meandering lunches with Dina B.; my GACKS who always have each other's backs; random acts of kindness by Greg Barbee; therapeutic nourishment with Mari Verano; gatherings with global adopted Koreans and local adoptees of color; validating Twitter vents with BIPOC; educational rants with domestic, intercountry, and transracial adoptees—too many to list by name, as I fear the harm of an omission.

Thanks to Zenobia Jeffries Warfield at *YES! Magazine* and the folks at *Plan A* for offering my voice a venue, and doing the important work that you do.

Thanks to Thomas Park Clement, Lee Herrick, Susan Major, Reshma McClintock, and all who've supported my previous books.

Thanks again to Lee Herrick *(Scar and Flower)*, Susan Ito *(A Ghost at Heart's Edge)*, Julayne Lee *(Not My White Savior)*, Lisa Marie Rollins *(Other Words for Grief)*, Marci Calabretta Cancio-Bello *(Hour of the Ox)*, SooJin Pate *(From Orphan to Adoptee)*, and all who've read and performed alongside me.

Thanks to my cousin Jennifer Burbank, AKASF, AAAW, the late Octopus Lounge, Owl and Company Bookstore, Beyond Baroque, and all who've hosted or sponsored events.

Thanks to Nicole Chung *(All You Can Ever Know)*, Angela Davis *(Freedom is a Constant Struggle)*, Ally Henny *(Armchair Commentary; Combing the Roots)*, Roxanne Gay *(Difficult Women)*, Deann Borshay Liem *(Geographies of Kinship)*, Audre Lorde *(Sister Outsider)*, Chanel Miller *(Know My Name)*, Chimamanda Ngozi Adichi *(Americanah)*, Ijeoma Oluo *(So You Want to Talk About Race)*, Alice Stephens *(Famous Adopted People)*, Helen Zia *(Asian American Dreams)*, and every BIPOC whose work has kept me going over the past few years.

Thanks to all the loud LGBT+ People of Color who refuse to be silenced. I hear you. I see you.

And to my readers: You give me life. I'm beyond thankful for your reads, social shares, and personal notes. Knowing my words have meant something to you means everything to me.

ABOUT THE AUTHOR

Since a young child growing up in a White family and community, JS LEE has sought refuge through art and storytelling. Through her work, she examines trauma survival, transracial adoption, the ill effects of racial isolation, and intersecting marginalization.

Beyond *Everyone Was Falling*, LEE is the author of the novels *Keurium* and *An Ode to the Humans Who've Loved and Left Me*, author and illustrator of its corresponding children's books *For All the Lives I've Loved and Lived* and *For All the Friends I've Found*, and the memoir *It Wasn't Love*. She currently lives in the Bay Area of California.

For updates and information, visit: jessicasunlee.com

Amazon and Goodreads reviews carry a lot of weight.

If you think this story is a worthwhile read,
it would mean the world to me if you'd so kindly
review it online. It will increase visibility, giving others a
chance to discover it. Feel free to share your favorite quotes
and spread the word—while omitting spoilers, of course.

Thank you!

CPSIA information can be obtained
at www.ICGtesting.com
Printed in the USA
LVHW051110290920
667372LV00002B/311

9 781732 094352